THE **OBSCURE**
TRUTH

THE **OBSCURE TRUTH**

JUELLE CHRISTIE

Cover Art by Fiona Jayde
Interior Design by The Deliberate Page

Manufactured in the United States of America

CHAPTER 1

THE WEIGHT OF HIS BODY SEEMED ALMOST TOO MUCH TO BEAR. A FAINT ODOR OF alcohol was on his breath, and it permeated through the layers of her skin. He slipped his hands back into his gloves and sealed his right hand over her mouth, allowing virtually no air to escape. She felt helpless and hopeless. The moment of dread and horror felt like an eternity, and scattered thoughts raced through her mind. She felt as if she was trapped in a nightmare with no doors or windows to escape. She wished it was a nightmare, but she knew it was reality, that this unwanted man was pressed against her body and she was defenseless. She thought about her family and how much she loved them. She wished that the last conversation with her mother had not ended so abruptly and she'd had the opportunity to say, "I love you."

Her thoughts rapidly shifted to a visual of her body lying cold and lifeless in a casket as her family and friends, dressed in black, mourned and comforted each other. Her focus suddenly shifted to the outline of her attacker's face, which was partly shadowed by his baseball cap. He had a light, unkempt beard, likely four to five days of growth. His eyes were partially obscured from her view, as the bill of his cap created a covering. She, however, was able to discern the piercing nature of his eyes. There was no conscience behind those dark, penetrating eyes.

The rain was coming down harder, and the thunder was almost deafening. The inclement weather seemed an appropriate backdrop to the horror that she was experiencing. The lightning flashed through her window, illuminating his face. She instantly realized that her perpetrator was that guy she'd encountered on her college campus on three or four occasions. She had playfully warded off his unwanted advances, and now he was determined to fulfill them. She clenched her teeth as he forcefully entered her. A stream of tears rolled down her cheeks. She tried to break free from his captivity, but the weight of his body was too burdensome. She tried to bite the palm of his hand, but the firm adherence of his gloved hand over her lips prevented her from opening her mouth. Only a whimper was allowed to escape. His tone of voice was chilling as he warned her to stay still or he would kill her. Her tears became uncontrollable.

She prayed to God to deliver her from this torment but also asked what she'd done in life to deserve this. She'd grown up a staunch Catholic, though her attendance at church had drastically declined when she'd moved away to college. She wished that she still wore the rosary around her neck. It had been blessed by her priest in her hometown of Laredo, Texas. During this moment of misery and torture, she felt alone. It was just her and this monster. She wanted his advances to end so badly, but she had no control. He had the power, and she was powerless.

After what felt like an endless period of time, he informed her that he was going to remove his hand from her mouth. He warned her that if she screamed, he would kill her. She nodded her head to convey understanding. He slowly removed his right hand from her lips. Her body was shaking like a leaf. She could not control the muscle movements of her body. A bolt of lightning flashed again, illuminating her apartment for a couple of seconds.

He asked in an expressionless voice, "Can I trust you to keep this a secret? I did not mean to hurt you."

Trying to regain her composure, she shakily responded, "Yes," in a voice that was almost inaudible.

"I did not hear you," he replied.

She gained a little bit more strength to her voice. Though her voice quivered, she managed to get the word "yes" out of her mouth.

"How do I know I can trust you?" he asked.

"I won't tell anyone. I promise," she managed to say, though with extreme difficulty.

Lightning again struck. His eyes looked empty, and there was no indication of remorse. His face suddenly changed from a vacant stare to a look of animation. He grinned and tilted his head back with an air of sadism. He then locked eyes with his victim. There was extreme fear and terror in her eyes, and he enjoyed every moment of it.

"Do you really expect me to believe that you will keep this a secret? Do you think I'm stupid? Do you?" he asked, demanding an answer.

She stuttered the word "no" out of her mouth while shaking her head, hoping to appear more believable.

He again grinned broadly, and without warning, he clenched his hands around her neck and squeezed as tightly as he could. She instantly grabbed his gloved hands while desperately trying to pull them away, but her efforts were futile. Lightning again illuminated his face, which amplified the bulging vein of the left side of his neck. She struggled, but with his full weight on top of her and the obstruction of her trachea with the powerful grasp of his hands, she succumbed to the effects of strangulation. Her arms fell to her side, and the life escaped her body.

CHAPTER 2

THE WAILING OF SIRENS WAS HEARD FROM A DISTANCE, AND THEY GRADUALLY GREW louder as they approached the crime scene. The loud, alarming sound cut through the quiet community of Shreveport, Louisiana. The October air was cool and crisp following a heavy outpouring of rain throughout the night. It was 10:42 am, and rays of sunlight were peeking through the clouds.

Moments before the arrival of the police, the victim's body had been discovered in her apartment by her friend and the building superintendent. Her friend Alison had become increasingly worried after Sofia had not picked her up for their ritual Saturday-morning cycling class that started at 9 am. Sofia was usually parked outside of her house at 8:45 am sharp.

Alison was born and raised in Shreveport and lived with her parents. She'd figured that she would save money if she continued to live at home, as opposed to venturing out on her own. She did take out some student loans and did some waitressing on the side two to three nights a week at a local diner. Her close friends that she'd graduated with from high school had been anxious to leave Shreveport and had moved to various parts of the country to fulfill their tertiary education. She had enrolled in pre-med courses and had picked up a major in biology. Her first chemistry lab class, she was partnered up with Sofia Valadez, and they both hit it off instantly. They both shared common interests. Sofia was also pre-med and was majoring in chemistry. Alison dreamed of becoming a gynecologist, while her good friend, Sofia, dreamed of becoming a neurosurgeon. They often studied together and joined each other in extracurricular activities, which included jogging, cycling, and occasionally tennis.

The last time she'd seen Sofia was the night before, around 8:00 pm, at the school library as they'd exchanged goodbyes in the parking lot. They'd both looked forward to burning calories in their cycling class the following morning. "See you at 8:45 am sharp," Sofia had shouted as she'd waved and positioned herself in the driver's seat of her 1984 silver Honda Civic.

Alison called Sofia's phone at 8:50 am, which rang six times and went to voicemail. The jovial voice on the voicemail stated, "You have reached Sofia. Leave a message, and I will get back to you." Alison called again at 8:55 am, and again, the phone went to voicemail after several rings. She called six more times at varying intervals, which all, again, went to Sofia's voicemail. Her last call was at 9:31 am. Something was wrong, and Alison knew it. Something was disturbingly wrong, and she could feel it her bones. She quickly grabbed her keys and handbag that were lying on the kitchen counter and bolted to her car after locking the front door.

Sofia's apartment was about four miles away from Alison's parents' house. She exceeded the speed limit of the back roads leading to her friend's apartment. She did not come to a complete stop at a stop sign, and she immediately looked around to ensure that there were no cops lurking in the background. This would be the most inconvenient time to be stopped and to be given a ticket, even though she could possibly persuade the cop to come to her friend's apartment to ensure that she was okay. "Stop it, Alison," she said, rebuking herself for thinking such negative thoughts. Maybe Sofia had just overslept and forgotten to turn on the ringer to her phone after leaving the library. After all, it had been a hectic week, and the subject material for their classes was becoming more intense.

She quickly turned into her friend's apartment complex and parked her 1982 maroon Toyota Corolla abruptly into one of the parking spaces. She jumped out of the driver's seat and ran up the stairs to the second level and made her way to apartment 208. She knocked on the door, but there was no answer. She forcefully knocked again, and then realized she was banging on the door. Still there was no answer. Alison quickly found her way to the office of the building superintendent. The superintendent was a tall black male about six foot one or six foot two in stature. He was well built and appeared to be in his mid-fifties. He had salt-and-pepper hair, but his clean-cut beard was mainly gray. His ID badge revealed that his name was John.

"Excuse me, sir," Alison said, almost out of breath. "Something is wrong with my friend. Something is wrong with her, and I know it," she finished, almost hysterical now. John noted her green eyes, and there was deep concern behind them. Her brunette hair was tied up into a bun. She had on exercise leggings and her lime green t-shirt had the words "Don't Quit" written across it.

"Slow down, young lady," John stated, trying to get control of the situation. "Tell me what happened."

"Sofia. She lives in 208. I've been trying to call her for almost an hour, and she's not responding. I need for you to open her door."

"Ma'am, there could be many explanations for her not answering her call. It has not even been an hour. I'm sure she's fine. Why don't you try calling her later?" John replied.

"Sir, you don't understand. This is not like Sofia. We had plans this morning. If, for some reason, she had to cancel our plans, she would have called. That's just the type of person she is. Could you please check up on her? Could you please open the door?" Alison begged.

"Your friend probably just overslept. It happens. I cannot just enter her apartment without prior notice unless it is an emergency," John responded.

"This is an emergency!" Alison was emotional. "Please, sir, I'm begging you. Please."

John looked into her eyes. She was scared. After a few-second pause, he gave into her request. They both made their way to room 208, with Alison leading the way a few steps ahead. She looked back twice, as if to indicate to the superintendent to hurry up. They were finally outside room 208. John knocked on the door with no response. He knocked again, harder and a little longer. "Sofia," he called out. He waited a few seconds, but there was no response. He knocked again and simultaneously called her name out, but with no response from inside the apartment. He pulled out his bundle of keys, inserted the key into the key hole, and unlocked the door. He slowly opened the door and called her name out again. He took a few steps in, with Alison close behind.

The small apartment was scantily furnished. To their immediate horror, there was Sofia, lying on her back, lifeless, on the floor. Her white underwear was around her ankles. Her jeans skirt was raised, barely covering her modesty. Alison repeatedly screamed, "Oh my God!" and was uncontrollable with tears. Her body would have fallen to the floor had it not been for the instant reaction of John.

He led her out of the apartment, and then he closed and locked the door. He guided her down the stairs to the first level for security reasons, as he did not know if the perpetrator was still inside the apartment. There were prominent marks around Sofia's neck, which had given him the assumption that she might have been strangled. Alison had reflexively grabbed on to him and was soaking his white linen shirt with tears. He reached his hand into the right pocket of his pants and grabbed his cell phone. He quickly dialed 911.

"911. What is your emergency?" a female voice said on the other end of the line.

"There's a dead girl on the floor of her apartment, and it looks like she was attacked," he exclaimed.

"What is the address?" the operator asked, and John told her. "The dispatchers have communicated with the appropriate authorities, and they are on their way," she continued. "Is she breathing? Does she have a pulse?"

John responded with panic in his voice, "I didn't touch her. She's ashy and blue. She's dead. She's definitely dead."

"Is there anyone else in the apartment?" the operator inquired.

"I don't know."

"What is your relationship to the female? Do you know what happened?" the operator continued.

"My name is John Watson, and I'm the superintendent of the building. I don't know what happened. I think she may have been attacked." He proceeded to explain what had led him to open the door to the apartment. He answered some more questions, and he was reassured that the police would be there shortly.

By this time, a small, scattered group of tenants had gathered to see what the commotion was about. John tried to encourage them to go back into their respective apartments. Some obliged, but others remained fixed out of curiosity.

Two police cars emblazoned with the title "Shreveport Police" pulled into the apartment complex. Two cops came out of the first car. The cop exiting the driver's seat was a white slender male about five foot seven who appeared to be in his early forties. He had raven black hair, and his face was clean shaven. His partner exiting from the passenger seat was a black male who also appeared to be in his forties and who was slightly taller than his counterpart. He had a goatee and a somewhat larger frame than his colleague.

The second police car that pulled up only had a driver. The policeman in the second car appeared to have slight difficulty exiting the car. He was about five foot three, which was probably a generous estimation of his height. He was rotund in appearance and had a protruding abdomen. The buttons on his shirt appeared to be holding on for dear life. He really could have gone up a size with his clothing. He was pale in complexion, with countless freckles. He was a redhead, and his mustache partly concealed his upper lip. He appeared to be in his early fifties. After successfully getting out of his car, he stood erect and tilted his head slightly upward as he walked to appear more authoritative.

The small group of individuals who had gathered started to whisper and speculate. The raven-haired police officer warned the spectators to go back inside their apartments. The policemen approached John and Alison. Alison was still crying uncontrollably. Her face was red, and her eyes were puffy. The black police officer, whose name was Jesse, inquired about what had taken place. John did his best to communicate what had transpired. Jesse took John's key to enter the apartment. Jesse and his counterpart, Danny, ran up the stairs to the second level and stationed themselves at the door of apartment 208. The intense wailing of ambulance sirens was heard approaching.

The portly red-headed police officer, whose name was Charlie, remained on the first level to interview John and Alison. He had a yellow writing pad that he fumbled through to a blank sheet. He took a pen from his pocket, bit the cap off, and replaced the cap on the other end while it was still in his mouth. He attempted to write the date, but no ink came onto the page. He scratched the tip of the pen vigorously back and forth until the ink came out of the pen.

Meanwhile, Jesse and Danny had entered the apartment with guns in their outstretched arms. The small one-bedroom apartment was open flooring with the exception of the bedroom. The victim's body was lying lifeless on the brown carpet of the living room floor. There was an old-looking beige sofa in the living room with a side table that held up a lamp and a couple of magazines. The small space between the living room and the kitchen consisted of a small round table with two wooden chairs at opposite ends. There were papers neatly piled on the table and what appeared to be a textbook. The officers positioned themselves each on opposite sides of the closed bedroom door.

"This is the police! If you're in there, put your hands up!" Danny shouted. The police officers looked at each other, communicating without words. After no response through the door and no activity heard, Jesse barged open the door, and the officers entered with their guns pointing. There was no one in sight. The small bedroom contained a twin bed that was made up with pink sheets. A small nightstand held up a lamp. There was also a picture in its frame on the nightstand that captured the smile of the victim. Contained in the picture were three other individuals of Hispanic heritage who appeared to be the victim's family. The policemen deduced that the older adults were the victim's parents and the young boy, who appeared fourteen or fifteen, was the victim's brother. The door to the small bathroom was ajar, and Danny entered. He quickly pulled aside the blue shower curtain, but there was no one hiding behind it. Jesse opened the closet, which housed a few shirts, dresses, skirts, and pants that were all categorized and neatly hung.

After eliminating further potential threats, the officers officially labeled the area a crime scene. The yellow crime scene tape was placed accordingly.

CHAPTER 3

JESSE, ONE OF THE FIRST OFFICERS TO ARRIVE AT THE SCENE, ESTABLISHED A SECURITY log and ensured that all visitors to the scene sign in and record the agency that he or she was with.

"What do we got?" Detective Young asked authoritatively to the crime scene investigator, Michael Bricks.

"We have an eighteen-year-old rape and murder victim of Hispanic origin by the name of Sofia Valadez. Her body was discovered by her friend and the superintendent of the building around 9:45 am this morning."

Detective Bernard Young was a middle-aged black male with a receding hairline. He'd been a police officer in Shreveport for almost a decade before making the transition to homicide detective. He'd wanted a change in his career, and he'd figured he could seamlessly transition into a career in detective work. He found it fascinating putting the pieces of the puzzle together and solving cases. The more difficult the case, the more exciting was his job. He envisioned himself as a modern-day Sherlock Holmes.

Giselle Bellamy listened as her mentor, crime scene investigator Michael Bricks, interacted with Detective Young and exchanged vital information. Mr. Bricks was well-built and stood around five foot ten, give or take an inch. He had a thick head of blonde hair and was clean shaven. He must have been in his middle to late forties. On arrival to the crime scene, Giselle had done a walk through with investigator Bricks to get a feel of the scene. Police

Officer Jesse had gone through the sequence of events and detailed their movements in the apartment.

Investigator Bricks mentally tried to put together the likely sequence of events. There was no evidence of forced entry. Did the victim know the perpetrator? There were no obvious shoe prints. There were no signs of blood spatter. There were two glasses on the kitchen counter. There was a prominent fingerprint on one of the glasses. Though the fingerprint likely belonged to the victim, Investigator Bricks hoped that this piece of evidence would be that of the perpetrator. The victim appeared to have been raped. Her white underwear was around her ankles. Her injuries appeared to be from strangulation. There was bruising around her neck. There were also comma-shaped impression marks on the victim's neck. It was deduced that the marks were from the victim's fingernails, likely the result of a defensive act to remove the perpetrator's grip from around her neck. Investigator Bricks formulated a strategy to collect the evidence. He again walked through with Detective Young, and they both discussed various scenarios and came up with a game plan.

Giselle was a twenty-year-old intern with the crime scene investigation unit at the police department in downtown Shreveport. She had earned an associate's degree in crime scene investigation at her community college. Giselle was of Creole heritage, and she was born in Baton Rouge. She wanted to be a crime scene investigator. The thrill of identifying and collecting evidence at the scene of a crime was captivating. The opportunity to be a part of bringing a perpetrator to justice would be rewarding. Her long-term goal was to be a forensic scientist. She wanted to eventually transition from gathering evidence to processing evidence. She thought of specializing in forensic toxicology, or maybe forensic DNA.

It was Giselle's first day on the job as an intern with the crime scene investigation unit. She was nervous yet excited. She'd barely slept in anticipation of what the day might hold. Nothing could have prepared her for what her eyes beheld. The vision of a young female about her age lying cold and lifeless on the floor was terrifying. She thought that the victim could have easily been her. She lived alone in an apartment similar to the victim's. She often came home late from studying at the library. Her apartment was at the very end of the building, which was lined by heavy shrubs and tall trees. The lighting of the walkways was dim. A stranger could easily be lurking in the shadows and attack her at a vulnerable moment. At that very moment, she made the decision to purchase a can of pepper spray. She had a fleeting thought about purchasing a gun. Her mind shifted back again to the victim. Who could have committed such a horrifying, heinous act? Did the victim know the perpetrator, or was this a random, vicious act? She thought about the dread and terror that the victim had experienced as she'd lived her final moments. She must have pleaded with her perpetrator to stop. Her eyes must have conveyed fear and helplessness. She'd been brutally violated and strangled. The feeling of suffocation was a cruel way to die. Giselle realized that her eyes were welling up with tears, and she tried to contain her emotions.

Giselle ensured that she was paying close attention to the investigative process. She heard her mentor's voice in her head repeatedly telling her not to contaminate the crime scene. She wore standard protection gear, which was comprised of protective gloves and booties over her shoes.

An investigator was taking photographs from outside of the scene, and he was now taking photographs of the actual scene. He wore standard protection gear in addition to a jumpsuit. He was taking photographs of the victim from multiple angles. He took photographs of the inside and outside surfaces of her hands and both surfaces of her feet. He was taking photographs of the evidence prior to its removal and of its relationship to the crime scene. He seemed to capture every inch of the apartment. He took at least two photographs of each item of evidence. He took overall views.

He took shots showing the item in relationship to its surroundings and close-up shots capturing the details.

She observed the manner in which the physical evidence was being collected at the crime scene. The lab people were dusting for prints and collecting trace evidence. There was a designated note-taker detailing the scene and describing each piece of evidence. The note-taker detailed the time that each piece of evidence had been found, where it had been found, and the name of the individual who had found it. There was an individual making sketches of the crime scene. Items were meticulously collected. The coroner, who was also a forensic pathologist, was on the scene. Detective Young, Investigator Brooks, and Giselle left the apartment and allowed the experts to proceed with their investigation.

Detective Young and his partner, Detective Roberto Sanchez, proceeded to interview John and Alison, who were sitting on the curb of the parking lot. John continued his attempt to console Alison with a gentle embrace. Alison's eyes were puffy from crying, and her face was red. They both stood up as the detectives approached them. Alison's nose was dripping, and she wiped her nose quickly with the back of her right hand. She tried to suppress her tears, which resulted in discomfort to her throat. John and Alison both relayed the information that they'd previously provided to the police officers.

Detectives Young and Sanchez interviewed other tenants in the building. The victim's neighbors in 207 were a married couple who appeared to be in their late twenties. The husband, whose name was Doug, was a tall, lanky male with jet-black, spiked hair. His left earlobe was stretched, and he had a tongue and a labret piercing. His neck and arms were covered with colorful tattoos. He worked in an auto repair shop on the other side of town. His wife, Jessica, was a college student studying art design. She had bright red hair and a pale complexion. She had at least five piercings on each earlobe and also had a tongue piercing. She had sleeve tattoos on her left arm. They both stated that they'd been out until 2 am this morning. They had met up with some friends at The Black Hole, which was a bar downtown. They reported that they'd arrived at the bar around 9:10 pm on Friday night. They'd kicked back a few beers and laughed with friends. They'd played several rounds of pool and had come home around 2 am. They had not seen or heard anything suspicious. They both stated that they'd passed out and been awoken by the commotion outside this morning.

"Did you know Ms. Valadez?" Detective Young inquired.

"Not personally," Doug responded. "I've seen her a few times going in or out of her apartment. The most we've said to each other is hello, how are you. That kind of thing. She seemed nice and quiet."

"Have you noticed anything suspicious recently? Have you ever seen anyone with her recently? Any men?" Detective Sanchez followed up.

"No," Jessica replied. "Have you?" Jessica turned to Doug, who shook his head no. "Usually she is by herself. I've seen her on occasion with a brunette girl. Cute girl. Other than that, I have not seen her with anyone."

"Thank you," Detective Sanchez replied, and he and his partner proceeded to interview other bystanders. Their interviews came up fruitless. None of the bystanders interviewed had seen or heard anything suspicious last night.

———————

"Good afternoon, detectives," said a male voice, and Detective Young and Detective Sanchez turned around simultaneously. "I have some information, and I don't know if it is helpful."

"You are?" Detective Young asked.

"My name is Jerry Frye, and I live in apartment 324." Jerry was about six feet tall and well built. He appeared to be of mixed race. Possibly one parent was black and one parent was white. He had a light complexion and greenish eyes. He had shaved his head flat. Jerry continued, "It was around 9:30 pm last night. I went to Henry's sports bar, ate a basket of their wings, drank a beer, and was coming back to my apartment. I was walking across the first level to the other set of stairs to get to my apartment. I walked by apartment 104, and there was that girl talking to that guy who lives in 104. I've seen that girl before, and I'm almost certain it's the same girl that lives in that apartment. Dark, long, straight hair. She looks Hispanic."

"How were they interacting?" Detective Sanchez inquired. "Did she appear scared? Were they arguing?"

"Not at all," Jerry responded. "She was smiling. It almost looked as if they were flirting with each other."

"Can you describe the guy?" Detective Young asked.

"Yes. White guy. About five ten, five eleven. Dark blonde hair. Glasses. Black rimmed."

"Do you remember what he was wearing?" Detective Young asked.

"Jeans. Black t-shirt."

"Did you see his shoes?" Detective Young continued.

"No. I did not get a look at his shoes."

"Anything else you can remember about this guy? Anything suspicious?" Detective Sanchez asked.

Jerry thought for a little bit. After a few seconds, he responded, "Not that I can think of."

Detective Sanchez replied, "Well, if anything else comes to mind, do not hesitate to call." Detective Sanchez handed Jerry Frye his card.

Detectives Young and Sanchez made their way to apartment 104. Detective Sanchez knocked on the door and waited. There was no answer. He knocked harder, pounding on the door. Again, there was no answer. The door was locked. Detectives Young and Sanchez now had the task of finding out who this guy who occupied apartment 104 was, starting with the superintendent. They needed to find this guy. They also needed to obtain a search warrant to go through his apartment.

By this time, the local news station was on the scene. The news reporter was animated as she described the scene and pointed in the direction of the apartment building.

CHAPTER 4

AFTER A LONG, TAXING DAY, GISELLE DROVE BACK TO HER APARTMENT. THE SUN WAS down. She made a stop at a convenient store before coming home, buying some pepper spray and a few other items. Images of the victim's body flashed periodically in her mind throughout the day. Once home, she sat in her car and observed her surroundings for a minute prior to exiting and locking the car doors. There was no one in sight. She had the pepper spray in her right hand and her keys and plastic bag of items in her left hand. She rapidly walked up the stairs to her apartment and quickly entered, immediately locking the door. She turned on the lights to the foyer and living room. She walked into the kitchen and turned on the lights. She grabbed a carving knife and slowly walked through her apartment. She slowly opened the door to her bedroom and turned on the light. Her bedroom was just the way that she'd left it. She opened the door to her closet. There was no one there; just her clothes and shoes. She walked into the bathroom and turned on the light. Empty. There was no one hiding in the bathroom. There was no one behind the shower curtain. She again walked to the front door and turned the knob several times to ensure that it was locked. She breathed a deep sigh of relief. "Get a grip on yourself, Giselle," she said and almost scolded herself. She thought to herself that she could not let her job get to her like this or she would never survive.

She took a shower. The warm water felt great running down her body, and it was helping to relieve some of the tension. She spent over half an hour in the shower, and the heat from the water started to disappear. The water was now getting cool, which was her indication to get out of the shower. She dried off her body and wrapped the towel around her. Her bathroom mirror had fogged up, and she wiped the mirror with her hand. She let out a scream but then realized that what she saw was a reflection of her brown robe hanging on the hook behind her. She tried to calm her breathing, and she observed her heartbeat as it slowed back down. "What is wrong with you, Giselle. You're going to drive yourself up a wall," she said, rebuking herself again. She flossed and brushed her teeth and got herself ready for bed.

She lay in bed and surfed through the television stations. She watched the local news for about twenty minutes, which did highlight the murder of Sofia Valadez and the ongoing investigation. The news reporter broadcasted an incident of a kidnapping in Monroe involving a four-year-old girl. A picture of the girl flashed across the screen. The suspected kidnapper was the child's father, and a picture of him flashed across the screen. A description of his vehicle was given in addition to the license plate number. The news reporter was asking the public to assist in the suspect's capture. A number to call moved across the bottom of the screen. The news also reported on an armed robbery and a domestic abuse case. The news was depressing, and Giselle flipped through the stations to something more lighthearted. She stumbled onto *The Golden Girls*. She had not seen that show in a while. She laughed as Rose told one of her silly St. Olaf stories and Dorothy made a sarcastic follow-up remark. And there came Blanche, dressed to the nines in anticipation of her date. You could always count on Sophia to have a witty response. She watched the entire episode and turned off the television.

She lay in bed and listened to the leaves rustling in the breeze. She thought about her life and her family. She'd moved to New Orleans from Baton Rouge at the age of two with her parents and her sister Bianca, who was four years her senior. Giselle had natural beauty without the need for makeup. Her skin was of an olive tone with a natural glow. She had long, enviable eyelashes, and her hazel eyes were warm and captivating. Her older sister, Bianca, who suffered from severe acne as a teenager, was envious of Giselle's natural beauty, which often resulted in fits of jealousy. Bianca's acne developed when she hit puberty and was prevalent on her forehead, around her mouth, and on her chest and back. Bianca's self-esteem was severely affected, to the point of not wanting to leave the house. She was teased at school and was nicknamed "pepperoni pizza," "measles monster," and other hurtful words that could be detrimental to a child's self-esteem. Forget about talking to boys! Bianca was painfully shy around the opposite sex. She felt as if everyone was staring at her acne. Bianca, over the years, visited four or five dermatologists. She tried several acne medications with benzoyl peroxide and salicylic acid formulations. She tried both topical and oral antibiotics without any significant improvement. Her dermatologist tried her on isotretinoin, and she noted some improvement after a month. Her mouth was extremely dry while on the medication, so she always ensured that she had chewing gum or hard candy in her purse. Her water intake increased dramatically while on the medication. Her mother Genevieve constantly tried to instill in her daughters that physical beauty was superficial and transitory.

Genevieve reminded her daughters that the true beauty of a person emanated from the heart, the mind, and the soul. Genevieve taught her daughters that true beauty was seen in how they treated others and how they viewed themselves. After years of torment, Bianca made a conscious decision to turn her life around. Her mother's words started to make a deep impression. She recalled her mother's words: "The way we live life is a choice. We can choose to be happy or we can choose to be unhappy. Don't let others make that choice for you." Bianca had a moment of clarity. She decided that she could not continue in the direction that she was going, as that direction led to pain, depression, and self-destruction. She decided that she had to choose another path.

After that revelation, Bianca decided to live life whole-heartedly and embrace her true beauty from within. It took an immense amount of work, and her efforts were initially met with a tremendous amount of self-doubt. She bought self-help books and tried daily to put the messages into practice. She recited positive affirmations to herself every day. Bianca once told Giselle that when a negative thought came into her mind, she cancelled it with a positive thought. Bianca constantly reminded herself that she could not allow others to dictate her level of happiness. She realized that individuals who made obnoxious and hateful comments were often not happy and content with their lives and found temporary gratification in tearing others down. Bianca forced a smile on her face daily until it became natural.

Giselle recalled her sister coming home from school one day with a big smile on her face, and she appeared happy as a lark. Giselle inquired about her day, and Bianca responded, "Today, Amanda called me 'pepperoni pizza face,' and I responded with a smile, 'I love pepperoni pizza. It's my favorite pizza in the world.' Amanda's grin was wiped off of her face, and she walked away." Giselle was so proud of Bianca and was thrilled to see the transformation of her sister into a positive, confident lady. It was tantamount to watching a beautiful butterfly break free from its cocoon. Her sister later graduated at the top of her class and pursued a degree in criminal justice at UCLA, and she was currently in law school at the same institution. She had been happily married for almost two years. Her husband was also in law school.

Giselle's parents still lived in New Orleans. Her father, Oliver, was a certified public accountant performing duties in auditing and tax activities. He'd celebrated his fiftieth birthday earlier this year in March. Giselle had gone home for her father's milestone celebration, which had had a Mardi Gras theme. Her father was a very handsome, dignified, older gentleman. He was of a medium brown complexion. He had worn a mustache for years. He'd fallen victim to early male pattern baldness and styled his wavy hair in a comb-over. Her parents owned a successful Cajun cuisine restaurant in the French Quarter that was known for its gumbo and po'boys. Genevieve ran the restaurant, and her homemade recipes, passed on from her grandmother, were listed on the menu. There was even a dish on the menu dedicated to Giselle's great-grandmother Cecile. The dish was named "Cecile's shrimp creole classic," and it was a favorite amongst customers. Genevieve took delight in the gratification of her customers. It was pleasing to witness her customers enjoying good food and wine with merriment and laughter.

Genevieve was born and raised in Baton Rouge. She'd met her husband Oliver when she was twenty years old. Oliver hailed from New Orleans, and he was a junior at Louisiana State University, majoring in finance, when they met. Oliver was a year older than her. Genevieve was a sophomore at the same university, majoring in sociology. Their paths crossed one Saturday morning at the library. Genevieve was sitting at a table, studying. Oliver, who was looking for a seat, asked if he could join her, and she obliged. After a few hours of studying, Genevieve collected her books to leave, and Oliver ended his studying at that moment. He followed her out of the library and proceeded to introduce himself. They engaged in conversation for over an hour outside of the library. She found him smart and charming, with a great sense of humor. They grabbed a bite to eat at a burger joint in the vicinity, and they talked and laughed for hours. She felt as if she'd known Oliver for years, and she was greatly enjoying the company. The rest was history. They got married three years later in a Catholic church, after they'd graduated. She had two miscarriages before Bianca was born, which was about two years after they tied the knot. Bianca was her parents' pride and joy. Giselle came four years after.

Oliver felt that he was working a dead end job, and he felt that there were more opportunities in New Orleans. The family uprooted and moved to New Orleans in the summer of 1994. Her father worked as an employed CPA for five years, and he worked hard and gained a great wealth of knowledge and experience. Oliver also gained a good reputation with his clients. He decided that it was time to nurture his entrepreneurial spirit and develop his own independent accounting firm. He established goals, started a market search, and developed a business plan. He calculated startup and operating costs and estimated projected revenue. He and Genevieve had savings, as they'd made it a priority to save ten percent of their income every month. Oliver decided that the best course of action would be to use his home as the business location. His search for clients included cold calling, direct mail advertising, and internet marketing. He catered to individuals and small businesses needing tax planning and preparation services. He offered invaluable financial advice, and he went beyond his clients' expectations. Oliver developed a strong customer following, and his clientele increased through word of mouth. His business was so profitable that he was able to move into a commercial space, and he vetted his employees. The business was recognized by local organizations, and the business continued to grow.

Oliver convinced Genevieve to start a restaurant business. When they'd met and Genevieve had cooked him a meal, from that moment, he'd been in love. The saying "The way to a man's heart is though his stomach" seemed to hit home. Oliver and Genevieve invested in a restaurant and named it Cecile's Kitchen in honor of Genevieve's grandmother. Genevieve ran the restaurant, and it was a success. Her grandmother, if still alive, would have been proud.

Giselle and her family moved to a four-bedroom Greek-revival-style home in a suburb of New Orleans. Giselle was very outgoing, while her older sister was introverted, which was likely related to her skin problems. However, after her sister gained a new sense of confidence, the sky was the limit. Giselle learned to play the piano and the violin, and she enjoyed playing tennis on the weekends. She was a voracious reader, particularly indulging in suspense and mystery novels. Giselle knew at a young age that she wanted to be a criminal investigator or a forensic scientist. She looked into forensic and crime scene investigation programs in the state of Louisiana. She wanted to stand on her own two feet, living outside of the confines of her parents' home. She, however, wanted to remain in the state and still be able to jump in her car and spend the weekend with her family if she so desired.

Her boyfriend of almost six months, Jeremy, had gotten into Southern Methodist University in Dallas on a football scholarship. After researching programs, Giselle thought that Shreveport would be a good location. She would be about three hours driving distance to Jeremy and about five hours driving distance to her parents. Her second visit to Jeremy was a surprise visit. She walked up to Jeremy's dorm room and found him outside of his door locking lips with a petite brunette, and his hands were secured around her tiny waist. Giselle froze, and her eyes welled up with tears so that her vision was blurred. Jeremy looked up and made eye contact with her. His smile immediately disappeared, and his expression was of someone who'd gotten caught. Giselle turned around and ran down the stairs. She jumped into her Volkswagen Jetta and drove all the way home to Shreveport in tears and disbelief. Jeremey tried calling her multiple times over the next four days, but she did not pick up. He left multiple messages on her voice mail indicating his remorse. Jeremy did not call after that, and she never heard from him again.

As Giselle lay in her bed, she wondered how Jeremy was doing. Her mind then returned to Sofia's body lying lifeless on the floor. She told herself that she had to remain strong and not let her job depress or debilitate her. She was a crime scene investigator, and her job was to locate, collect, and process evidence and work with a team to solve the case and bring about justice. Even though she was only a lowly intern, she was going to do everything in her power to see that the victim's perpetrator was brought to justice.

CHAPTER 5

THE FORENSIC PATHOLOGIST, DR. AASHNA KAPOOR, WAS EXAMINING THE BODY OF SOFIA Valadez. This was an eighteen-year-old Hispanic female, five foot five inches, 125 pounds. Dr. Kapoor examined the outside of the victim's body. The hair was examined for any evidence of fibers. There were no fractures or bruising to the skull. There were facial petechiae, notably around the eyes, indicative of physical trauma. This could have been a sign of choking or strangulation. Subconjunctival hemorrhages were noted in both eyes. There were bruising and engorgement of tissues around the neck. Fingernail marks were noted on the neck. This appeared to be from the victim and likely resulted from the victim trying to remove the assailant's hands. Her fingernails were medium length with round-tip nails. Two of her nails were broken. Swabs underneath her fingernails were taken. There was bruising around both of her wrists. There were no needle marks. There were bruising and tearing around her genital region. She had a one-inch birthmark on the anterior aspect of her upper right thigh. Livor mortis revealed that the victim died on her back, which was the position that she was found.

Fingerprints of the victim were taken. Blood and urine samples were taken. Hair samples from the scalp were obtained. Pubic hair samples were also obtained to examine for any evidence of semen or bodily fluids and for potential hair from the attacker. Trace evidence was obtained from the victim's body, including four strands of hair on her chest. Swabs were performed of the genital region.

Dr. Kapoor used a scalpel to dissect the body. She removed the top of the skull and removed the brain. She weighed it and took a sample. She noted that the hyoid bone in the neck was broken, verifying that the victim was strangled. She opened up the body cavity, examining the heart and the lungs. She took another blood sample from the heart. She examined the abdominal organs. She assessed for any injuries to the organs and weighed them. Gastric contents and tissue samples were obtained. The samples were labeled to go to the crime lab.

CHAPTER 6

TWO POLICE CARS PULLED INTO THE FRONT YARD OF AN OLD BUNGALOW-STYLE HOME. The grass was dry and sparse. The garage was open and housed a 1969 light blue Cadillac. Detective Young and Detective Sanchez hopped out of one vehicle. Officer James Grady, from the Monroe Police Department, was in the other vehicle. A brown Labrador retriever was lying lazily on the porch. Detective Sanchez opened the screen door and knocked on the door. After a few seconds, an elderly woman opened the door.

"Good morning. I'm Detective Sanchez, and this in my partner, Detective Young. This is Officer Grady. We're looking for Nathaniel Wellington."

The elderly lady had deep concern in her eyes, and the wrinkles on her forehead became more pronounced. Her gray hair was combed into a bun. "He's my grandson. Is he in trouble?" she asked.

"We just need to talk to him," Detective Young answered. "Is he here?"

"Nate!" the elderly lady called out. "Nate!"

"Yes, Mamaw," said a male voice. A young male in his early twenties came into view. He was tall and slender. He had dark blonde hair and black-rimmed oval glasses. He wore jeans and a white t-shirt with an image of the band Led Zeppelin. He stood behind his grandmother. "What's going on?" Nate inquired.

"Are you Nathaniel Wellington?" Detective Young asked.

"Yes I am. What is this all about?"

"We're going to need you to come with us," Detective Young responded.

"What! Why?" Nate said defensively.

"What's going on?" Nate's grandmother started to cry and held onto her grandson's arm.

"Can you at least tell me what this is all about?" Nate demanded.

"This is about Sofia Valadez and her murder," Detective Sanchez stated.

"What! Who?" Nate said in disbelief. "I don't know what you're talking about! You must have the wrong person!"

"We have a witness who identified you with Ms. Valadez Friday night," Detective Sanchez continued. "We just need to ask you a few questions."

"I don't know anyone by that name. I'm telling you. You have the wrong person!" Nate pleaded.

"Mr. Wellington, you can either come with us voluntarily, or we will be forced to arrest you," Detective Young stated authoritatively.

Nate looked at his grandmother, who was still holding onto his arm. "It's okay, Mamaw. Everything will be okay. I'm going to clear this up. I love you."

"I love you too," Nate's grandmother said in a choked voice as she watched her grandson walk away with the detectives.

———

Nathaniel Wellington sat across from Detective Sanchez in the interrogation room at the police station in downtown Shreveport. It was a small soundproof room with a desk and two armless chairs. The room was otherwise bare. The walls were painted gray, with no windows. There was a one-way mirror from which Detective Young and Captain Witherspoon observed the interrogation. A light from the ceiling illuminated the room. The room was at least ten degrees colder than the rest of the building.

Detective Sanchez observed Nate intently. He observed every facial expression, eye movement and gesture. He observed Nate's body posture. "You seem nervous," Detective Sanchez said, interrupting the silence.

"I don't know what's going on. I have told you a hundred times that I don't know this girl. I keep telling you that you have the wrong person."

"Where were you the night of Friday, October 16th?" Detective Sanchez inquired.

"I was at home," Nate replied. "I left my class at 5 pm. I grabbed a bite to eat at Bonanza Burgers, and I got home a little after 6 pm. I spoke to Mamaw Daisy for about half an hour. I told her that I was coming to visit that night, and I asked her to make her famous apple pie. I packed some clothes in a bag for the weekend, and I left my apartment to head to Monroe around 8:45 pm or minutes to 9."

"At what time were you with Sofia Valadez?"

"For the last time, I don't know a Sofia Valadez," Nate said defensively. He sat back in his chair and started biting his fingernails.

"Why are you biting your nails? Are you nervous?"

"I bite my nails sometimes. Wouldn't you be nervous if a cop knocked on your door and dragged you out of your house to the police station and on top of that accused you of murder?" Nate asked rhetorically.

Captain Witherspoon and Detective Young continued to observe the interrogation behind the one-way mirror. "Who is this guy?" Captain Witherspoon asked. The captain's bald head was always shiny, as if he'd rubbed oil over his scalp. He crossed his arms, left over right, and with his left hand, he gently tugged his strawberry blond mustache, which was something he often did when he was in deep thought.

"Nathaniel Wellington," Detective Young responded. "He's a twenty-year-old engineering student. He is from Monroe. He is an only child. His mother lost her battle to breast cancer when he was fifteen years old. He was devastated and suffered a major depressive episode. He cut his wrist with a knife, and he was found by his cousin bleeding profusely on the bathroom floor. His cousin called 911, and he was treated for his injuries. He spent a few weeks in an inpatient psychiatric facility. He reportedly has been stable on his medications since then. He was raised by his grandmother, Daisy Lane. His father was a drug addict and has not been in the picture. He has been excelling in his classes. His classmates describe him as a nice person but that he keeps mainly to himself. He has not been in trouble with the law."

Back in the interrogation room, Detective Sanchez's eyes were affixed to Nate's face. "Why don't you believe me?" Nate asked.

"An eyewitness saw you with the victim last night around 9:30 pm outside your apartment. Can you explain that?"

"No, I can't explain it because it wasn't me. I don't know her. I've never met her. I was not talking to a girl outside of my apartment. I told you what I did last night three times. Are you hoping that I will change my story?"

"No. I'm not hoping that you will change your story. I just want you to tell the truth," Detective Sanchez responded.

"I am telling the truth!" Nate noticed that his voice was raised. He took a deep breath. "Am I being charged?"

"No. We have nothing to charge you with."

"Then, can I go?"

"I have no other reason to keep you. But before you go, I'm sure you don't have any problems providing us with your fingerprints and a DNA sample," Detective Sanchez replied.

"No, I don't. If that's what it takes to settle this matter," Nate said wearily.

"Great!" Detective Sanchez stood up. He led Nate out of the interrogation room.

CHAPTER 7

DETECTIVE ROBERTO SANCHEZ WAS A MEXICAN AMERICAN BORN IN EL PASO, TEXAS. His parents, Jorge and Guadeloupe, were immigrants from Ciudad Juarez, Mexico. His parents were store owners in Juarez, selling clothes, shoes, and souvenirs such as mini Mexican flags. He had an older brother, Julio, who was born in Juarez. His father was a skilled guitar player, and he'd formed a band comprised of his best friends, Alejandro and Miguel. They called themselves Los Tres Mejores, and they were well known around Juarez.

The city was a dangerous place to live. The drug cartels were everywhere, and crime was rampant. There were police officers that were corrupted and citizens were living in fear. Jorge had learned that his wife was pregnant with their second child, and he wanted a better life for his family. He wanted his children to have endless opportunities, and America was the dream. His decision to take the risk with his family to cross the border was cemented after he witnessed his brother-in-law killed execution style in front of his home. Jorge's brother-in-law Fernando, who was his wife's brother, was involved in the drug cartel. He wanted to get out, but once you were in, there was no escaping. Fernando needed a place to stay. Jorge did not want him anywhere near his family, but his wife was insistent that she could not abandon her brother. She convinced him that family should always be there for family. Reluctantly, Jorge agreed that Fernando could stay with them temporarily.

It was a beautiful cloudless day in Juarez and Jorge was teaching his son to play the guitar on the front step. Fernando was in the front yard, carving wood to make a souvenir of an eagle, similar to the one on the Mexican flag. A military-style jeep slowed down in front of his home. The jeep's three passengers wore camouflage clothing and red bandanas tied around their faces that covered their noses and mouths. A passenger carrying an AK-47 opened fire in the direction of Fernando, and he was shot in his stomach. He turned around to escape, and he was shot several times in his back before falling face forward onto the ground. Jorge's son Julio, who was only five years old, witnessed the horror as Jorge grabbed him and brought him into the house. He locked the door behind them and held his son closely as the boy cried. Guadeloupe, who was in the kitchen making a pot of soup, dropped what she was doing and rushed into the living room. She'd heard the shots fired. Julio rushed into his mother's arms, and she tried to console him. She asked her husband what happened, but he did not answer. He demanded that she take Julio into the bedroom and instructed her not to come out until he said it was safe to come out. She asked about Fernando, but he ignored her question and again demanded that she go into the bedroom with the child. She followed his instructions and took Julio into the bedroom.

Jorge pulled the curtain slightly open and peeked out. There were no vehicles in sight, and the men were gone. He saw Fernando's bloody body lying on the front lawn. He opened the front door and walked towards the body. The grass was soaking up the blood. He turned the body over, and he noticed that Fernando was not breathing. Jorge laid his fingers on his brother-in-law's neck. There was no pulse. Fernando's eyes were open. Jorge looked at Fernando and knew he was dead. Jorge lowered his head and started crying. He knew at that very moment that he had to get his family out of Juarez.

Jorge had money saved from the family business and from his gigs as a guitarrista. There was a man by the name of Manuel

Gutierrez who ran a restaurant business in El Paso. He was often referred to as Dinero. He was secretly known as someone who would help smuggle you into America for the right price. Jorge was willing to find out that price. Through connections, he had a meeting with Dinero. The amount that Dinero was requesting would have cleaned out Jorge's savings. He had a long discussion with his wife, which kept them up the majority of the night. By that time, Guadeloupe was four months pregnant. After several hours of going back and forth, they made the decision to go along with Dinero. It was a huge risk that they were undertaking. They were giving away their entire life savings and could not be guaranteed entrance into America. Dinero's plan was to smuggle them in. There was a huge chance of them being captured by border patrol, and if they were, they would be sent back to Juarez with no money. There was also a slim chance of them getting over into America safely and having a chance of a better life for their children. That glimmer of hope was worth the risk.

What was their plan if they made it to America? Jorge had a friend he'd grown up with who lived in El Paso with his wife and two children. They were legal citizens. His friend Pablo had been sponsored for a green card by his job, and after several years, he'd applied for his citizenship. He'd also sponsored his wife, who later became a citizen. His children were both born in El Paso. His friend was willing to put Jorge and his family up until Jorge was able to stand on his own two feet.

Dinero's plan worked. They made it into America and avoided capture. All they had to their names were two suitcases containing some clothes, one pair of shoes each, and some toiletry items such as soap and toothpaste. Pablo picked them up at a meeting point on the outskirts of El Paso. Pablo and Jorge embraced tightly. They had not seen each other in years. Pablo hugged Guadeloupe and lifted Julio playfully in the air. Pablo loaded the trunk with the tattered suitcases, and they were on their way through the dusty roads. They interacted in Spanish as they spoke about the risky journey over the border. Jorge updated his friend about the latest events in Juarez. Jorge made the conscious decision not to bring up Fernando's horrific murder. Guadeloupe was still unable to talk about her brother without breaking down.

Pablo was bilingual, speaking both Spanish and English. Jorge spoke a little bit of English. He understood more than he could speak. Guadeloupe spoke no English at all. Fortunately, El Paso had a sizeable proportion of Hispanics who spoke Spanish. Pablo, however, encouraged his friend to make it a priority to learn English. He stated that he had a very good Spanish to English translation pocket book and suggested that Jorge carry it around with him and attempt to speak English at every opportunity. Pablo also knew of an English tutor that Jorge should consider once he got his feet wet.

They turned on to the main road, and the Rio Grande could be seen in the distance. There was Juarez on the other side. A chill went through Jorge's spine as he recalled the fear and terror his family had left behind. He thought about Fernando, who'd never gotten a proper burial. He looked behind from the front passenger seat. Guadeloupe and Julio were both staring out of the window. He turned back around and gazed into the distance. He took in the desert terrain and the mountains in the backdrop. He thought about Fernando again. His mind transitioned to the future of his family. How was he going to get a job? Would he be able to provide for his family? His thoughts were interrupted by the sound of Pablo's voice. Pablo was telling him that his wife was preparing carne asada with tortillas.

Pablo's wife Maria opened the door as she heard the car pull up. She welcomed Jorge and Guadeloupe with open arms. She stooped down and gave Julio a kiss on his cheek. The aroma of the food cooking greeted them at the door. Pablo lifted both suitcases and led his guests to the room that all three of them would be staying in. It was a modest bedroom with a queen-sized bed, a side table, and a dresser with four drawers. Pablo and Maria's sons came running out of another bedroom. The younger one had a toy truck in his hand, and the older one was trying to take it away from him. Pablo had to separate his boys and told them to share. Pablo introduced his two sons. The older one was Matthew, who was six. The younger one was Thomas, who was four.

Pablo and Maria were very welcoming. Jorge, however, did not want to overstay his welcome, and he knew he had to find a job as soon as possible. He was hired for a job as a janitor at a mom-and-pop Mexican restaurant. He also did janitorial work at a medical clinic. Guadeloupe was hired by a cleaning agency and started cleaning residential homes. They were able to move into a low-rent apartment. Maria stepped in to help with Julio when needed. Guadeloupe was moving further along in her pregnancy, and Jorge urged her to stop cleaning. Jorge worked diligently on learning English. He chose to speak English when interacting with a fellow Hispanic who was bilingual. He was picking up the language rather quickly, and he was able to have a basic conversation in English. He made it a duty to learn ten additional words daily to build his vocabulary. Jorge picked up another job in which he did drywall installation and roofing. He even picked up a gig where he sang and played the guitar at a lounge on Saturday nights.

One night, Guadeloupe was rushed to labor and delivery. She gave birth to a healthy boy, who was named Roberto Jorge Sanchez. Growing up, Roberto thought of his dad as the hardest working person he knew. His dad constantly reminded Roberto and his brother Julio to work hard and to make something of themselves. Julio was more studious than Roberto, and his nose was always buried in a book. Roberto, on the other hand, would much rather play cops and robbers. Jorge always wanted to see Roberto's homework when he got home, even if he was physically and mentally exhausted from working all day in the blistering heat.

Jorge continued with his words of encouragement to his boys. He reminded them that they could be anything that they dreamt of becoming.

After graduating high school, Julio was able to obtain state-based financial aid. He enrolled in college and followed a pre-med track. He got straight A's his first semester, and it was cause for big celebration in the Sanchez household. It was just as big of a celebration as the one they'd had when Julio had received his acceptance letter into college.

Roberto opted to join the police academy. He envisioned himself as a police officer at a young age. He wanted to be on the side of justice and protect the citizens of his country. Jorge was just as proud of Roberto, as he felt his son was living his dream. Jorge knew that his sons would never have had these opportunities had they remained in Juarez. He beamed with pride when he thought about his sons.

CHAPTER 8

DETECTIVE ROBERTO SANCHEZ AND HIS WIFE, JUANITA, ATTENDED SUNDAY SERVICE at the Catholic church downtown. There was a special part of the regular Sunday service dedicated to remembering the life of Sofia Valadez. Sofia's parents and her brother were sitting on the third pew on the right side of the church. Detective Sanchez and his wife were sitting in a pew on the left, towards the back of the church. His eyes frequently deflected in the direction of the Valadez family. Mrs. Valadez wore a lace veil. Mr. Valadez, who sat to the left of his wife, had his arm around her shoulder. The boy sat on the right side of his mother. Detective Sanchez had met Mr. and Mrs. Valadez briefly when they'd come to identify the body of their daughter. Not many things affected Roberto emotionally, but the agony and heartache that he was witnessing tore him to pieces. He felt their pain. It was bad enough to have to bury a child, but having to bury a child under these circumstances was unimaginable. The plan was to transport the body back to Laredo, Texas, for the burial.

The priest asked God to bless and guide all those involved in seeking the truth and carrying out justice for Sofia. The second reading was from the Book of Revelation. An elderly man, who looked to be in his late seventies, read the lesson. Roberto tuned back into the reading. The elderly man's voice came though the microphone on the podium: "But as for the cowardly, the faithless, the detestable, as for murderers, the sexually immoral, sorcerers, idolaters, and all liars, their portion will be in the lake that burns with fire and sulfur, which is the second death."

Roberto listened to his thoughts, which centered on the words "burn with fire." He thought that the perpetrator deserved to burn in the depths of hell. He deserved to be tortured infinitely with no mercy. One thought led to the other. He then realized the priest was at the pulpit and had started his sermon. He thought to himself that judgement should be left to the Lord. Roberto's mind drifted in and out of the sermon.

The congregation was asked to kneel. The priest prayed from the prayer book, "In your hands, O Lord, we humbly entrust our sister Sofia. In this life, you embraced her with your tender love. Deliver her from every evil and bid her eternal rest. The old order has passed away. Welcome her into paradise, where there will be no sorrow, no weeping or pain, but fullness of peace and joy with your son and the Holy Spirit forever and ever."

"Amen," the congregation replied in unison.

The priest continued, "O Lord, whose ways are beyond understanding, listen to the prayers of your faithful people, that those weighed down by grief at the loss of this child may find reassurance in your infinite goodness, through Christ our Lord."

"Amen."

The service continued. In addition to the regular collection, a special collection was passed around for Sofia to go towards her burial. Roberto opened his wallet and gave every bill he had, which amounted to $162. Numerous members of the congregation approached the Valadez family during the peace portion of the service. There were many hugs and members offering their support. Mrs. Valadez appeared overwhelmed.

Roberto approached the Valadez family at the end of the service. He introduced his wife, and they both offered their support. Roberto promised them that whoever had done this would be found and brought to justice.

Almost two weeks had passed, but the official results were not in yet for the Sofia Valadez case. Detective Sanchez was growing impatient. He'd been repeatedly told that the process takes time. Reasons for the delay included a substantial DNA backlog, an inadequate number of qualified DNA analysts, and new cases that were constantly coming in. Detective Sanchez, through his connections, requested that the Sofia Valadez case get moved up the pile. During this waiting period, he flew to Laredo, Texas, to attend the funeral of Sofia Valadez. The funeral service was well attended, with standing room only. The love and support for the Valadez family was overpowering. Mr. Valadez had to hold his wife back as Sofia's casket was descending into the ground.

On return to Shreveport, Detective Sanchez was thrilled to hear that the results of the crime scene investigation and the DNA testing had come in. He and his partner, Detective Young, made their way to meet up with the forensic pathologist, who was also the coroner. Dr. Aashna Kapoor met up with the detectives and led them to her office. She walked assertively, and her lab coat was white and starched. She had a very thick Indian accent. Dr. Kapoor took a seat behind her desk, and the detectives each took a seat opposite her. Dr. Kapoor proceeded to review the findings with the detectives.

The coroner stated that the victim had considerable tearing to the genital region, leading her to believe that the victim might have been raped. Unfortunately, they'd been unable to extract semen from any of the samples. It was deduced that the perpetrator had likely used a condom. There were no pubic hairs from the perpetrator identified. Her blood and urine tests did not reveal any alcohol or drugs. There were no poisons detected. The victim had significant bruising and other visual signs suggestive of strangulation. The fracture of her hyoid bone and other neck findings led to the conclusion that she was manually strangled. Her time of death was estimated to be between 9 pm to midnight on Friday, October 16th. The manner of death was deemed to be homicide, and the cause of death was determined to be a result of asphyxia from strangulation.

Dr. Kapoor revealed that a fingerprint from a drinking glass had been recovered from the crime scene. She also mentioned that four strands of hair had been collected from the victim's body that did not belong to the victim. Dr. Kapoor revealed that it was fortunate that one of the strands identified contained the hair root, as they'd been able to extract DNA from it.

Dr. Kapoor paused for a moment. After a few seconds, she stated that the fingerprint and the DNA sample were an exact match with the evidence she'd received of the suspect Nathaniel Wellington.

CHAPTER 9

NATE WAS COMING OUT OF THE DOUBLE DOORS OF HIS PHYSICS CLASS WHEN HE WAS approached by Detective Young and Detective Sanchez.

"Nathaniel Wellington, you are under arrest," Detective Young stated authoritatively.

"What! You're making a big mistake! I didn't do anything!" Nate said defensively. His peers looked on in shock as handcuffs were placed on him. The whispers created a wave through the campus.

Detective Young read Nate his Miranda rights: "You have the right to remain silent. Anything you say may be used against you in a court of law. You have the right to consult an attorney before speaking to the police and to have an attorney present during questioning. If you cannot afford an attorney, one will be appointed to you before any questioning if you wish. If you decide to answer questions now without an attorney present, you have the right to stop answering at any time until you talk to an attorney. Do you understand your rights?" Nate did not answer the question. "Do you understand your rights?" Detective Young repeated.

"Yes," Nate responded solemnly.

Detective Sanchez placed the suspect in the back of the police car and jumped into the front passenger seat as Detective Young drove off in the direction of the jail.

"I didn't do it!" Nate stated in a raised voice. "Why are you doing this to me?" he pleaded.

"Nate, it's over," Detective Sanchez chimed in. "You're not fooling anyone. Your prints and DNA were found all over the crime scene."

"What!" Nate replied in disbelief. "That can't be. I don't know this girl, and I sure as hell have never been in her apartment. It must be someone else. You have to believe me."

"What I will believe is the evidence. The evidence does not lie, but you lied to us," Detective Sanchez responded.

"I did not lie!" Nate shouted.

"We're going to need you to calm down," advised Detective Sanchez.

"This has to be a nightmare! This can't be real!" Nate said, shaken up. "I didn't do it. Please. I didn't do it. Please. Please," Nate begged as streams of tears rolled down his cheek. He started to breathe rapidly, as if he was having a panic attack.

"Mr. Wellington, I suggest that you try to calm down, and I advise that you get yourself a lawyer," Detective Young said.

Nate peered outside of the window as the police car took a left turn towards the jail. The police car pulled into a parking space, and Nate was led in handcuffs into the jail. Booking procedures were followed. Nate provided basic information, including his full name, home address, and date of birth. His personal items, including his wallet, were taken from him. The items listed were written on a piece of paper. Nate was asked to review the inventory and sign it, which he did. Another set of fingerprints were obtained, and he was photographed. Nate opted for an attorney to be appointed to him.

After the booking procedures were completed, Nate was placed behind bars. He looked around at his six-by-eight-foot cell. There was a narrow pipe frame bed with a pillow and stained sheets. There was a sink and a toilet that looked as if they had not been cleaned in years. Nate stared through the bars. *This can't be happening to me*, he thought. Reality had not yet set in. He thought about Mamaw Daisy. Less than a month ago, Mamaw had been rushed to the hospital with chest pain and been diagnosed as having had a massive heart attack. She'd been rushed to the catheterization lab, and two stents had been placed in her coronary arteries. Mamaw would not be able to handle the stress of him being in jail, let alone being charged for murder.

He thought to himself, *How could my fingerprints and DNA be at the scene of the crime? Could I be a part of a set up? Who will believe me? Can my attorney possibly get me off?* Questions circled through his mind, questions that seemed to have no answers. He thought to himself, *My life is over.* There was no way he could integrate back into this world. He sat on the bed, avoiding the stain. He crossed his arms over his bent knees. He lowered his head onto his arms and cried.

―――――――――

Nathaniel Wellington was set for arraignment in two days. No bail was allowed, and he was required to appear in court to enter a plea based on the charges set against him. At that time, bail would be determined by the judge. He sat in his cell and refused to eat. He did not sleep his first night in jail. He was becoming numb and emotionless.

"You have a visitor," a burly guard shouted from the other side of the bars. Nate was brought out of his daze. *A visitor*, he thought. He was bewildered. The guard opened the bars to his confinement, and he was led to the visitation area. He did not see anyone he recognized. He was led to a small round table. There sat a physically attractive lady with cascading dark curls framing her face.

"Good morning, Mr. Wellington. My name is Giselle Bellamy, and I'm with the crime scene investigation department."

Nate reluctantly sat down. He was worn out. His hair was disheveled, and the stress was evident on his face. He looked at the stranger across from him. He was uncertain why she was there at the jail and wanting to speak with him. The nightmare seemed never ending. On another thought, could she potentially be his savior? Could she be his light at the end of this dark tunnel?

"Why did you do it?" Giselle asked. The glimmer of light that he thought he'd seen had gone out.

"What?" he asked.

"Why did you do it? Why did you take her life?"

Nate was about to reach his breaking point. Who is this person who thought she had the authority to demand his presence and then make these baseless allegations? He questioned whether she was also a part of a plot to tear him down and destroy him. Nate was about to stand up and call for the guard to lead him back to his cell, but then he had a change of mind. He thought to himself that he probably should not speak to her. Could she use anything he said against him? He then thought that he had nothing to hide. He had nothing to tell. He looked wearily at the stranger, and after a sigh, he stated, "I didn't do it."

"Can you explain why your DNA and fingerprints were found at the scene of the crime? Did you have a relationship with her?" Giselle asked calmly.

"Ma'am, I've never had a relationship with her. I've never met her. At least, to my knowledge, I don't think our paths have ever crossed. I wish I could give you your answers, but I can't because I do not have the answers. I don't know why and how my fingerprints and DNA could have been in her apartment. I've never been inside her apartment. I feel as though someone is setting me up. I know you don't believe me, but I'm telling the truth," Nate replied.

Giselle stared at him for a few moments. She then proceeded with her line of questioning, "Who do you think would set you up? Do you have any enemies?"

"Since I was arrested, that's all I've been thinking about. I did not sleep a wink last night. I don't know who would do this, but that's the only explanation I could come up with. I know it seems far-fetched. It seemed incredulous to me also that someone would go through such great lengths to murder someone and frame another person. I know you don't believe me. It's hard to believe, and I understand that. It's the only explanation I have. I didn't murder that girl."

Nate paused for a moment. "I will be honest with you. I've suffered from depression for many years. A few years ago, I tried to kill myself after my mother died. My mother was my world. She was my comfort and my rock. I never had a father. He was more concerned about his next high. My mom had to take his place as a father and had to carry out the role as a mother. She did the best job that she possibly could. She was the best mother in the world. She was diagnosed with breast cancer. She underwent surgery and had chemotherapy and radiation. She went into remission and was doing well. A couple years later, she started to experience these terrible headaches that were not getting better. One day, she had a seizure right in front of me. She was shaking and foaming at the mouth. Blood was coming out of her mouth. I think she bit her tongue. I was terrified and called an ambulance. The few minutes that the ambulance took before arriving felt like an eternity. She was brought to the emergency room. She had a CT scan of her head, which looked like she had a brain mass. She underwent further testing, which revealed that her breast cancer had returned and metastasized. The cancer had also spread to her lungs and liver." Nate stopped talking for a moment. His eyes were welling up, "I watched my mother suffer."

Nate paused again for a moment. He tried to gain his composure, but his emotions were overpowering him. "I wish I could have taken her pain. I wish it was me. My mother's request was not to be resuscitated. She said that she was not going to go against God's plan. I didn't understand why she would say that. Why would God's plan be for my mother to suffer? Why would He take her away from me? She urged me to stay strong and to remain faithful. She asked me to take care of Mamaw Daisy. She told me she loved me. I was with her in her hospital room the night that she passed away. The nurses rushed into the room. Mom's blood pressure was dropping. She was leaving me. Her last words were 'I love you, Nate.' The nurses were unable to get a blood pressure. She lost her pulse. A physician was called in, and the doctor pronounced my mother dead. I have never felt such loss in my life. I felt as if my heart was ripped out of my chest. I lay on my mother's chest and cried. I looked at her face, and she looked to be at peace. I did not have peace. My mother's words urging me to be strong replayed in my head, but I was not strong. I felt a huge sense of loss. I did not want to live. I fell into a deep depression. One day, I took a knife out of the kitchen drawer at Mamaw's house. I sat on the cold tiles of the bathroom floor. I felt helpless. I held the handle of the knife and quickly moved the sharp blade across my left wrist." Nate showed Giselle the scar on his wrist.

Nate continued, "I was bleeding, and the gushing of the blood would not stop. At that moment, my cousin Patrick found me. He screamed for Mamaw and called 911. I was rushed to the hospital. I was going in and out of consciousness from losing so much blood. I was rushed to surgery, and I required four pints of blood. I recovered well in the hospital. I had to go to a psychiatric facility for a few weeks. I progressed well. I was started on an anti-depressant, which stabilized my mood. I went back to live with Mamaw Daisy. She became a second mother to me. I love her with all of my heart. She was so proud when I got into college. I have been following an engineering track. She said to me that my mother would have been proud. Even though my mother's not physically here with me anymore, I still feel her presence. I want her to be proud of me. I've been doing very well in school. I have gotten all A's so far, with the exception of one B in biology. My plans are to be a successful chemical engineer. My mother now would be disappointed to know that I'm in jail. I dread to think what Mamaw is going through right now. I would never want to hurt my family, and I would never hurt that girl," Nate stated with deep emotion.

Giselle looked into Nate's eyes as he wiped the tears away. The evidence said one thing, but his eyes said another. His eyes told another story. She felt like she could see into his soul. She just was not sure anymore, and she wished that her first words to him hadn't been ones of accusation.

"Time is up!" the guard called out, which interrupted Giselle's thoughts. Nate stood up, and he was led away by the guard. Giselle watched Nate walk away.

Giselle followed procedure and left the walls of the jail. She drove away. Her mind kept focusing on Nate's eyes. Despair had been behind those eyes. She had also seen truth and sincerity. She was confused. It was lunch time, and she pulled into her favorite deli.

"The usual?" Mr. Morrison smiled from behind the counter.

"You got it." Giselle smiled back. Mr. Morrison fixed Giselle a turkey sandwich on whole wheat bread, with mayonnaise, lettuce, tomatoes, and extra pickles, and with black pepper sprinkled on top. Giselle grabbed herself a bottle of water, paid for her meal, and sat down at a table next to the window.

She observed the people walking by. She usually looked forward to her sandwich at her favorite deli, but today, she was not enjoying her lunch. She could not stop thinking about Nate. What if he really was telling the truth? She finished her meal, waved goodbye to Mr. Morrison, and went on her way. She ran some errands for the rest of the day. Investigator Michael Bricks, whom Giselle was interning under, was in Lafayette for a meeting, and he'd given her the day off. Investigator Bricks was returning tonight.

Giselle went to work the next morning, and she wondered what the day would bring. She thought about Nate and wondered how he'd survived his second night in jail. She knew his arraignment was scheduled for this afternoon.

"How are you liking this job so far?" Investigator Bricks inquired. He poured himself a cup of coffee and drank it black.

"It's pretty intense," Giselle responded. "It can be a shock to your system at first."

"You'll get used to it," Investigator Bricks replied before taking another sip of his coffee. "So, what are your ultimate plans?" Investigator Bricks sat behind his desk and offered Giselle a seat across from him. She obliged and sat down.

"I'm hoping to get into a forensic science program and obtain a bachelor's degree. I would like to specialize in forensic toxicology, or maybe forensic DNA. I've applied to some programs in New York City. I've also applied to programs in New Jersey."

"New York, huh. The Big Apple. Why New York?"

"I've always been fascinated with New York City. I've never actually been there. It just seems like there is no other city like it. I've researched the city, and there's so much to see and do. The experiences seem endless. What better place to study and practice forensics? Besides, I've never lived outside of Louisiana, and I think it would be an exciting change."

"Well, good luck," Investigator Bricks responded with a smile.

"Thank you." Giselle smiled back. Then she switched gears. "Nathaniel Wellington's arraignment is this afternoon."

"Yes, it is."

"I think he may be innocent."

"Why do you think that?" Investigator Bricks had a quizzical look on his face.

"I went to see Mr. Wellington yesterday morning," Giselle continued.

Investigator Bricks sat back in his chair, and Giselle had his full attention. He asked, "Why did you go to visit him?"

"I felt like I needed answers. That case has been bothering me. I still sometimes see Sofia's face and her body lying on the ground. She was just a young girl attending college to better herself and follow her dreams. I heard that she wanted to be a neurosurgeon. I felt like her hopes and dreams were just taken from her. Some deviant came into her life and ripped it all away in such a tragic manner."

"Well, it's up to the judge to decide and set bail accordingly for Mr. Wellington. If this case goes to trial, it will be up to the jury," Investigator Bricks responded. "So, why do you think he is innocent?"

"There was something genuine about him and his emotions. I can't explain it, but it is something that I felt. Almost like an intuition."

"Well, Ms. Bellamy, our line of work is not based on intuition. It is based on facts. It's all about what you can prove. That will be your job in forensics. It will be about what you can prove."

"I know that, Mr. Bricks. I really do. It's just that this case feels different. Mr. Wellington thinks that someone framed him."

"Ha!" Investigator Bricks let out sarcastically. "Framed him? So he thinks that someone planted his DNA and prints in the apartment? This guy is a nutcase! He spent time in the loony bin." He leaned forward with his arms on the desk. "Look, Ms. Bellamy, you cannot let your emotions cloud your judgement. Criminals—and I'm not pointing my finger at Mr. Wellington because he is only a suspect at this point in time—criminals are very cunning and deceitful. That's who they are. It is a pathology. They will prey on anyone who appears weak. You cannot let them get to you. Keep your mind focused on the facts. Let the facts lead you in the investigation."

The phone on the desk rang. "Michael Bricks," he said through the receiver. "Yes. Uh-huh. Uh-huh. Okay. What!" Giselle observed him while he was on the phone and noted that his facial expression had dramatically changed. "How did this happen?" Several minutes went by as Investigator Bricks listened to the caller. "Well, thank you for informing me." He hung up the phone and paused for a moment. "Nathaniel Wellington committed suicide in the jail."

"What!" Giselle responded in disbelief. "What happened?"

"A guard found him dead this morning. He committed suicide by strangulation. He tied his bed sheet around an overhead pipe. They suspect that he stood on the bed to do this. He had a firm knot around his neck."

Giselle's mouth was open. She was speechless.

A man appearing to be in his early fifties stuck his head in the door. He said, in the direction of Investigator Bricks, "We have a case of a woman found dead outside the Hunny Bunny Motel downtown. She appears to be a prostitute."

"Duty calls, Ms. Bellamy. Let's go." Investigator Bricks stood up and motioned, and Giselle followed behind.

CHAPTER 10

JERRY FRYE SAT IN HIS RECLINER, DRINKING A BEER. HE WAS WATCHING THE LOCAL EVENING news. The big story of the day was about Nathaniel Wellington and his suicide at the jail. The reporter summarized the events leading up to Nathaniel's body being found dead with a sheet knotted around his neck. He highlighted Sofia Valadez's murder and the investigation findings leading to the arrest of Nathaniel Wellington.

The screen switched to a female reporter broadcasting the news out of Monroe. The reporter was stationed outside the residence of Nathaniel Wellington's grandmother. The reporter interviewed Ms. Daisy Lane. "What is your reaction to the news of your grandson's death?"

Ms. Lane paused briefly before responding. Her eyes welled up with tears. She replied, "This is a tragedy. I can't begin to describe to you the loss that my family and I are feeling right now."

"What are your thoughts about your grandson being a suspect in the Sofia Valadez's murder?" the reporter continued.

"I know my grandson, and I know he would never do what he is being accused of. He would never rape or commit murder. It's not him. He has one of the biggest, kindest hearts of anyone I know, and I'm not saying that because he's my grandson. He is the type of person to deny himself and give to others. There is no way he could have ever done something like this."

"How do you respond to reports that his DNA and fingerprints were found at the scene of the crime?" the reporter asked.

"I don't know how to explain that. There has to be another explanation, but I know Nate did not rape or kill her."

"What are your thoughts on his history of depression and the frame of mind that he may have been in?" the reporter asked.

"Yes, he had a history of depression. There are millions of people suffering from depression, but it does not make them bad people. It does not mean that they would commit a crime. Nate was doing well. He was enjoying life. He was doing well with his studies. He was physically active and enjoyed swimming. He was doing volunteer work, trying to give back to the community. He was doing well. I sincerely believe that these accusations and the arrest brought back the depression and he was pushed over the edge," Ms. Lane replied.

The camera switched focus to Nate's cousin, Patrick Green. Patrick had positive things to say about his cousin. He re-emphasized his grandmother's sentiments. He stated that Nathaniel was incapable of committing such a crime.

Jerry Frye was listening intently. He was fixated on the praiseworthy and admirable words of Nathaniel's family. It was evident that Nathaniel's family truly loved him. Jerry's eyes moved away from the television screen. He thought about his family. What family? He did not know what it was like to have a real family. He did not know what it felt like to be wanted. He did not know what it felt like to be loved.

Jerry was twenty-one years old. He acknowledged that he was a monster. He was vile and horrid. He was cold and callous. How had he become this evil person? How had the course of his life brought him to this moment? A moment where he was listening to the news about a young woman whom he'd raped and murdered and the suicide of the innocent man that he'd framed. He had tipped off the investigators, leading them in the direction of Nathaniel Wellington.

Jerry chugged the remaining contents of the beer bottle. He got up out of the recliner and went to the bathroom with the beer bottle still in his hand. He looked in the mirror, and he hated the reflection. He despised the person he had become. He was empty inside and soulless. After a few moments staring at his reflection, he forcefully threw the bottle at the mirror, shattering it. The broken pieces of the bottle dispersed onto the bathroom counter and the bathroom floor.

CHAPTER 11

JERRY FRYE WAS BORN IN GREENVILLE, MISSISSIPPI. HE GREW UP POOR, AND THERE were nights that he went to bed hungry. He lived with his mother, brother, and his mother's boyfriend, Fletcher. His older brother, Robert, was four years his senior. Jerry and Robert had different fathers. His mom had once been married to Robert's father, Gary, who'd been killed in the Vietnam War. Robert was only two years old at the time of his father's death. Jerry's mother, Matilda, spoke about Gary affectionately, and it was evident that Gary was the love of her life. Her world had been torn apart when she'd received the news of Gary's death, and life had been downhill since then.

Jerry had been born about two years later. His mother never spoke about Jerry's father. She would never reveal the identity of his father despite his pleas. Once, when Jerry asked his mother about his father, she became furious and scolded him. She warned him never to ask about his father again. Jerry was terrified and stuttered an apology to his mother. He never again asked about his father.

Jerry looked very different than his brother. His brother was dark-skinned, and Jerry was very fair. Jerry had greenish eyes and brown hair with natural golden highlights. On many occasions, strangers were surprised that he and Robert were brothers.

Jerry despised his mother's boyfriend, Fletcher, who was a drunk and a parasite. His mother worked two cleaning jobs, and the family lived paycheck to paycheck. There was barely enough to pay the rent and utilities. Fletcher did not work, and he would leave the shotgun-style house in the morning after Matilda left for work. Fletcher would then wobble into the house late in the evenings, drunk. He also smoked like a chimney, and the smoke seemed to penetrate his pores. On one occasion, Fletcher took some money that Matilda hid under the mattress to buy booze and who knows what. The family barely had anything to eat until Matilda got paid two weeks later. Portions of food had to be rationed out, and Jerry went to bed hungry while Fletcher sat in front of the television with his six-pack of beer. Matilda got herself a third job to ensure that bills were paid and food was on the table. Jerry could not understand why his mother would allow Fletcher to be in their home and a part of their lives. His mother would constantly make excuses for Fletcher. She would describe him as a good man who was influenced by the negative effects of alcohol. She told Jerry and his brother that Fletcher was trying to change, and she believed that she could help him change.

Once, Jerry overheard his mother and Fletcher arguing in the bedroom. Fletcher's voice was drowning out his mother's voice as he yelled and screamed behind the closed door. There was a loud noise and the sound of broken glass. Moments later, his mother ran out of the bedroom with her left hand pressed against her cheek. She grabbed a napkin from the kitchen and briefly exposed her lower lip, which was bleeding. She pressed the napkin firmly against her lower lip to stop the bleeding. She turned around and locked eyes with Jerry, who was motionless. Jerry was scared, and his eyes welled up with tears. His mother had a look of surprise and embarrassment. She told Jerry to go in his bedroom and do his homework, and Jerry reluctantly obeyed. He abhorred the sight of Fletcher. If there was a word stronger than hate, that is how he felt towards Fletcher.

Despite the dysfunction at home, Jerry did very well in school. He thought of school and his books as an escape from the miserable existence at home. Jerry had natural ability, and he was gifted especially in math. He scored high on an IQ test. His brother also did well in school but much greater effort was needed. Robert viewed his education as a way to get out of Greenville, maybe his only means out, and he studied diligently. Jerry admired his brother tremendously, and his brother was all that he had. Robert got a college scholarship, and he planned to move to Tennessee. Jerry pleaded with his brother to go to a college nearby in Mississippi. Robert tried to explain to him that he had to take advantage of this opportunity. It was his only way out. "What about me?" Jerry pleaded. His brother told him that he would one day find himself out of Greenville. His brother encouraged him to continue studying and to do well in school. Jerry was only thirteen years old at the time. He was devastated when his brother left. He had no one.

The next two years continued to be unbearable. His mother still worked three jobs, and Fletcher was still around. He was still a drunk, and nothing had changed. Jerry did not see his brother after he moved away to Tennessee. He received one letter from his brother telling him how much he was enjoying his studies at Fisk University. He had no correspondence from his brother after that.

One night, Jerry was asleep in his room when he was awoken by the sound of his bedroom door opening. The door creaked on its hinges as it slowly opened, which caused Jerry to let out a loud gasp. He immediately sat upright on his bed, and the outline of a man was in view. Jerry instinctively knew that it was Fletcher. The silhouette instructed him in a low tone of voice to be quiet.

Jerry's first inclination was to scream, but Fletcher had predicted this, and he gave Jerry a stern warning: "If you scream, I will kill your mother." The silhouette inched closer to the bed, and Jerry's body quivered with fear. Fletcher again warned Jerry to remain quiet as he sat on the bed. The cigarette smoke from Fletcher's clothing entered Jerry's nostrils, causing him to cough a couple of times.

"What I'm going to do will be our little secret," Fletcher whispered. He then proceeded to tug at the drawstrings of Jerry's pajama pants, and Jerry forcefully pushed Fletcher's hand away. Fletcher made another attempt to tug at Jerry's drawstrings, and Jerry again pushed Fletcher's hand away. "Do you want your mother dead?" Fletcher asked in a low tone of voice. "Do you? Because that's what she will be if you keep resisting me." Fletcher paused for a moment to let his words take effect. "Now just relax and be quiet," Fletcher instructed. Jerry felt helpless, and the night was interminable. He prayed for the sun to come up to shed light on Fletcher's actions. A better option would be for his life to end and never see the sun rise again.

After that horrifying incident, Jerry went out of his way to avoid Fletcher. He started to lock his bedroom door at night, and he was awoken suddenly by any noise. Jerry's mother, Matilda, noted a change is his behavior and inquired whether he was all right. Jerry lied to his mother, stating that he was fine, but Matilda knew that something was wrong. She probed Jerry until he finally confessed that he'd been sexually violated by Fletcher. Matilda looked away, and Jerry sensed that his mother either did not believe him or she did not want to believe him. "It's true," Jerry stated defensively. "He said he would kill you if I didn't let him. He made me promise not to tell."

"Stop this nonsense!" Matilda warned him. "Fletcher would never do that." Matilda threw down the dishcloth in the sink, and she went into her bedroom and closed the door. Jerry stood in the kitchen in disbelief. He was dumbfounded that his mother would take up for Fletcher and ignore the terrifying ordeal that he'd had to endure.

Jerry realized that he was building a wall up around himself, and he started to have little regard for the feelings of others. He got involved with the wrong crowd. He started smoking cigarettes and marijuana. He and his group of guy friends picked up girls, and they made a bet on who could sleep with a particular girl first. Their reward was cigarettes. Whoever won that week would be rewarded with a cigarette from the four remaining losers. Jerry won two weeks in a row. He would dump the girl afterwards, which would result in heartache or anger from the victim. He did not care. Why should he care? He'd never felt loved or supported, not even from his own mother. Why should he care about others when no one cared about him?

One Tuesday afternoon, Jerry came home from school and met Fletcher on the couch watching television. Fletcher was home earlier than usual. Typically, he would be hanging out with friends. Maybe he even had a girlfriend or two on the side. Jerry would not put it past him. His mother had not come home yet from work, and he did not expect her home for several more hours. There were five empty beer bottles on the table, and Fletcher was drinking the sixth one.

Fletcher taunted Jerry, telling him that his mother needed to get a fourth job. He accused Matilda of not working hard enough and belted out a laugh. Jerry was infuriated, and his blood was boiling through his veins. He shot back at Fletcher, telling him that he needed to get a job. Jerry proceeded to call him lazy and a fat slob. Fletcher put down his beer bottle on the table and asked Jerry to repeat himself. Fletcher's eyebrows came closer together as he scowled. Jerry repeated himself, and Fletcher angrily stood up. Fletcher thrust himself towards Jerry, and Jerry dodged him. They were on opposite sides of the kitchen table.

Fletcher started screaming profanities, and he threatened to have Jerry's mother put him out on the street. Jerry was scared, as he did not know what Fletcher was about to do. Fletcher saw the fear in his eyes and started to laugh. He asked Jerry if he knew who his father was, but Jerry did not reply and stared straight at him. Jerry tried to conceal his fear, but Fletcher could read it clearly on his face. Fletcher belted out another laugh and looked directly into Jerry's eyes. Fletcher enjoyed every moment of his dominance. In a hateful voice, he told Jerry that his mother had been raped by a trailer park honkey. He spoke slowly, but the hate in his voice was still the same. "You're a bastard child from a trailer park honkey who raped your mother."

The rage intensified in Jerry's body, and the fear was gone temporarily. He grabbed a knife from the kitchen counter and lunged towards Fletcher, stabbing him in his arm. After realizing what he had done, he ran out the door into the front yard. He heard Fletcher screaming profanities from inside. He did not want to face Fletcher, and he took off running down the street.

Jerry ran until he was out of breath. He ran through dirt roads sprinkled along the way with shotgun-style homes, and he had nothing on him except the clothes on his back. His legs seemed unable to take him further at that speed. He slowed down and started to walk. Jerry turned around a few times, expecting to see an angry Fletcher behind him. There was no Fletcher. He was a safe distance from home. He was terrified as he recalled his explosive interaction with Fletcher. It did not seem real. He felt as if he was trapped in a nightmare, but he knew what he'd just experienced was real. It was too real. He could still smell the heavy odor of alcohol on Fletcher's breath. The smoke from the cigarettes had seeped into his clothing. Jerry still felt the knife in his hand as he'd pierced Fletcher's flesh. The screaming and profanity-laden yelling were deafening and still rang in his ears.

He thought of the result of his act. Would Fletcher lose his arm? Had he killed Fletcher? What would his mother say or do when she found out? What would happen to him? He had nowhere to go. He had no money. Where would he sleep? He thought about the shocking revelation of the identity of his father. He could picture Fletcher's face clearly as he'd divulged that secret. How did Fletcher know? Why would his mother trust him with that information?

Fletcher had reveled in the moment as he'd divulged this forbidden secret. The loathing had been written all over his face, and it was an image that Jerry would never forget. He understood why his mother did not want this closeted information to ever see the light of day. It was now evident why his mother would experience negative emotions when he'd asked about the identity of his father. It took his mother to a dark and angry place. He created probable images of the rape in his mind, and it was horrifying. He tried to imagine the face of the man who'd attacked his mother. What had he looked like? He imagined how terrified and helpless his mother must have felt. The thoughts sent chills down his spine. He was aware of his heart racing.

Questions continued to race through his mind in a circular manner, which almost made him dizzy. It was difficult for him to grasp the idea that he was a product of rape. He felt defiled. He felt broken. His mother likely viewed him as repulsive and unclean. She was probably ashamed of his existence. He'd never felt a close connection to his mother. Could he have been a constant reminder of the rape? He almost wished that he did not know this information. He hated Fletcher. He despised him for this revelation. He hoped that Fletcher would lose his arm. Better yet, he hoped that Fletcher was dead.

Jerry alternated between running and walking, and he covered a lot of ground. Hours passed, and he was getting hungry. He was physically drained. The sun had gone down, and he wondered if his mother was home yet. Had she found out what he'd done? Had Fletcher gone to the hospital, or was he lying on the kitchen floor? Could Fletcher be dead? Could he really have killed him? Would the police lock him up and throw away the key? The possibilities scared him.

He recognized Mrs. Jackson's home in the distance. Mrs. Myra Jackson was a friend of his mother. She was twice divorced, and she was on her third marriage. Her husband, Lester, was a slender man, and Mrs. Jackson was literally three times his size. Lester was very quiet, and he had a gentle spirit. He was the complete opposite of his wife, who was loud spoken, outgoing and sociable.

Jerry realized that he had two options. He could either sleep underneath a tree or knock on Mrs. Jackson's door. The night breeze was rustling the leaves, and the temperature was likely going to drop further. His cotton shirt was not enough to keep him warm. His stomach was growling, and he needed something to eat and a place to lay his head for the night. Meanwhile, he would figure out his next step. He needed to get as far away from Fletcher as possible.

Jerry took a deep breath and walked up to Mrs. Jackson's door. He opened the screen door and knocked on the door. He knocked again, and after several seconds, a light from the living room came through the window. An irritated female voice inquired who was at the door, and Jerry identified himself. The door opened, and Mrs. Jackson, who was a rather large woman, was in view. She had on a long floral night gown and pink slippers, and it was evident that she was not wearing a bra. Gravity had taken full effect. She had pink rollers in her hair that were secured with a hair net.

Mrs. Jackson pointed out to Jerry that it was late and inquired what he was doing on her side of town. Jerry lied to Mrs. Jackson and told her that he'd been out with friends and had lost track of time. He then realized it was getting dark, and he had no way of getting home. It was too late for him to walk home alone. Mrs. Jackson suggested calling his mother to inform her of his where-abouts, but Jerry informed her that his mother would still be at work. Jerry asked if he could sleep on her couch for the night, and he would be on his way in the morning. Mrs. Jackson obliged. Her husband was already sleeping.

She made Jerry a bologna and cheese sandwich and poured him a glass of sweet tea. She brought him a pillow and placed a folded blanket on the couch. She gave him a lecture and advised him to be more cognizant of the time in the future. She pointed out that a young boy should not be out of the house at these hours of the night. She expected that his mother would be worried sick when she found out that he was not at home in his bed. Mrs. Jackson inquired about the company he was keeping and had questions about his friends. After several rounds of questioning, Mrs. Jackson retired to bed.

Jerry tossed and turned all night. He drifted in and out of sleep. He had visions of Fletcher's face when he closed his eyes, and awoke in a cold sweat. He lay awake for an uncertain amount of time. He envisioned a life outside of Greenville. He wanted a life outside of Mississippi. What would be his next step? He had no money. He did not have a penny in his pocket. How would he carry out a plan to leave Mississippi without money? He had limited time to figure this out before he was on his way.

Jerry awoke to a knock at the door. He was lying on a couch about ten feet away from the door. He immediately jumped up from the couch in a panic. It was dawn outside. Mrs. Jackson emerged from one of the rooms wearing her floral night gown and pink slippers. The rollers were still in her hair, though a couple were falling out. As she was walking to the door, she informed Jerry that she had called his mother's house about twenty minutes ago to notify her of his whereabouts. She stated that Fletcher had answered the phone and he'd said he would relay the information to his mother.

Mrs. Jackson opened the door and was surprised to see the police at the door. One of the officers inquired if Jerry Frye was in the home. Jerry immediately took off running and bolted through the back door, which was observed by the police officers. He'd had no time to put on his shoes.

One of the police officers, who had a muscular frame, ran through the house, following Jerry. The other police officer, who was lanky in appearance, ran around the house to the back. Jerry stumped his right big toe forcefully on a jagged rock jutting out of the soil. He went face down onto the ground. The police officer who'd followed him through the house apprehended him. His hands were placed in handcuffs behind his back.

Mrs. Jackson emerged through the back door, and she was horrified. She was speechless for a moment, which was unusual for Mrs. Jackson. She then demanded to know what was going on. The officer who had apprehended Jerry notified Mrs. Jackson of the charges. Jerry was accused of aggravated assault with a deadly weapon. The officer also informed Jerry of his rights. Mrs. Jackson was in disbelief. She stood up for Jerry, informing the officers that he was a good boy.

Lester had awoken from his sleep and came to the door to witness the commotion. He was alarmed to see Jerry in handcuffs. Mrs. Jackson updated her husband in a low voice. Both officers helped Jerry to his feet. Jerry's right big toe was painful and throbbing, and a trickle of blood escaped from a wound created by the injury. The front of his shirt and his pants were soiled. He was patted down by the lanky officer, who found and removed a wad of cash from his pants pocket. The officer asked him where he'd gotten the cash. Jerry did not answer. His head was hung in shame. He caught a glimpse of Mrs. Jackson, who was staring straight at him. Mrs. Jackson went back into her house and entered the kitchen. She reached into the top cupboard and grabbed a can that had previously contained soup. The can was empty. The money was gone. She stormed back out and accused Jerry of being a little thief. Jerry was ashamed. Lester, who was usually very quiet, echoed his wife's disdain and referred to him as a little thief.

He had not wanted to steal from Mrs. Jackson. He'd had no money, and he'd felt as if he'd had no other choice. He'd once overheard Mrs. Jackson giving advice to his mother. She'd advised his mother to keep money that was stored at home in containers that a thief would never suspect. Mrs. Jackson had surprisingly admitted that she stored extra money in a container in the kitchen. This advice had come after Jerry's mother had lied about someone breaking into her house and stealing the money she had hidden underneath the mattress. The thief was Fletcher, and his mother knew it.

The lanky officer gave Mrs. Jackson back the money. Jerry now had a charge of theft against him. Mrs. Jackson's eyes were fixed on him as he was led away by the officers. If looks could kill, he would have been dead. The lanky officer retrieved Jerry's shoes as he was brought barefooted by the other officer to the police car. Jerry was placed in the back seat of the car, and the lanky officer drove off.

Jerry was taken into custody. Due to the gravity of the offense, he was detained in the county jail and was separated from the adult inmates. He was assigned a probation officer. He remained in the jail for about six hours before he was transported to meet with the probation officer, with whom a juvenile assessment was completed. The assessment incorporated details of the crimes committed. The assault charge with a deadly weapon was considered a felony charge. The theft charge was considered a misdemeanor.

The probation officer had also received a statement obtained from Fletcher. Fletcher had accused Jerry of being a bad kid with a nasty temper. He stated that Jerry had a rotten attitude and had no respect for authority. Fletcher reported that Jerry was quickly going down the wrong path. He revealed that Jerry had been caught smoking cigarettes and marijuana. Fletcher reported that on the afternoon of the stabbing, he'd wanted to have a mature conversation with Jerry about the identity of his father. He'd wanted Jerry to know that he loved him and he would be there as a father if he needed him. Fletcher reported that after he'd told Jerry the secret about his father, Jerry had become enraged and threatened to kill him. He reported that Jerry had grabbed a knife and stabbed him in the arm before running out of the house.

Jerry was getting angry as he learned about Fletcher's fabricated story. He acknowledged in his mind that he'd been smoking cigarettes and marijuana, but everything else that Fletcher had reported was a big fat lie. He was not a troublemaker at home. He was deathly afraid of Fletcher, and he went to great lengths to avoid him. He spent most of his time locked up in his bedroom when he was at home. Prior to the stabbing that had led to his arrest, he had never been in trouble with the law.

Jerry was informed that Fletcher's medical condition was stable. He'd been brought to the emergency room by a neighbor, with the knife still embedded in his arm. The emergency room physician had been able to stop the bleeding. The wound had been closed, and he'd been sent home with antibiotics and pain pills.

After hearing that Fletcher was okay, Jerry realized that he was getting angrier by the moment. He thought that he would be relieved, but it was the complete opposite. He tried to suppress his emotions, but he became more infuriated. He felt as if he was going to explode. Almost subconsciously, he blurted out his hatred for Fletcher. He accused Fletcher of being a liar, and he wished that Fletcher was dead. The probation officer was shocked at the outburst. The officer deemed Jerry to be a danger to the public, and he was ordered to remain in a detention facility and appear before a juvenile court judge.

Jerry stood before a judge the following day for his detention hearing, and he was sworn in. The judge informed Jerry of his constitutional rights and his right to an attorney. The judge reiterated the charges set forth against him in addition to the testimony of the probation officer. Given the severe allegations, it was determined that Jerry would be held in a secure detention facility while awaiting his next court date, which was set for a plea.

The juvenile detention center was a large brick building surrounded by a chain-link fence topped with barbed wire. The inside of the building was cold and depressing. The walls were painted white, and there was a peculiar smell that greeted him upon entry into the facility. It was an unpleasant odor that he could not describe. There were visible cameras throughout the building. Jerry was informed of the rules and regulations of the facility. He was strip-searched by the correctional officer. He was ordered to take a shower, and he was given a khaki detention uniform.

Jerry was given an opportunity to contact his mother, but he refused. He was angry at his mother. He was almost as angry with her as he was with Fletcher. Fletcher was a nobody to him. Fletcher was a complete waste of space. He was a poor excuse of a human being. His mother, on the other hand, should have protected him. Her blood ran through his veins. She should have never allowed Fletcher into the house. She should have never made excuses for him time and time again. She was probably still making excuses for him. She probably believed Fletcher's version of the story. Now Fletcher was at the house healing from his injuries. His mother was probably waiting on him hand and foot. She was likely attending to his every need. If Jerry had owned a dollar, he would have bet that Fletcher was in front of the television with a beer in his good hand. Meanwhile, he was locked up in a facility with no means of escape. He would have to wait until his next court date. He had no one. He felt betrayed and abandoned. He felt rejected. His own mother had rejected him.

Thirteen days later, Jerry had his first court date. The bailiff escorted him in handcuffs into the courtroom. His mother was seated in the courtroom. She was the only spectator present. He made eye contact with his mother and quickly looked away. His handcuffs were removed, and he sat next to his lawyer, who'd been appointed to him. The prosecutor sat at an adjacent table in the courtroom. The bailiff took his place, and the judge was front and center.

The judge appeared to be in his early sixties. He was a heavyset white male with salt-and-pepper hair, and he wore his reading spectacles on the tip of his nose. There was no one else present in the room. Jerry was asked by the judge to stand and raise his right hand, and he was sworn in. Jerry took his seat. The judge informed Jerry of the charges filed against him. He was told that one of the charges against him was very serious. The judge informed him that a conviction of assault with a deadly weapon was a felony and he could face the possibility of state prison. The judge noted that Jerry could possibly be tried as an adult. Jerry acknowledged that he understood the charges. He was asked by the judge to enter a plea. He entered a plea of no contest.

Jerry's appointed attorney was a slender white male who appeared to be in his late thirties. His name was Lance Braiseworth. He had dark brown hair and was clean shaven. He stated that his client had no previous arrests or encounters with the law. He communicated to the judge that placement in an adult system would only be detrimental to his client. He stated that his client would not receive the treatment and the rehabilitation that he needed if he was sentenced to an adult prison. The attorney urged the judge to consider a juvenile detention facility that would help to rehabilitate his client.

The prosecutor was a black male of average height. He appeared to be in his early forties. He had a light beard and wore glasses. His name was Marcus Jones. Mr. Jones acknowledged that this was the defendant's first arrest and encounter with the law, and he also acknowledged that one of the charges filed was a felony. Mr. Jones agreed that an adult system would be disadvantageous, and he agreed that the defendant should receive rehabilitation. He requested that the defendant be fingerprinted and DNA obtained given the fact that a felony had been committed. Mr. Jones agreed that the defendant should be sentenced to a detention center.

The judge summarized the statements of the defense attorney and the prosecutor. The judge sentenced Jerry to fourteen months at a juvenile detention facility. The bailiff approached Jerry and escorted him out of the courtroom in handcuffs. Jerry did not look in the direction of his mother. He was transported back to the juvenile detention facility.

––––––––

Jerry turned seventeen shortly after his sentence commenced at the detention facility. There was no cake or candles. But then again, he'd never had a birthday cake. A birthday was just another day in his household. There was no cause for celebration. Jerry was notified by one of the guards that his mother had come to visit, but he refused to meet with her. He was delivered an envelope from his mother that appeared to contain a card. The front of the envelope had lettering in black ink that read "Happy Birthday Jerry." He stared at the envelope for a few seconds while he sat on his bed. Without opening it, he tossed the letter to the side. He lay on his bed with his hands behind his head and stared up at the ceiling. He began the countdown to his day of freedom.

Life at the detention center was rigid. The facility housed only juvenile boys, and he was confined to pod C. His cell contained a cot bed anchored to the wall and the ground, with a thin mattress. The bedding was changed every Saturday, and the juveniles were expected to make up their beds every morning. The cell also had a toilet that was adjoined to the sink. There was a square table made of wood adjoined to the wall in a perpendicular manner that served as a desk. A few inches beyond the desk was a wooden stool affixed to the ground. There was a small window at the back wall of the cell with vertical steel bars. The view through the window revealed a barbed wire fence that reminded Jerry of his loss of freedom. Beyond the barbed wire fence was an expanse of grass towards the horizon. The solid door of the cell had a window that allowed the guards to observe him from the outside.

He and the other juveniles were awoken by guards at 6:30 am sharp every morning. They were allowed one short shower daily, and clean facility clothing was provided on a daily basis. This included clean underwear, socks, a t-shirt, and a towel. The juveniles were led through the electronically secured doors that separated the pods from the hallways, and they were ushered to the cafeteria. Breakfast was served in the cafeteria at 7 am. After breakfast, the juveniles were taken to the school room, and classes started at 7:30 am. There were bathroom breaks incorporated into the schedule. There was a lunch break followed by classes in the afternoon.

After classes, they were allowed some free time. The juveniles were taken outdoors within the confines of the razor wire fence, and they were monitored closely by the guards. Most of the juveniles opted to play basketball. Others huddled in small groups as they laughed and joked around. It was evident that there were some cliques that had formed. Jerry sat alone on a bench and read through the pages of a book on business and finance. He'd found the book tucked away on one of the shelves in the library. Jerry was gifted in math. He loved numbers. He did not know what it was like to have money, but he envisioned himself with money. He envisioned his life someday in a big city managing large amounts of money. He occasionally looked up from the pages and observed the basketball game. Two teenagers on the court got into a fight over the ball. Two guards ran onto the court and separated the boys, and the boys were removed from the court by the guards.

Jerry refocused on the words in the book. After several more minutes of reading, his book was forcefully knocked out of his hands by someone's hand. The book hit the pavement, which bent a few of the pages. Jerry looked up, and there was a tall white boy casting a shadow over him. The act seemed to have gone unnoticed by the guards. The bully had a wide grin on his face that revealed his poor dentition. He had straggly shoulder-length brown hair and facial stubble. His neck was wide, and his shoulders were broad. He was known at the facility as Big Harry. He was reportedly seventeen years old, but he looked twenty-seven. He relished his ability to cast fear in his fellow inmates. He heckled Jerry about reading a book in his free time. In a strong Southern drawl, he called Jerry a sissy and a wimp, which made Big Harry erupt in laughter.

There were two other juvenile boys who seemed to emerge from the shadows of Big Harry. One was a black boy with light skin and unkempt braided hair. The other boy was white with curly red hair, and his face was covered with freckles. The two boys laughed at Jerry as Big Harry continued to jeer at him. Jerry did not know how to react. He was frozen in fear, and he wanted the ridiculing to end. After repeated rounds of taunting, Big Harry seemed content and moved on to his next victim, and his two sidekicks followed closely behind. Jerry picked up his book and dusted it off.

At 5 pm, the juveniles were led into the cafeteria for dinner. The juveniles were a mixture of whites, blacks, and a small percentage of Hispanics. They sat with their respected cliques. Jerry took a plate that had a serving of carved turkey, mashed potatoes with gravy, a side of green beans, and a roll. He placed the plate on a tray with sweet tea, and he sat down at a table in the corner of the room. A fellow juvenile sat at his table uninvited. He was a slender black boy, about five foot eight. He introduced himself to Jerry as Gregory Wilson, but he went by Greg. He tried to make small talk, but Jerry was not interested. He had no desire to make friends. He wanted to finish his sentence and get out of the confines of the juvenile detention center. Despite Jerry's dismissiveness, Greg continued his line of questioning. He asked Jerry why he was in "juvy," but Jerry did not reply. He just stared at Greg and took a big bite of his roll.

Jerry looked around and observed the other juveniles. The boys appeared to have made friends. There was loud laughter and intense discussions. At an adjacent table, there was a discussion in which the juveniles were ranking the hottest actresses on television. They each argued their point, making their fellow inmates laugh uncontrollably. The discussion, at one point, became very vulgar. Some of the boys agreed with each other, and some were in opposition. At another table, towards the center of the cafeteria, Big Harry sat with his two sidekicks and two other boys. Big Harry was obviously the center of attention. His audience appeared to laugh at anything that came out of his mouth. There were other tables at which boys were interacting.

Jerry refocused on Greg, who was staring directly at him. Jerry figured that he might as well make friends, as he would be in juvy for what appeared to be an eternity. He answered Greg's question. He told him that he'd stabbed his mother's boyfriend and stolen from his mom's friend. Jerry asked Greg the same question. Greg revealed that he'd been caught shoplifting at a clothing store downtown and the cops had discovered weed on him. He'd been sentenced to juvenile detention for twelve months, and he had already served two months.

Greg asked about Jerry's parents. After a brief pause, Jerry stated that he did not know his father. Jerry noticed that he was starting to get angry as he recalled the revelation of his mother's rape by Fletcher. He envisioned Fletcher sitting on the couch, drinking a beer, and watching television. The thought made him sick to his stomach, and he started to lose his appetite. He took a deep breath and tried to remove Fletcher from his thoughts. He told Greg that he did not have a mother. He stated that his mother had rejected and abandoned him.

Greg revealed that his parents had divorced when he was six years old, and he had not seen his father since then. He admitted that his mother was addicted to crack cocaine, and he too felt as if he did not have a mother. Greg stated that most of the boys in the facility had very difficult upbringings. He revealed that Big Harry's father had shot his mother dead in a fit of jealousy when he'd come home early from work and found her in bed with the neighbor. Big Harry's father had then turned the gun on himself. Big Harry was an only child, and he'd only been ten years old when the murder-suicide had occurred. Big Harry had been taken in by an aunt, but his aunt hadn't been able to tolerate his behavior. He was smoking cigarettes, drinking alcohol, and he was constantly getting in trouble with the law. He had offenses that included vandalizing public property and fighting in a public place, and he'd also been arrested for stealing a bicycle leaning against a lamppost outside a convenience store.

Greg shared stories with Jerry about his life in the detention center over the past two months. He spoke about "the hole," which was solitary confinement. A juvenile was placed in the hole if he acted out or if he was at risk of harming himself or fellow juveniles and staff. It was a padded cell located directly off of the control room. The youth would be under twenty-four-hour direct supervision. A psychological evaluation would then be put in place, and the youth would also be screened for suicidal thoughts. A conflict resolution was required before the juvenile was able to go back to his cell and interact with the other juveniles. Greg pointed out some of the juveniles that spent time in the hole. Greg had never experienced the hole, and he did not plan to experience it.

Greg gave Jerry background information on the other juveniles. He revealed the crimes that some of them had committed and that had landed them in juvy. He described some of their personalities and advised Jerry of the juveniles to avoid. He particularly warned Jerry about Darryl Greene. Darryl had a very tough exterior, but he had an eye for the boys. Greg revealed that Darryl had once made a pass at him, but he had been able to escape his unwanted advances. Jerry absorbed all of the information that Greg provided. He was also happy that he'd made himself a new friend.

The guards announced that dinnertime was over. The boys were led back to their cells in their respective pods. A snack was provided at 8 pm. Jerry brushed his teeth, washed his face, and got ready for bed. The day was almost over, and he would be one day closer to freedom.

Jerry awoke the following morning to the same routine. After breakfast, the juveniles were led into the classroom. Classes were from 7:30 am to 3 pm, with scheduled breaks. Ms. Jenny Meloncamp was one of the teachers, and she taught language arts and social studies. She also taught the students how to construct a resume and job interviewing skills. Mr. Pierce Rogers taught math and computer skills. Mr. Bernard James, who was also a counselor, taught personal development and social skills. Mr. James's curriculum included anger control and behavioral modification. The juveniles also had study hall, in which they were expected to do their homework.

It was evident to the teachers that Jerry was an intelligent boy. He grasped concepts very quickly, and his ability surpassed the other boys. Ms. Meloncamp and Mr. Rogers gave Jerry more advanced work and additional assignments tailored to his needs and ability. Jerry spent a good portion of his free time in the library. He enjoyed reading books and would read any book he got his hands on. He would often help his buddy Greg with his homework during study hall.

Greg and Jerry became very good friends, and they spoke often about their plans once they got out of juvy. Greg hoped to get his GED and go to vocational school. He wanted to be a mechanical engineering technician. Jerry wanted to get his GED and go to a career college. He planned to study business administration and then pursue an MBA. Jerry envisioned himself working for a firm on Wall Street. He pictured an adult version of himself in a sharp black suit, driving a nice expensive car, and living in a condo in Manhattan. Until then, he would have to complete his time in juvy.

Jerry was in the library, reading a book in the corner of the room. Darryl Greene sat next to him and invaded his personal space. Darryl introduced himself and extended his right hand towards Jerry. Darryl's hand floated in the air for several seconds before Jerry reluctantly shook his hand. Jerry introduced himself and then buried his head back in his book. Darryl proceeded to talk, and he asked if they could be friends. Jerry lowered his book and stared at Darryl. He was very dark-skinned, which contrasted the whiteness of his teeth as he grinned. Jerry replied that he was not interested in making friends and he wanted to be left alone. Darryl did not take the cue to leave, and he tried to convince Jerry that they all need friends to survive juvy. Jerry closed his book, stood up, and walked out of the library. After that incident, he went out of his way to avoid Darryl.

During a lunch hour, Jerry was standing in line in the cafeteria. Greg was in front of him, and they were engaged in conversation. Unbeknownst to Jerry, Darryl had fallen in line behind him. Darryl brushed his hand over Jerry's rear end. Jerry turned around and locked eyes with Darryl, who was wearing a broad grin. An intense anger erupted in him, and he punched Darryl in the face, knocking him to the ground. Jerry got on top of him and continued punching him repeatedly until blood started to spatter. Some of the juveniles were cheering him on. Greg tried unsuccessfully to pull Jerry off of Darryl. The guards rushed to Darryl's rescue and tore Jerry away from him. Darryl's face was covered in blood, and he moaned as he lay helpless on the floor.

Jerry was placed in the hole. Darryl was brought to the hospital, where he was found to have a broken nose. The doctor apparently was able to realign the bones and cartilage in his nose. Darryl had tremendous facial bruising and a facial laceration above his left eyebrow that required stitches. Darryl was instructed to apply ice packs or cold compresses to reduce the swelling. He was advised to take anti-inflammatory medications for the pain.

Jerry was under close supervision while in solitary confinement. The walls and the floor were padded, including the inside of the solid-steel door. The door had an observation port that allowed the staff to have a full view of the occupant. The isolation room was also under constant video surveillance. Jerry felt like a helpless caged animal. He remained in confinement for twenty-two hours each day. He was allowed out of his cell to take a shower and to briefly get some fresh air. He was closely guarded during that narrow window of time that he was out of the padded cell. His meals were provided to him in his cell.

Jerry had virtually no human interaction, and he felt as if he was going crazy. He was not allowed to attend classes or interact with the other juveniles. It was just him and the confines of the padded cell. He was not provided reading material to pass the time. The minutes and hours seemed frozen in time. He did not know when it was day or night. His emotions became a roller coaster, with unexpected twist and turns. He found himself screaming and kicking aimlessly at the padded walls. He sometimes screamed for hours, until his vocal cords were fatigued and the sounds would not escape. The heightened screams often alerted the guards, who would bang vigorously on the steel door. The guards would instruct him to stop screaming. He would then fall into a deep depression and curl himself into a ball in one of the corners of the cell. He would cry until he could no longer produce tears. He could not go any longer under solitary confinement, and death seemed like a better option. The mental, emotional, and physical stress took an extreme toll on his body, and he started to feel numb. He was held in solitary confinement for fourteen days, but it felt like an eternity.

After two weeks of solitary confinement, Jerry was evaluated by Ms. Gina Lall in a closely guarded room. The room also had video surveillance. Ms. Lall was one of the juvenile detention counselors. She was a very attractive woman with long strawberry blonde hair. She asked Jerry to recount the fight between himself and Darryl. Jerry detailed the fight and revealed the specifics leading up to the altercation. Jerry was rather calm and dismissive as he summarized the incident, and it was evident that he was putting up an emotional wall as a defense mechanism. Ms. Lall was determined to break that wall down. She encouraged him to acknowledge his emotions, but he was reluctant and remained quiet.

Ms. Lall was gentle and patient. She tried to reassure him that her goal was to offer support and direction. She acknowledged that Jerry was experiencing hurt and deep emotional pain. She challenged him to confront his emotions and embrace new, healthy emotions.

Several minutes passed by in silence. Finally, Jerry broke the silence, admitting that he felt angry and bitter. He was angry at his mother and his current situation. He was angry at the world. Jerry's eyes were squinted, his lips were pursed, and his body was tense. Ms. Lall listened intently as he spoke, and she observed his facial expressions, tone of voice, and body movements.

Ms. Lall affirmed that anger was a normal human emotion and often masked another emotion. She was quick to point out that anger could be destructive once it became irrational and got out of control. Ms. Lall asked Jerry about his upbringing. Jerry was very hesitant at first to divulge this information, but Ms. Lall's encouraging voice allowed him to be more vulnerable. Jerry's body relaxed, and his body was almost in a drooping state. His lips occasionally trembled as he spoke, and he tried to suppress his tears. He expressed to Ms. Lall that he missed his brother Robert and stated that his brother was the only person he had in the world. Jerry stated that he'd been extremely close to his brother growing up and looked up to him. He'd heard from his brother once, through a letter, after his brother had left for college. It had been more than four years since he'd had any correspondence with his brother.

Jerry and Ms. Lall spoke for almost three hours, during which Jerry had a brief bathroom break. Ms. Lall felt that some bricks had been removed from the wall that Jerry had created around himself. Ms. Lall gave him exercises to do. She encouraged him to keep an anger journal and to document his emotions in the journal. She told him that she would get him a journal to document his emotional journey and progress. Ms. Lall encouraged him to be specific by identifying the cause of his anger, how he reacted to the situation, how it made him feel afterwards, and what he could do differently if he was placed in a similar situation. She also demonstrated relaxation techniques, such as breathing exercises. Ms. Lall encouraged Jerry to practice the act of substituting negative thoughts with positive thoughts. She conveyed to him that the changes would not occur overnight, but required practice. Jerry was receptive to Ms. Lall's recommendations, and he verbalized that he never wanted to be placed in the hole again. It had been a traumatic experience that he would never want to revisit.

Ms. Lall was sympathetic towards Jerry. She realized that a lot of his negative emotions stemmed from deep pain that caused him to act out. Ms. Lall had worked as a counselor at the detention facility for almost eight years, and she had counseled hundreds of juvenile boys. She had genuine compassion for the boys at the facility, and she wanted to have a positive impact in their lives. She did see progress in some of the juvenile boys, but there were some boys who were resistant to change. It gave her great pride when she heard of success stories where juveniles made positive changes in their lives upon release from the facility. Unfortunately, there was a significant percentage of boys that got themselves into trouble again after being released just to find themselves back in juvenile detention.

Ms. Lall concluded that Jerry was ready to go back to his original cell block and integrate with the other boys. She did not like the idea of solitary confinement for juveniles, as she believed that this form of punishment could cause adverse psychological effects. The facility had made progress, as juveniles had previously been held in solitary confinement for a month or even longer. Now the maximum amount of time that a juvenile could be held in solitary confinement was two weeks. This posed a challenge in identifying the proper disciplinary actions for a misbehaving juvenile while considering the safety of the other juveniles and staff.

As much as Jerry despised being locked up in a juvenile detention facility, he was happy to be out of solitary confinement and back on his cell block with the other boys. It felt strangely like semi-freedom, given the alternative. He was happy to see his friend Greg, and as always, Greg wanted to get the scoop. He wanted to know all of the details of Jerry's experience in the hole.

Jerry recounted the emotional agony of the past two weeks. He referred to the experience as a prison inside of a prison. Greg admitted that he'd missed his buddy and he was glad that Jerry was out of solitary confinement. He updated Jerry on the day-to-day occurrences while he'd been in the hole. Big Harry was still Big Harry, and he and his loyal sidekicks continued to heckle and tease the boys that were perceived as weak. Darryl was one of the victims that Big Harry targeted. Big Harry and some of the other boys reminded him daily about the punches that had sent him to the emergency room. It was still just as amusing to the bullies as it had been on the day that the altercation had occurred.

On a brighter note, Greg stated that he was keeping himself occupied by studying for his GED. The friends made plans to resume studying together at the library the following day. Jerry had missed classes for the day, and it was time to head to the cafeteria for dinner. The scene was the same as it had been before he was placed in solitary confinement. It was the same spectacle, just a different day. The boys were divided into their respective cliques. The talking and laughter filled the room of the cafeteria, and Jerry welcomed the noise. It surely beat having three meals a day alone while locked up in a small space.

Big Harry stood up out of his seat and grabbed the attention of Jerry from across the cafeteria. In a raised voice, he directed his speech towards Jerry and congratulated him for "knocking Darryl's lights out." The noise in the room subsided, and the attention was directed between Big Harry and Jerry. Big Harry ridiculed Darryl, who was sitting at a table alone in the corner of the cafeteria. There were bursts of laughter throughout the room. Once Big Harry felt that his jeering had taken effect, he moved onto a discussion amongst his friends at his table. The other boys refocused on their previous conversations.

Darryl's head hung low, and he barely touched his food. Jerry had caught a closer glimpse of Darryl earlier, and though his skin was dark, there were signs of bruising evident on his face. There was a laceration above his left eyebrow that was healing.

The following morning, Jerry followed the same routine. After breakfast, the juveniles were led into their classes. He enjoyed getting back in the books. He and his friend Greg were determined to make something of their lives.

Night came, and day came again. The days, weeks, and months passed, and Jerry was getting closer to freedom.

Greg's time in juvy was winding down. Greg had taken the GED exam and passed. He had started the application process to get into a vocational school. He hoped to get into a program with the goal of becoming a mechanical engineering technician. Greg had his release interview, and it was unanimously decided amongst the members of the panel that he was ready to be released. Greg was ecstatic about the news. It had been a long road, but his time at the detention facility was coming to an end. He could clearly see the light at the end of the tunnel. Greg's aunt and uncle were scheduled to pick him up the next morning. As happy as Jerry was for his friend, he was also saddened. He was going to miss his friend tremendously. It was a bittersweet moment. The friends made plans to stay in touch. Jerry had no one but Greg when the time came for him to be released from juvy. Greg promised to pick him up from juvy after the completion of his stay.

Greg had breakfast for one last time with the group of boys. Several of the boys approached him and wished him luck. Jerry embraced his friend, and they reassured each other that they would remain in touch. Jerry watched as Greg was escorted out of the room by a guard. He looked forward to the day when he would be escorted out of the walls of the facility. He had four more months to go before he was eligible for release.

Jerry had made some other friends among the juvenile boys in the facility, but these were not the same as the friendship that he had formed with Greg. He stayed mainly to himself, and he spent a good portion of his free time in the library. Jerry took interest in Mr. Bernard James's classes. Mr. James was a counselor who taught personal development and social skills. He wanted to raise self-esteem in the boys. He encouraged them to take responsibility for their actions. He urged the boys to stop blaming others for their decisions and misfortunes in life and challenged them to take control of their lives.

Mr. Bernard James was a light-skinned black male, and he had dark curly hair and striking hazel eyes. He appeared to be of mixed race. Jerry looked up to him with strong admiration. Mr. James was old enough to be his father, and Jerry envisioned him as the father he never had. He often sought advice from Mr. James.

Jerry was struggling to deal with rejection. He felt as though he'd been rejected his entire life. He realized that a lot of his anger stemmed from the hurt of deep emotional wounds caused by the feeling of rejection. He did not feel loved, and he had a hard time loving himself. Mr. James's advice to him was to learn forgiveness. He urged Jerry to forgive everyone in life who had hurt him along the way, especially his mother. He also urged Jerry to forgive himself. Mr. James warned him that if he refused to forgive himself and others, he would forever remain imprisoned, even after release from the confines of the detention facility. Mr. James inquired whether he believed in God. Jerry stated that he did not know if there was a God. He wanted to believe in a higher power, but he had a hard time accepting this idea. Mr. James encouraged him to meet with Father Angelino. He was a Catholic priest who periodically made visitations to the detention facility. Jerry heard of Father Angelino and knew that he offered pastoral services to the juvenile boys who were interested. There was a small percentage of boys who were willing to receive pastoral care, but Jerry was not one of them. However, he had a change of heart. If Mr. James recommended that he meet with Father Angelino, then that's exactly what he was going to do.

Father Angelino was born in the Italian town of Montalcino in Tuscany. He was in his late sixties. He'd dedicated the majority of his life to the service of others and traveled to several countries as an evangelist. He'd spent a significant amount of time in countries such as Vietnam, Cambodia, Uganda, and the island nation of Haiti. He'd also done a lot of spiritual work through several towns in his native Italy. As he'd advanced in age, his evangelic travels had slowed down. He was now a priest at St. James Catholic Church downtown. He frequently visited the boys' and girls' juvenile detention facilities to offer spiritual guidance and direction.

It was a Saturday, and Jerry had his first meeting with Father Angelino. He did not know what to expect. The word "God" was not a word mentioned in his house much growing up. The one and only time he recalled stepping foot in a church was when he'd attended the funeral of Nana Violet, his mother's mother.

Father Angelino greeted Jerry with a warm smile. He was about five foot six, and his hair was fully gray. In a thick Italian accent, he congratulated Jerry on taking the first step towards learning about God and hopefully building a relationship with God. They sat at a round table. Father Angelino asked Jerry about himself. He asked Jerry about his family, his upbringing, and his life growing up. He asked Jerry about the path he had taken that had led him to where he was at the moment. Jerry had divulged this information to Ms. Lall and Mr. James. Somehow, it was a little bit easier to share this information with Father Angelino.

Father Angelino wanted to know what was important to him in life and the type of person he wanted to be. Jerry admitted that he wanted to get as far away from his old life as possible. He wanted to leave Mississippi and become successful. Father Angelino was curious about Jerry's definition of success and asked him to explain. Jerry stated that he wanted to be in a profession that made him a lot of money. He wanted to be well respected and to make it to the top. He wanted to eventually get married and have children. He vowed to be a better parent to his child than his mother was to him.

There was a brief moment of silence. Father Angelino broke the silence and asked Jerry his feelings about spirituality and making moral choices. Jerry did not know how to answer the question, and he stuttered an incoherent response. Father Angelino advised him that it was just as important to nurture the spiritual component of his being as it was to nourish his body with food. He encouraged Jerry to develop a relationship with God and emphasized that a relationship takes time, persistence, and effort to build. Father Angelino described God as loving and kind. He looked directly into Jerry's eyes and slowly stated, "God loves you." Jerry was dubious and questioned Father Angelino's words. Jerry asked that if he was loved by God, then why had so many bad things happened to him? Why was he hurting? Why was he locked up?

Father Angelino gave Jerry another warm smile. He revealed that faith in God did not mean that the road would be paved smoothly. He told Jerry that there would be a lot of valleys along the way but God would carry him through. Father Angelino confidently stated that God guaranteed a perfect eternity for those who loved Him and did what was right. He went on to state that God gave every person a choice. Father Angelino noted that moral laws were written on human hearts and were universal. He stated that human beings know right from wrong, and he challenged Jerry to love his enemies and those who hurt him. He warned Jerry that whatever choices he made in life, he must be willing to deal with the consequences.

Jerry spoke with the priest for over two hours. At the conclusion of their discussion, Father Angelino reached into his bag and gave Jerry a black leather-bound Bible. He opened the pages to Psalm 23 and instructed Jerry to read it and memorize it. Father Angelino invited him to church after he was released from the juvenile detention facility. Jerry thanked Father Angelino as he accepted the Bible. It was a step in the right direction for him, but it was going to be a long road.

Jerry took his GED and passed. He discussed his plans with Mr. James to go to a four-year college. Mr. James provided him with material to study for the SAT, and he studied diligently. Four months passed, and he was ready for his release interview. The members of the panel congratulated him on making it through his stay at the detention facility. After Jerry's altercation with Darryl, he remained out of trouble, and several of the counselors and staff had positive things to say about him. The panel unanimously decided that he was ready to be released. Jerry could not contain his excitement. A huge weight was removed from off his shoulders, and he was less than twenty-four hours away from freedom.

After breakfast, Jerry was escorted out of the cafeteria by a guard. He was given his clothes that he'd worn upon entry into the facility. The clothes were washed and folded. He put on his clothes, which still fit him, though the shirt was a little tighter than what he'd remembered. He was escorted out of the building by a guard. Jerry felt as if he was in a dream. He prayed that it was not a dream. He took a deep breath and filled his lungs with air, and he felt the warm sunshine on his forehead. It was a beautiful day and a cloudless sky. He looked in the distance, and he spotted Greg waiting for him as he'd promised.

Greg playfully punched Jerry's shoulder and then gave him a hug. Jerry was excited to see his friend. He hopped into the passenger seat of Greg's old white Toyota Corolla. The exterior of the car had several rusty spots. The polyester seats were worn, and the passenger seat had a dark stain. Greg stated that he'd purchased the car for five hundred dollars at a used car dealership.

The two friends caught up on the last four months. Jerry tried to summarize the remainder of his stay after Greg had left, but Greg wanted to know every detail. Jerry divulged as much information that he could recall. He spoke about his meeting with

Father Angelino, and at that moment, he realized that he'd left his Bible underneath the bed in his cell. Jerry spoke about the advice that he'd received from the priest, and he told his friend that he'd been invited by Father Angelino to attend church service. The discussion later transitioned to Greg's life over the past four months. Greg had gotten into a two-year mechanical engineering program at a vocational school, and he was enjoying the hands-on skills he was receiving in the program. Greg had received financial aid and a grant, and he used the money towards his tuition and living expenses. He'd moved out of his aunt and uncle's house and moved into an apartment.

Greg turned his car down a main street, and there were dilapidated buildings in view. They drove past a dollar store and a consignment shop. Then Greg took a right onto Hancock street. He drove for about half a mile before making a left onto Hickory lane. There was a sign that read "Hickory Apartments," and Greg pulled into the parking lot of the building and then into a parking space. Greg admitted that the exterior of the building could use a fresh set of paint, but he was proud to call the building his home. This was the first time that he'd taken control of his life and accepted responsibilities.

Greg led his friend to his apartment. He fumbled with the key for a few seconds before successfully opening the door. He turned on a dim light, which revealed the paint peeling off of the walls. It was a small apartment with scant furniture. There was an upholstered couch that looked as though the seats were sunken in. Greg offered the couch to Jerry to sleep on. It was not going to be a comfortable sleep, but it sure beat the alternative. Greg showed Jerry the rest of the apartment. The kitchen was very small, with little room to navigate. The cupboards were old, and some of the knobs to the kitchen drawers were missing. Greg reached and opened one of the cupboards, which contained several cans and packets of ramen noodle soup. He told Jerry that he could help himself to the food. He then opened the fridge, which was almost bare. There was a carton of milk, several cans of Coca-Cola and condiments.

Greg proceeded to show Jerry his bedroom, which was also very small. Jerry stood outside the door and observed the room. The walls were painted a hideous shade of blue, and the paint was cracking. The ceiling revealed a water stain with a brown rim. The double bed, which seemed to take up most of the room, was unmade, and there were several items of clothing strewn across it. The side table to the left of the bed held up a lamp, an alarm clock that was blinking with the wrong time, and an opened can of Coca-Cola.

Greg exited his bedroom and directly across from the bedroom was a small bathroom. The sink had remnants of hair, which appeared to be from shaving. There was also a clump of blue toothpaste in the sink close to the drain. The shaver was on the countertop, and it was plugged into the wall. There were also several bathroom items occupying space on the countertop, which was already limited.

Greg apologized for the mess. Jerry welcomed the mess. He would rather sleep under a bridge than go back to juvy. Greg's small, dilapidated apartment was a much better deal than sleeping under a bridge. Jerry knew his lodging would only be temporary, and it was imperative that he find a way to support himself. His ultimate goal was to get into a college. Any college would be welcomed as long as it was out of the state of Mississippi. He'd done very well on his GED exam. He desperately wanted to leave his old life behind and begin a new chapter in his life. The first step in supporting himself was to get a job.

As Greg was preparing them a bowl of ramen noodles in the kitchen, Jerry sank himself into the couch. He picked up the newspaper that was sprawled across the center table. He paged immediately to the classified section and scrolled through job postings. He was willing to do any job as long as it put money in his pocket. There were a wide variety of jobs listed, but there were several jobs that he did not possess the skill set for. He did find some opportunities that were promising. There was a listing for a customer service representative job for a beauty supply company. There was a listing for a security job at the mall downtown. There were several cleaning jobs. There was also a position as a library assistant. Jerry also considered applying for a job at a fast-food restaurant or one of the local grocery stores.

Jerry gulped down the bowl of ramen noodles. He was still hungry, and he craved a juicy cheeseburger and french fries. The friends talked for hours and revisited their dreams. Jerry's first order of business the next day was to find a job and to find a job fast.

Jerry was hired as a cashier at a local grocery store. He was also hired for a weekend job as a library assistant, which benefited him. He had access to limitless books and materials while at work, and he used the opportunity to study for his SAT.

Jerry was thrilled when he received his first paycheck. He experienced a sense of pride and accomplishment. It was not much by any stretch of the imagination, but he'd earned it. The first thing he bought was a cheeseburger and fries at a popular spot downtown. His craving was satisfied as he sank his teeth into the mouthwatering burger.

Jerry bought groceries and filled Greg's fridge. He had eaten enough ramen noodles to last him a lifetime. He also paid the electrical bill for the month. As his paychecks became more consistent, he increased his contributions to the monthly bills and paid a portion of the rent. He also made sure he saved the remainder of his pay.

Jerry studied diligently in preparation for his SAT exam. He learned test-taking strategies and timed himself when taking a mock exam. The moment came when he sat down to take the exam. He was anxious, and he'd barely slept the night before. He'd tried desperately to fall asleep, but his nerves had been on edge. Jerry had tried to calm his thoughts by convincing himself that he was prepared. He'd eventually fallen asleep sometime during the middle of the night. After taking the exam, he felt surprisingly confident.

After weeks of anticipation, the SAT results were in the mail. Jerry placed the envelope on the center table in the living room. He paced back and forth before gaining the courage to open the envelope. He stared at the test results printed on the paper. His heart, which had been beating at a fast pace, felt as if it stopped momentarily. His jaw dropped as he beheld the words on the paper. His dropped jaw elevated and formed a wide grin. The anxiety escaped his body, and he was filled with elation. He screamed with excitement as he gleefully ran through the small apartment. He could not wait to tell Greg the good news. He'd scored a 1540 out of 1600 on the test. This was cause for celebration, and he planned to take Greg out to their favorite burger joint downtown.

Jerry started applying for scholarships. He applied to colleges in the surrounding states of Mississippi. A high school diploma was preferred by many of the colleges and universities, and it did not help that he had a juvenile record. Just for good measure, he applied to a college in New York. He could have considered a community college, but he was determined to go straight into a four-year college. Jerry obtained his transcript from the juvenile detention center. He had excellent grades and had earned a 4.0. He worked tirelessly on his application essay. His hard work paid off, and several weeks later, he received his first acceptance letter to a college in Shreveport, Louisiana. The hopes of leaving Mississippi had transformed into a reality. He did not care if he received acceptance letters from the other colleges that he'd applied to. He was on cloud nine, and he was heading to Shreveport.

After a couple of weeks, he was ready to make the move to Shreveport. Greg dropped him off at the bus station. The friends embraced each other, and then Jerry boarded the bus. He made his way down the middle of the bus before sitting at a window seat. He gazed down at Greg through the window and waved. He'd never had a friend like Greg, and he was eternally grateful.

The bus made its way to Shreveport, Louisiana. It made a few stops along the way, dropping off people and replacing the seats with new passengers. Jerry stared through the window as he observed the scenery. There were wide-open spaces of land, and it was imagery that mirrored his new sense of freedom. It was exciting, but at the same time, there was a fear of the unknown. Whatever his life would encounter, it had to be better than the life he was leaving behind in Mississippi. He propped his head back on the headrest, closed his eyes, and dreamt of his future.

The bus pulled into the station in Shreveport. Jerry gathered his black bag, which contained his life. He had some articles of clothing and toiletries, and hidden in an inside pocket was all of the money that he'd saved from his jobs. He took a local bus that dropped him off close to the college. He found a small apartment in close proximity to the college. Jerry went on the college campus. He felt as if he was in a dream and prayed that he would not wake up and find himself back in Mississippi. He applied for student loans and financial aid, and he signed up for college courses. The reality then set in that he was a college freshman. He was on the road to making his dreams a reality.

The following day, he went out and bought himself a used car. The passenger door was difficult to open, and there were several dents to the body of the vehicle. Despite it's less-than-ideal condition, it was a deal that he could not pass up. His friend Greg had taught him to drive. He looked at his Mississippi driver's license, which still had Greg's address on it. He looked at the person in the picture. It was a horrible picture, and it did not do him any justice. He thought to himself that he would replace the card with a Louisiana driver's license as soon as possible.

Jerry settled into his new apartment. It was just as small as Greg's apartment, but thankfully, it was in better condition. His classes did not start for another week, and he decided to take a road trip to New Orleans. It was a city that he'd always hoped to visit as a kid. He'd had a classmate in middle school whose family was from New Orleans. The boy, whose name escaped him at the moment, had spoken about New Orleans as though it was the greatest city in the world. It had been the first time that he'd heard about Mardi Gras.

Jerry ventured off to New Orleans. He admired the surrounding landscape as he drove in the direction of the city. His car took him through wetlands and swampy territory, and he took in every moment of his journey. It took him a little under six hours to reach his destination, which included rest stops. He got off the interstate at an exit that led him to the Central Business District of New Orleans. He made his way to Canal Street, and after driving around for several minutes, he decided to park his car in a paid parking lot. The city was bustling with people. He was already excited as he moved himself through the crowds. He stopped and peered through a store window that displayed Mardi Gras masks and t-shirts emblazoned with the words "New Orleans." There was an adjacent store that had a mannequin behind the window dressed up as a gypsy, with her headdress decorated with coins and wearing a free-flowing dress. The mannequin appeared to be staring into a crystal ball. He walked further down Canal Street and watched as a street car went by.

Jerry made his way through the French Quarter to Jackson Square. The square was full of entertainment, and there were street performers dancing and playing a variety of musical instruments. Several artists displayed their work along the square. Jerry watched as an artist sketched a woman on a canvas that was propped up on an easel. He observed the magnificent facade of the Cathedral-Basilica of Saint Louis, and the lawns surrounding the cathedral were impeccable. A horse connected to a carriage galloped through the streets and transported a middle-aged couple who were engaged in an embrace. Jerry crossed the street and joined the long line leading into Café du Monde. It was worth the wait as he indulged in a beignet and a hot cup of café au lait.

Jerry walked through the French Market and bought himself a souvenir. He continued his touring through the French Quarter. He passed a vagrant and his dog lying on the sidewalk. He maneuvered up and down the streets of the French Quarter and relished in the architecture. There were ironwork balconies adorned with plants, and the courtyards were comprised of lush greenery. He started to get hungry, and he walked into a restaurant with a sign that read "Cecile's Kitchen," and he was led to a seat by the window. His waiter was very friendly and energetic. Jerry proceeded to order Cecile's Shrimp Creole Classic, which was a dish highly recommended by the waiter. Jerry was not disappointed, and he savored every bite. The manager, who introduced herself as Genevieve Bellamy, inquired whether he had enjoyed the meal, and Jerry was very complimentary in his response. He paid for his meal and left the restaurant.

The sun started to set, and he made his way to Bourbon Street, which had a different vibe. The street was boisterous and possessed a party atmosphere. The street was lined with bars, restaurants, and strip clubs. He stopped in front of a club that advertised itself with a sign saying "Girls, Girls, Girls." He hesitated for a moment, but his curiosity got the better of him. He walked into the dim room and paid an entrance fee. His first sight was a topless woman gyrating seductively next to a pole. Jerry felt as if he had entered another world as he sat at a small round table. He observed the men in the room, and some were engaged in heavy talks and laughter as they consumed alcoholic beverages. There were others that lined themselves around the stage as they parted ways with their money. He also spotted a sprinkle of female customers throughout the room. There was a man towards the front of the room who appeared to be enjoying a lap dance. Jerry stayed at the club for a little over an hour before deciding to leave. He retrieved his car and checked into a cheap motel on the outskirts of the city. He made his way back to Shreveport the following morning.

CHAPTER 12

JERRY ENROLLED IN A BUSINESS TRACK IN COLLEGE. HE ENJOYED HIS CLASSES, AND HIS ritual was to go to the library after his last class for the day. He would spend roughly three hours at the library and then burn off some calories at the college gym. He noticed a gradual change in his physique as his efforts became more consistent. His biceps and quadriceps became more toned, and the ripples of his abdomen were more pronounced. He modified his diet and subscribed to the magazine *Healthy Living*. Jerry had developed an excitement about life, and he was optimistic about his future. He was friendly with some of his classmates, though he had not yet developed a close friendship with them as he had with Greg.

One Saturday, Jerry was driving down a side street, and his attention was drawn to a church sign that read "St. James Catholic Church." He was instantly reminded of Father Angelino and the invitation he'd received to attend a church service. A second sign, below the church sign, noted the hours of service. The Sunday church services were at 7:30 am and at 10 am. He decided to attend the 10 am service. He bought himself a pair of black slacks and a white short-sleeved button-down shirt. He also bought himself a cheap pair of black dress shoes.

The following morning, he prepared himself to go to church. He shaved off his light beard and then ironed his shirt and slacks. He arrived at the church ten minutes early. He walked through the church doors, and he was welcomed by the usher and given a program. Jerry felt like a fish out of water. The idea of going to church was a foreign concept. He sat on the last pew towards the right side of the church, and he observed the people walking into the church. They either walked in separately or in small groups as they filed into their pews. There was a family of four sitting three rows in front of him, and the mother had difficulty consoling her newborn baby. The pacifier dropped repeatedly out of the baby's mouth as he wailed inconsolably. The high-pitched noise pierced through the inner confines of the church. The mother gave up and scurried out of the church while clutching her newborn. The baby's crying became softer and softer as the mother moved towards the rear doors, and their departure was followed by instant silence.

The organ came to life as the organist's fingers moved up and down the keys. The congregation immediately stood up on cue and sang to the accompanying music. Jerry was delayed in his response, and he fumbled through the pages of the hymnal to the designated page. A large cross, held up by a teenage boy, was guided down the center aisle. Several individuals dressed in white robes filed behind the cross, walking in pairs. At the end of the procession walked the priest. Jerry did not know the hymn but followed the words written on the page.

The priest stood behind the altar, and his voice projected as he read the prayers. The service carried on, and passages from the Old Testament, Psalms, and the New Testament were read by three separate individuals at the pulpit. This was followed by a hymn, and Jerry was able to find it in the hymnal fairly quickly. The congregation sang, "Amazing Grace, how sweet the sound, that saved a wretch like me. I once was lost, but now I'm found, was blind but now I see." Jerry followed along in the hymnal. He picked up the tune, and he was able to sing the last verse.

The priest made his way to the pulpit. He announced that the gospel reading had been taken from Luke, chapter 15, verses 11 through 32. The priest read the lesson, which was titled "The

Parable of the Prodigal Son." Jerry listened to the gospel intently, and the priest continued, "But the father said to his servants, 'Bring quickly the best robe and put it on him, and put a ring on his hand and shoes on his feet. And bring the fattened calf and kill it, and let us eat and celebrate. For this my son was dead and is alive again; he was lost and is found.'" The priest continued the reading and ended with the acknowledgment, "This is the word of the Lord," to which the congregation responded, "Thanks be to God."

Jerry was attentive to the sermon and absorbed every word coming forth from the priest's mouth. The priest was a black male who appeared to be in his sixties. His receding hair and beard were white as snow. He spoke gently and deliberately. He paused momentarily as a few latecomers, who tried to be inconspicuous, slid into the back pews.

The priest continued his sermon. He likened the prodigal son to sinners who had alienated themselves from God. He noted that all had sinned in the eyes of God and all were in need of repentance. The priest acknowledged that God was a loving and a forgiving God. He assured the congregation that a life through God brought hope and provided sustenance. The priest likened the father in the scripture to God. The priest pointed out that the father had watched and waited patiently for his son to return. It was noted that the return of the son, or the sinner, was cause for celebration. The priest urged the congregation to acknowledge their sinful state and to seek forgiveness. He reassured the congregation that God kept no record of wrongdoing if a person repented and wholeheartedly sought forgiveness. He challenged the congregation to exercise forgiveness towards their enemies.

The priest concluded his sermon, and the words struck a major cord in Jerry. There were several prayers that followed and led into the peace offering. A man and a woman sitting directly in front of him turned around almost simultaneously and extended a friendly hand towards him. The gesture was unexpected, but Jerry, in turn, shook their hands. There were other individuals in the church who approached Jerry and offered him a warm smile and an amicable handshake. The congregation then took their seats, and the service continued.

A collection plate attached to a long stick was directed down each pew. Jerry opened up his wallet, which contained a five-dollar bill and several one-dollar bills. He was uncertain about the amount he was expected to throw in. He observed the people around him and noted that some individuals threw money into the collection plate while others kept their heads down as if the collection plate did not exist. The plate stopped in front of him, and he threw in a one-dollar bill.

The service continued, and the priest recited prayers, referring to the bread and wine. Jerry was not sure that he understood the significance of the bread and wine. He remained seated in his pew and observed the people as they joined the line to receive communion. There were prayers that followed, which led into the final hymn. Afterwards, the teenage boy took his place behind the cross and led the procession of robed individuals down the center aisle of the church. The priest gave his final blessing, and the service concluded. Most of the congregation made their way to the rear doors, while some lingered and engaged in discussion. Jerry shook the priest's hand and then made his way to his car.

He replayed the sermon in his mind as he drove back to his apartment. The idea that he could be forgiven for all of his sins was hopeful, but he was uncertain that God would actually forgive him for all the bad things that he had done in life. Would God forgive him for stabbing Fletcher in the arm and for stealing money from Mrs. Jackson? Would God forgive him for punching Darryl repeatedly in the face and sending him to the emergency room? It just seemed like a lot to ask for and a lot for God to forgive. He reminded himself of the priest's words, which had declared that God kept no record of wrongdoing if a person repented and wholeheartedly sought forgiveness. Jerry desperately wanted to believe that his slate could be wiped clean and he could be offered a fresh new start. He pondered the words that had instructed him to forgive his enemies. That concept seemed like a hard pill to swallow. Should he forgive Fletcher for making his life a living hell? The rejection of his mother had shattered his soul, but should he forgive his mother for creating this feeling of rejection? How could he expect God to forgive him but not forgive others? The thought of forgiving his mother and Fletcher seemed easier said than done, but he was willing to make the first step.

Jerry was uncertain how to communicate with God and about how he should ask for forgiveness. Should he look up at the sky and talk to God, or should he just speak freely? Jerry had a few more minutes in his car before reaching his apartment complex. He decided to talk to God openly, but initially, he felt silly. He gained courage and resumed his conversation with God. He expressed the feelings he had bottled up inside, and he started to feel a weight gradually being lifted from his body. Tears streamed down his cheek, and he wiped the tears away.

CHAPTER 13

JERRY WAS IN THE LIBRARY ONE EVENING FOLLOWING HIS LAST CLASS OF THE DAY. FOR some reason, he felt very tired, and the desire to take a nap had fallen heavily upon him. He desperately needed a large cup of caffeinated coffee. He lifted his eyes from the pages, and instantly, the sleep escaped him. In his line of vision was arguably the most beautiful girl he had ever seen. He thought to himself that she must have been a freshman. He did not recall seeing her on campus, and surely, he would have noticed such a radiant beauty. She appeared to be of Hispanic origin. Her straight dark hair, parted in the middle, framed her face and fell to the mid-portion of her back. She sat with a friend, who had her brown hair up in a loose bun. She was a white female and was thin, though she appeared to be toned judging from her arms. She would be considered average looking, depending on who was asked.

Jerry's eyes diverted back to the female that had gripped his body and caused his heart to palpitate. He had never experienced this feeling before, and it felt awkward. He felt like a giddy schoolgirl who had a major crush. Even though he was now fully awake, he had difficulty resuming his studies with the knowledge that she was ten feet in front of him. About an hour went by, and the beauty and her friend gathered their books and left the library. Jerry could not stop thinking about her, and he hoped that their paths would cross again.

Approximately two weeks later, Jerry was exiting his finance class when he spotted the beauty seated alone on a bench several feet away. He immediately stopped in his tracks, and he noticed his heart was beating faster. He took a deep breath, and he tried to calm himself down. He could not believe that a female could have this much effect on him. He wanted desperately to talk to her, but he had difficulty mustering the courage. He wanted her to acknowledge his existence, and he envisioned her as his girlfriend. He again took a deep breath, and he walked towards her direction.

He sat on a bench that was in close proximity to the bench that the beauty had claimed. Her head was down as she paged through a novel. Jerry, at one point, realized that he was staring at her. The beauty looked up from the page, locked eyes with Jerry, and gave him a warm smile. Her smile was angelic, and it lit up her face. He was taken off guard and returned an awkward smile. The beauty went back to reading her novel.

Jerry tried numerous times to stand up and walk over to her bench, but the fear of the beauty rejecting him caused his body to feel heavy. He counted in his head from one to ten, and then he immediately got up and walked over to her bench. There was no turning back. He was able to voice a hello, and he surprisingly sounded confident, though he was experiencing a different feeling inside. He asked permission to sit on the bench, and she smiled and obliged. The beauty moved closer to the edge of the bench to allow more room for him to sit down, and then she returned to reading her book.

He introduced himself as Jerry Frye. The beauty then introduced herself as Sofia Valadez. Jerry began small talk, inquiring where she was from and what she was studying in college. Sofia engaged herself in the conversation and shared with Jerry that she was from Laredo, Texas. She also revealed that she was a college freshman majoring in chemistry. Sofia stated that she was following a pre-med curriculum and her ultimate goal was to become a neurosurgeon.

She admitted that she was already looking into medical schools and her number one choice was Yale. Jerry, in turn, told her that he was majoring in finance and business administration. He had plans to pursue an MBA with the ultimate goal of moving to Manhattan and getting a job on Wall Street.

Jerry lied to Sofia and told her that he was from New Orleans. Sofia had never been to New Orleans, and Jerry spoke about the city as if he'd lived there his entire life. He saw the interest in Sofia's eyes, which gave him more enthusiasm and confidence. He flirtatiously told Sofia that he would take her to Café du Monde one day for a beignet and a cup of café au lait. The intimidation of talking with her had gone away, and he felt very relaxed and comfortable during their conversation.

They spoke for about twenty minutes before Jerry asked to take her out for a bite to eat. Sofia hesitated for a moment and appeared to be searching for the right words. She then told him that she was very busy with her studies, and she had an organic chemistry test coming up soon. Jerry's heart sank like a ship, and the confidence he'd been able to generate sank with it also. He thought it was a poor excuse, as she was sitting on the bench reading a novel, which she appeared to be halfway through with judging by her bookmark. He extended the invitation for lunch or dinner after she finished her exam. Sofia told Jerry that she would think about it and get back to him. She told him that she was off to her biology class, and she placed the novel in her bag and waved goodbye. Jerry remained on the bench, motionless. He was still in shock after the conversation with Sofia had taken an unexpected turn. In his mind, they seemed to have hit it off, but apparently, he'd been wrong. He watched her as she walked away and the distance between them got wider and wider.

Jerry had a hard time getting Sofia out of his mind. It felt like she had a tight hold on him, and he could not escape her grip. He was vigilant when walking through the campus, and he hoped that he would run into her again. Several days passed, and on one late afternoon, he spotted her coming through the doors of the science building. He jogged up to her, and in an elated voice, he asked whether she remembered him. She assured Jerry that she remembered him and asked him how he was doing. He was relieved that she showed some interest, and he was happy to tell her that he was doing well. He inquired about her organic chemistry test, and she was excited to share that she'd scored an A.

After congratulating her for her accomplishment, Jerry invited her out to dinner to celebrate. Again, Sofia hesitated and gently turned down his invitation. It was evident that she did not want to hurt his feelings, but at the same time, she wanted it to be clear that she was not interested in his advances. Jerry felt as if a knife had been driven through his heart and twisted several times, which added to the pain and injury. Sofia told him that she would see him around, and she went on her way in the direction of the library.

Jerry's body felt paralyzed, and he stood motionless in the central area of the campus. The moment did not seem real, and he tried to grasp the last few minutes that had passed. He felt disappointed, hurt, and rejected. The hurt started to shift to indignation and anger as he felt his body seething. He felt like screaming at the top of his lungs. How dare she reject him? He felt as if his body had been taken over by a devious force that he could not control. He walked towards the direction of the library, and he became cognizant that his hands were clenched into fists.

He walked through the doors of the library, and immediately, he noticed Sofia seated at a table on the right side of the room. She was seated with the brown-haired girl that she'd been with previously on the day that he'd first seen her. They were both buried in their books and appeared to be oblivious to their surroundings. Jerry found a desk in the right corner of the room, facing Sofia's rear. He removed his finance book from his bag and attempted to appear as if he was studying. He frequently looked up from the pages and peered in Sofia's direction. He must have had his eyes in his book for a longer period of time than he'd thought, as Sofia and her friend were no longer sitting at the table and their books were gone.

Jerry swiftly got up from his chair, picked up his belongings, and walked through the first floor of the library. The friends were nowhere to be found. He walked briskly through the front door of the library, and he noticed the friends talking in the distance. It was already dark outside, but they were illuminated by the lamppost. They stood next to a car with the driver-side door open, and it appeared as if Sofia was getting ready to jump in.

Jerry walked through the parking lot and found his way to his car, which was parked three rows away. The headlights of Sofia's car went on, and the car was backed out of the parking space. She maneuvered her way out of the parking lot, and Jerry followed at a safe distance behind her. He realized that he was following a familiar route as he trailed her for about seven to eight minutes. When Sofia pulled into an apartment complex, he was shocked to learn that they resided in the same complex. Jerry parked a few spaces away and turned off his engine and headlights. He appeared to have gone unnoticed, and he observed Sofia as she walked up the stairs and walked through a door on the second level. Jerry sat in his car for about fifteen minutes and stared at the door of the apartment. He then drove around the complex to the lot directly in front of his apartment. He went up the stairs to the third floor and entered apartment 324.

Time passed, and Jerry could not get Sofia out of his mind. His thoughts were consumed with her, and the obsession affected his sleep. The diligence that he'd once exercised with his studies had taken a drastic turn, and he found it immensely difficult to concentrate on his schoolwork. He would park his car in view of her apartment door, and he would stare at the door for prolonged periods of time. He wondered what she was doing behind the closed door, and the possibilities seemed endless. He periodically observed the other tenants as they moved in and out of their respective apartments. Jerry was aware that his thoughts and behavior were unhealthy and bordered on insanity. He scolded himself every time he sat in his car looking out at her apartment door, but he could not resist the temptation. He wanted Sofia to acknowledge him. He wanted her to accept and appreciate him. He wanted her to be attracted to him. If she loved him, he would give her the world.

It was roughly 5 pm on a Friday afternoon when Jerry saw Sofia sitting on a bench, again reading a novel. He approached her and asked permission to sit down. Sofia gave him a smile but told him that she had taken a short break to relax and she needed to head to the library to study. She got up from the bench and waved goodbye. Jerry watched as she walked in the direction of the library. In her path, she stopped briefly to speak to a male student. They appeared to share a joke, as she tilted her head back with laughter. She waved to the male student and continued on her way in the direction of the library. Jerry felt himself getting angry. His jaw clenched, and his body quivered. He felt every muscle in his body become tense. He was aggravated that she'd had a few moments to spare to speak to someone else, and a male at that. He continued to stare at her until she was no longer in sight. He despised her, and she was going to pay for the way she'd treated him. He looked up at the sky and observed the dark clouds looming in the distance. He expected that it would be a night of heavy rain.

Sofia concluded her studies at the library, and she waved goodbye to her brown-haired friend in the parking lot. The October sky was dark as Jerry followed Sofia to the apartment complex. He parked a few spots away from her, and he watched closely as she walked up the stairs and entered apartment 208. He reached into his glove compartment for his baseball cap, and he placed it on his head. He reclined the driver's seat and pondered his next move.

A slender male about five foot eleven, with dark blonde hair and dark-rimmed glasses, emerged from apartment 104. He had a small suitcase in his hand, and he placed it in the trunk of his car. Jerry suspected that he was going out of town, possibly for the weekend. He'd observed this guy before, and he seemed to follow a similar routine with his comings and goings. Jerry hadn't observed other occupants in apartment 104. He'd actually never seen anyone else enter or leave that apartment. The slender male walked back into his apartment for a couple of minutes. He then walked out and appeared to lock the door. He jumped into the driver's seat of his car, turned on the engine and headlights, and drove away.

Jerry remained seated in his car in a reclined position. He wondered what Sofia was doing in her apartment. He wanted her to feel pain, because she'd caused him pain. He wanted to look deep into her eyes and see the terror and fear. He wanted her to know who was in control. Jerry needed someone else to take the fall for the devious act he was going to commit, and the slender male in apartment 104 was the perfect scapegoat.

Jerry had some black gloves in the glove compartment of his car. He drove to a nearby retail store that sold home improvement and construction products, and he bought a lock pick and a tension wrench. He then made his way back to the apartment complex. He left his tools in the car, and he made a quick stop at his apartment to retrieve a few items. He grabbed four small, clear plastic bags from a box in the kitchen. He found a tweezer in the bathroom, which he took with him. He located an unopened box of condoms in the top drawer of his nightstand. He'd purchased the box at a gas station several months before so that he would be prepared in case an opportunity presented itself. He also pulled a jacket from the hanger in his closet, and it conveniently had two inner pockets. He was very uneasy and apprehensive and needed something to calm his nerves. Jerry opened the bottle of whiskey on the kitchen counter and chugged about half a pint down. He was not a big drinker, and it felt as if it was boring a hole though the lining of his stomach.

Jerry exited his apartment, and he was very vigilant as he made his way back to his car. There was no one in sight, and it was imperative that he remain inconspicuous during the entire operation. He drove around to the side of the lot near apartment 104. He remained in his car, in a reclined position, and he thought about his next steps. He planned to break into apartment 104 and retrieve something that he could plant as evidence in Sofia's apartment. Another option would be to abort the plan and return to his apartment. His emotions ran high, and the logical approach took a back seat.

As he continued to ponder his plan, his thoughts were interrupted as a car pulled up three spaces to the right of him. A man and a woman exited the car, and they were immersed in talks and laughter. They made their way down the hall of the first level of the apartment building, and they entered one of the apartment doors. Jerry looked around, and there was no one else visible. He placed the pick, wrench, plastic bags, tweezer, and the wrapped condom in his inner jacket pockets. He put the gloves on and walked up to the door of apartment 104.

He looked around, and there was no one in sight. He removed the pick and the wrench out of his pocket, and he positioned himself in a manner to block his actions. He inserted the tension wrench into the bottom of the key hole and applied gentle pressure and light torque. He inserted the pick at the top of the lock and gently pushed the pins up. He used the tension wrench to turn the cylinder, and he successfully unlocked the door. Jerry looked around again, and still there was no one in sight. He entered the apartment and closed the door behind him.

All of the lights were off, and he heard no sounds. There was a silhouette of a lamp in the living room area. Jerry slowly and cautiously walked to the stand that was holding up the lamp. He reached his gloved right hand underneath the lamp shade, and after two clicks of the socket knob, a dim light shone through the room. He looked around the small apartment, and the layout was familiar and appeared to be an exact replica of his apartment. He walked into the bathroom, and on the counter was a nylon paddle brush webbed with countless strands of dark blonde hair. Jerry carefully took out one of the plastic bags and the tweezer. He meticulously separated and pulled some strands out of the brush with the tweezer, and he deliberately placed the strands into the plastic bag. He zipped up the plastic bag and placed it in his right inner jacket pocket.

Jerry walked into the bedroom, which had a twin-size bed that was unmade. There was not much else in the room except for a few items of clothing on hangers in the closet. He made his way into the kitchen, and there were dishes in the sink. There was a glass on the kitchen counter, and on close inspection, there was a visible fingerprint on the glass. The likelihood of the fingerprint belonging to the tenant was extremely high given the fact that the tenant lived alone. Jerry took the chance, and he placed the glass into one of the plastic bags. He opened the cupboards in the kitchen and found an identical glass. The glass appeared clean, but for certainty, he wiped the glass with a kitchen towel and placed it in a separate plastic bag. He wanted to position both glasses in Sofia's apartment so that it would appear as if she'd been drinking with the presumed perpetrator. Jerry removed the pick and wrench from his pockets, and fortunately for him, the inner pockets of his jacket were wide and deep enough to hide and secure the glasses.

Jerry turned off the light and peered through the window in the living area, and there was still no one in sight. He held the pick and tension wrench in his left hand and crossed his arm to hide the objects underneath the right front part of his jacket. He opened the door, locked it from the inside, and closed the door with his gloved hand.

Jerry's heart started to beat faster as he made his way up the stairs to apartment 208. A roar of thunder broke through the silence, accompanied by a bolt of lightning. The rain started to trickle down, and this was soon followed by a heavy downpour. He stopped in front of apartment 208. He looked around, and there was no one in view. He felt as if his heart was beating out of his chest. There was still time to go back to his apartment, but he had gone too far, and he seemed to be at a point of no return. Jerry used the pick and tension wrench to unlock the door. He turned the cylinder, and he knew at that moment that he had gained entry into the apartment. He gently turned the knob and slowly opened the door. He quietly walked into the apartment and closed the door behind him.

The room was dark, and he debated whether he should turn the light switch on. The lightning illuminated the room, and he caught an image of Sofia sleeping on the couch. He laid the pick and tension wrench gently on the floor. Then he removed the clear bags with the glasses, which he also placed lightly on the floor. He walked cautiously towards Sofia, who still appeared to be sound asleep. He stood above her, and she looked peaceful despite the tempestuous weather outside. Jerry thought that things could have been different, but she'd ruined it for the both of them. Everything was her fault. The lightning flashed again, illuminating Sofia's face, and at that moment, he quickly sealed his gloved hand over her mouth.

Sofia immediately woke up, and she tried unsuccessfully to remove his hand from her mouth. Her arms whaled on her attacker, as the strength of his body was too much to bear and she felt defenseless. She felt like she was suffocating as his forearm obstructed her trachea. Her last breath was imminent. Jerry lightened the intensity of his grip and warned her that if she made a sound, he would kill her. Sofia shook her head to convey under-standing. The tears rolled down her cheeks, and her throat felt like it was on fire. Jerry instructed her to get up slowly and lie on the floor. He warned her again that if she made a sound or tried to attack him, he would kill her. Sofia did as she was told, and she lay on her back on the ground. Her tears were uncontrollable and dripped onto the carpet.

The lightning flashed again, and Sofia recognized Jerry's face underneath the baseball cap. Jerry blamed her for the position she was in and told her that it could have all been avoided if she'd treated him better. He boasted that he was now the one in control. The lightning illuminated Sofia's face, and Jerry saw the fear and terror in her eyes. His lips formed a broad grin as he witnessed her facial expression and the panic behind her dark eyes. He pulled down her underwear, and then he removed the gloves. He reached for the condom in his pocket, removed it from the wrapper, and then he placed it over his manhood. He put both gloves back on and then proceeded to take advantage of her.

After completing the heinous act, he deviously asked her whether she would keep the act a secret. Sofia agreed to keep the act a secret, but Jerry indicated that he did not believe her. Without warning, he clenched his hands around her neck and squeezed tightly. She grabbed his gloved hands, but she was unable to loosen the grip. His full weight was on top of her, and he obstructed her trachea, causing her to gasp for air. She succumbed to the effects of strangulation, and her arms fell to her side.

Jerry stood up and watched the lifeless body on the floor. He switched on a lamp and then meticulously gathered up the incriminating evidence. He strategically placed the blonde hairs from the plastic bag onto the lifeless body. He removed the glasses from the plastic bags and placed them on the kitchen counter, and he examined the area again to ensure there were no signs of incriminating evidence. He peered out of the window, and there was no one in sight. The rain was still falling down heavily. He closed the door behind him and made his way to his car.

CHAPTER 14

JERRY LOOKED AT THE BROKEN MIRROR IN HIS BATHROOM, WHICH HE'D SHATTERED with a beer bottle. He was unrecognizable, and he despised the reflection. He did not know who he was anymore. He had watched the news, which had broadcasted Nathaniel Wellington's suicide in the jail. The news reporter had stated that Nathaniel's DNA and fingerprint had been found at the scene of the crime. Nathaniel's battle with depression had been displayed on the screen, and it had been speculated that the depression had driven him to commit the crime and compelled him to commit suicide.

Jerry looked at his hands, and he knew he was a monster. He had the bloodstains of two people on his hands that he could not wash off. There were family and friends crying and wailing because of the heinous acts that he'd committed. Hopes and dreams had been shattered because of him. He reluctantly looked at himself again in the broken mirror. His facial hair was stubbly, and he desperately needed to shave. His eyes were bloodshot from the alcohol and his inability to sleep. The nights had been met with terror as he'd envisioned the lifeless body of Sofia when he'd closed his eyes.

Jerry went into the kitchen and made himself a cup of coffee. He felt like a zombie as he moved stiffly throughout the kitchen. He felt like he was walking around in a defiled body without a heart and a soul. He realized that he had to make a change and that he could not keep himself cooped up in the small apartment day and night. He poured himself a second cup of coffee, which seemed to perk him up a little bit. Jerry took a broom and swept up the remnants of the glass that had shattered from the mirror. He brushed his teeth and shaved off his facial stubble. He took a cold shower, which infused some life into him. He had missed some of his classes, and he was ready to make the first step out of his apartment and face the outside world.

Jerry threw on a pair of jeans and a white t-shirt, and he emerged from his apartment. The sun was shining brightly, and he squinted his eyes from the penetrating light. He walked across the third level to the stairwell, and a gentle breeze brushed against his skin. He made his way to his car, and it took three attempts at turning the key before the engine came to life. He needed a new car, and the first big splurge he would make would be to buy a luxury car when he became a wealthy, successful businessman. He drove his car around the side of the complex to the scene of the crime. It felt like any other day. There were no crowds of people hovering outside the complex, and the yellow crime scene tape was no longer present.

He drove his car to the school campus and parked in a lot adjacent to the library. He walked through the campus, and there was nothing that appeared out of the ordinary. Students walked in different directions as they made their way to their varying destinations. Jerry walked into his finance class fifteen minutes early, and he found a seat in the back row of the classroom. An Asian boy by the name of Jian sat next to him in the back row. Jian was first-generation Chinese American, and he'd moved to Shreveport from San Francisco. He and Jerry shared a few classes together, as they both were following a business track. They weren't exactly friends, but they did converse before or after classes or if they met each other around campus.

"Where have you been?" Jian asked Jerry. "Did you hear about that girl that got murdered? She was a student on this campus."

Jerry was taken off guard, and he did not know how to respond. His heart rate started to accelerate, and he tried to compose himself. "I've been sick for the past few days," Jerry responded as he tried to appear as calm as possible. "I think I came down with the flu or something." Jerry paused momentarily and then resumed his response to Jian's questions. "I did hear about that girl on the news. Her name, I think, was Sofia. Sofia Valadez." Jerry then cleared his throat for a couple of seconds. "I was shocked to find out that the murder happened in my apartment complex. Could you imagine watching the news and seeing something like that happening in your building?"

"That's insane," Jian responded. "I heard she was a very nice girl. Did you know her?"

"Not exactly," Jerry answered. "I've seen her once or twice around campus."

"They say that this crazy guy named Nathaniel Wellington raped and killed her. He was also a student on campus. He committed suicide in the jail, you know." Jian shook his head in disgust and continued sharing the details. "They say that he hung himself in the jail cell by a sheet he tied into a knot. That is such a cowardly way out. What kind of sicko rapes and murders an innocent girl? I'm assuming she's innocent. But who cares! What kind of sick bastard does something like that? I hope he rots and burns in hell."

The conversation was making Jerry very uneasy, but he tried to remain as calm as possible. "You're right. Nathaniel is a sicko," Jerry responded. The professor was gearing up to start the class, and Jerry could not have been more relieved. He tried to concentrate on the lecture, but his thoughts would periodically wander, and images of Sofia's dead body would flash through his mind.

The moment the lecture ended, Jerry got up from his seat and made his way out of the classroom. He did not want to stick around and resume the conversation with Jian. He told Jian that he would catch up with him later and then made a beeline to his car. He felt as if everyone in his path was looking at him and they knew that he had committed this abominable crime and had framed an innocent man. Jerry desperately wanted to get away for a moment and be by himself. He decided to forgo his afternoon classes. He felt as if everything was closing in on him and that if he did not get away soon, he would suffocate. He jumped into the driver's seat, and after two turns of the key, his engine started. *Why can't the car start after the first turn of the key?* he thought. Jerry drove out of the library's parking lot and maneuvered his way onto the main road.

He drove until he was on the outskirts of the city. He then took a side road and drove through some back roads until he was near the river.

He parked his car, got out of the driver's seat, and walked through the wooded area until he reached the bank of the river. He was alone, and he felt like he could breathe. There was no one around to judge him. He sat on a log and looked out into the distance. The stream of water flowed openly and freely without any hindrance. He took off his shoes and socks and submerged his feet in the cool rippling water. He felt a sense of security in the moment even though it was only temporary. The sun started to set, and the sky was painted an extraordinary shade of orange. He wished he could remain in the safe haven of his surroundings, but it was time to go back and face reality. Jerry positioned himself in the driver's seat, and he turned the key three times in the ignition before the engine turned on. He drove back into the city in the direction of his apartment.

Jerry slept for about two hours, and then he woke up in a cold sweat. The image of Sofia's face had entered his dream, and it had turned into a nightmare. He felt as if he was having a panic attack. His heart was pounding, and his chest felt tight, almost as if he was having a heart attack. A wave of intense fear flooded his body, and he started to hyperventilate. He got out of the bed and abruptly made his way to the kitchen and grabbed a paper bag. He felt lightheaded, and he knew that if he did not sit down soon, he would pass out. He started to experience a tingling sensation around his mouth, and his fingertips were numb and tingly. He slowly sat on the kitchen floor. His body was drenched with sweat, and his t-shirt clung to his body. He placed the paper bag over his nose and mouth, and he took about ten breaths. He removed the paper bag and deliberately slowed down his rate of breathing. His heart rate slowly decreased, and the chest pressure grew less. The tingling around his mouth and the numbness of his fingertips went away. He sat on the kitchen floor for about thirty minutes before gathering the strength to pull his weight off of the ground. He was in the process of making himself a cup of coffee but decided against it after deducing that his palpitations might return.

Jerry spent the rest of the night on the couch. The rays of the sun streamed through the living room blinds and fell onto his face. He was uncertain whether he'd slept. If he had, it might have been only for a few minutes. He contemplated going to class, but he knew that he would not be focused and his efforts would be in vain. It was Friday, and he was glad the weekend was approaching. He had already missed a lot of his lectures, and he needed the weekend off to just clear his mind without worrying about missing more classes. He decided to take the three days to himself and hopefully have a fresh start on Monday.

Jerry knew that if he did not get himself out of his apartment and interact with others, he would drive himself crazy. He went downtown to Henry's sports bar and ordered himself a basket of wings, onion rings, and a beer. It was karaoke night, and there were three girls on stage singing "Born in the USA" by Bruce Springsteen. The words and the tune were completely off, and the girls appeared to have had one too many to drink. Jerry sat on a stool at a round table by himself and observed his surroundings. It seemed like a typical Friday night at Henry's.

"Jerry!" a loud voice shouted. "What's going on, man?" The words had come out of the mouth of Matthew Van Long. "I haven't seen you in a while. What's shakin'?"

"Hanging in there," Jerry responded. Matthew was a student on campus, and he was in Jerry's statistics and calculus class. He pulled up a stool at Jerry's table and sat down uninvited. He fingered his hand through his blonde curly hair and looked at Jerry with his intense blue eyes.

"Things are finally starting to get back to normal around here after that murder," Matthew commented. "Who would have thought something like that would happen around here. I guess you never know who's crazy."

"Uh-huh," Jerry responded as he took a big gulp from the beer can. This was not the conversation that he'd wanted to entertain. He wished Matthew would get up from his table and leave him alone.

Matthew quickly changed the subject to football. He was from Houston, and he was a big Texans fan. Jerry knew a little bit about football, and he was able to engage Matthew in conversation. The discussion ran its course, and Matthew made his way to a circle of friends at another table. Jerry ate the rest of his wings and left the sports bar.

Jerry made his way back to his apartment. He was relieved that he'd been able to make it through a meal in public without panicking and searching for a way out. He slept about six hours that night, which was the most sleep he'd had since he'd committed the murder. He went to the grocery store on Saturday morning and ran some errands throughout the day. It seemed like an ordinary Saturday, and people were going through their business of the day. The day was uneventful, and Jerry decided to attend church the following morning.

Jerry walked through the wooden doors of the church. There were members of the congregation scattered throughout the pews. He felt uneasy as he situated himself in a back pew. He felt as if his sins were inscribed on his forehead for all to see. He felt as if God was watching him and judging him for his sins. Beads of sweat formed on his forehead, and his body was restless. He took a slow, deep breath, and he tried to calm his nerves. He recalled the priest's sermon on the prodigal son, a sinner who'd sought forgiveness from a loving God. Jerry likened himself to the prodigal son, and he wanted to be forgiven and absolved of his sins. He wanted a clean slate, and he promised to be a better person.

The service commenced, and the order of the service followed. A hymn was sung, and prayers were read in unison. The Old Testament passage and the psalm were read, and then an elderly lady made her way up to the podium to read the New Testament passage. She was a thin lady of short stature, and the lens of her glasses seemed to encompass most of her face. She pulled the microphone down to accommodate her height, and she proceeded to read the scripture. "The second reading is taken from 1 John, chapter 3, verses 12 through 15," the elderly woman began. "Do not be like Cain, who belonged to the evil one and murdered his brother. And why did he murder him? Because his own actions were evil and his brother's were righteous. Do not be surprised, my brothers and sisters, if the world hates you. We know that we have passed from death to life, because we love each other. Anyone who does not love remains in death. Anyone who hates a brother or sister is a murderer, and you know that no murderer has eternal life residing in him."

Jerry felt nauseated, and he was about to lose the contents of his breakfast. He got up out of the pew, and he felt dizzy. The walls of the church seemed to be closing in on him, and he needed to escape. He was able to avoid attention, as he was the only one seated in the last pew. He stumbled out of the building and made his way unsteadily to his car. The parking lot had a few cars, but there was no one in sight. He bent over some shrubs, and the contents of his stomach projected out of his mouth. He realized that he was breathing heavily, and he tried to slow down his respirations. After several minutes, his breathing and heart rate slowed down. He sat in the driver's seat of his car, and after a few attempts, the engine started, and he made his way to his apartment complex. *Could the scripture reading be a coincidence?* Jerry thought. Did someone know about the crime he'd committed and added the reading to the service? The words shook him to his core, and the guilt was weighing heavily upon him.

Jerry sat on the couch in the living room of his apartment. He reprimanded himself for allowing his emotions to overwhelm him and prevent him from functioning. He acknowledged that he'd committed a horrendous act, but he had to move on with his life, or he might as well be dead. No one suspected him, he thought. Everyone thought that the crime had been committed by Nathaniel Wellington. After all, his DNA and fingerprints had been found at the scene of the crime. Jerry recalled the moment when he'd approached the detectives and led their investigation in the direction of Nathaniel Wellington. He was remorseful about framing an innocent person, but there was nothing that he could do about it, and he had to move on. Sure, the right thing to do would be to own up to the crime and exonerate Nathaniel Wellington, but that was not an option. He told himself that he had to move on with his life.

Jerry resumed his classes on campus. He had missed several classes, and as a result, he got a C on his finance exam and a D on his accounting exam. Jerry was alarmed at the grades, but he was not surprised, as he'd gone through a period where he could not focus and study.

A couple of weeks passed, and the talk of the rape and murder had died down. Jerry was convinced that he'd gotten away with the crime and that now he could focus on his studies and move on with his life. He needed additional money to supplement his financial aid, and he found a job as a patient transporter in the local hospital.

It was late November, and Thanksgiving Day was approaching. Jerry always detested the holidays. For many, it was a time of love, warmth, family, and togetherness. For him, it was a time of sadness and aloneness. The holidays always reminded him of the family he'd never had. He picked up a rotisserie chicken at the grocery store on the day before Thanksgiving. The campus was desolate, as most students had traveled to spend the holiday with their families. There were many students in his apartment complex who had also left to spend the holidays with their loved ones. Jerry slept in on Thanksgiving Day and got up almost at noon. He heated the rotisserie chicken in the microwave and heated a can of corn and green beans on top of the stove. He sat down on the couch in the living room and ate his meal. He flipped through the television stations and settled on football.

About four weeks passed, and it was Christmas Day. The day was a repeat of Thanksgiving, and Jerry found himself alone in his apartment. He did not recall ever getting a gift for Christmas. It was a holiday that his mother had never celebrated in their house, and this had not been for any religious purposes. He'd had a friend growing up whose family was Jehovah's Witness, and they had not celebrated holidays or birthdays. He, on the other hand, was not a Jehovah's Witness, and his family had never celebrated holidays or birthdays.

He flipped through the television channels while he ate his dinner on the couch, and he stopped on a channel that displayed a family sitting around the Christmas tree. The family looked happy as they exchanged gifts. It was an image that he dreamed of experiencing, even though he was twenty-one years old and soon to be twenty-two. He changed the channel, and the television screen displayed *Charlie Brown's Christmas Carol*. He quickly changed the channel to a program that was not reminiscent of Christmas. He was looking forward to the holidays being over and to getting a fresh start in the new year.

CHAPTER 15

A NEW YEAR HAD BEGUN, AND JERRY WAS FEELING LIKE A NEW PERSON. HIS SLEEP pattern had normalized, and he had not experienced any more panic attacks. He even started going back to the gym. The crime he'd committed was in the past, and he could now focus on the future. His grades the last semester had not been ideal, but this semester was going to be different. He was determined to study hard and get straight A's at the end of the semester.

Jerry was studying in the library when he looked up from his book and saw the brown-haired friend of Sofia Valadez. The friend was sitting at a table about ten feet in front of him, and she was studying alone. Jerry's mind shifted to the dead body of Sofia lying on her living room floor, but he was quickly able to shed the thought, and he returned to his studies. He completed three hours of solid studying, and then he made his way back to his car and to his apartment.

The weeks passed, and he was excelling in his schoolwork again. It was Friday night, and it was time to relax and have some fun. Jerry went to Henry's, and this time, he sat at the bar. The joint was buzzing with college students, and it was karaoke night. He ordered a basket of wings, onion rings, and a beer. An African American female with curly shoulder-length hair approached the barstool next to him and inquired whether the seat was taken. After Jerry assured her that the seat was not claimed, she hung her black leather jacket on the back of the chair and sat next to him. She ordered a basket of wings and a Diet Coke, and she then focused on the television screen above the head of the bartender, which was broadcasting a football game. She was quite attractive, and from Jerry's view, her body appeared to be in great shape. She wore a white tank top and fitted jeans that accentuated her curves. She turned her head briefly towards Jerry and smiled, which revealed a perfect set of teeth.

"Hi. I'm Jerry." He extended a hand toward her.

"Hi. I'm Morgan," she responded and shook his hand.

"I haven't seen you around here before. Are you from around here?"

"I'm from Phoenix, but I've been in Shreveport for about a year. And you?"

"I'm from New Orleans. I'm up here for college," Jerry replied.

"I love New Orleans." Morgan's eyes lit up. "I know it very well. What part of New Orleans are you from? I'm sure I'll know the school you attended."

Jerry realized that he had put his foot in his mouth. "You have such beautiful teeth and a beautiful smile," he said, changing the subject. Morgan's smile widened, and she started to blush. "I'm sure I'm not the first person to have told you that."

"Thank you," she replied modestly. "What are you studying?" Morgan seemed to have forgotten her original question, and Jerry was relieved.

"I'm in business school," he said proudly. "One day, I'm going to be a successful businessman. Who knows, I may end up on Wall Street one day." Jerry paused for a moment and then continued, "Phoenix, huh. So, what brought you out to Shreveport?"

"Work. I work with mentally and physically handicapped children."

"Oh, okay. Do you enjoy it?" Jerry asked and then took a sip of his beer.

"I do. I really do. It can be a challenge, but it is rewarding."

"Do you have family around here?" The moment Jerry asked the question, he wished he could have taken it back. He did not want Morgan to inquire about his family.

"Nope," she answered. "My parents and sister are in Phoenix. Most of my family are out in California. What about your family? Are they in New Orleans?"

On the spur of the moment, Jerry responded, "My parents are dead. They died in a tragic car accident. I was an only child."

"I'm so sorry to hear that," Morgan replied, saddened. "I'm so sorry to have brought it up. Are you okay?"

"I'm fine," Jerry answered. "So, tell me a little bit about yourself. How old are you, if you don't mind me asking?"

"I'm twenty-two. And yourself?"

"I'm twenty-one," he replied. "So, what kind of stuff do you like to do? What are your hobbies?"

"I love to work out, whether it's jogging, cycling, yoga, you name it. It makes me feel good about myself. I literally feel sick to my stomach if I go more than three days without working out."

"Well, it certainly shows," Jerry said flirtatiously, and Morgan flashed him a smile. "I enjoy working out myself. I briefly fell into a rut, but I'm back on track. Maybe we can go jogging together sometime."

"That would be great," Morgan replied excitedly. "I welcome a jogging partner. Just as long as you can keep up."

"Oh, don't worry about that. I'll keep up. So, what other things do you like to do? Do you like going to the movies?"

"I do, but I haven't gone to the movies since I moved here. I guess I haven't had anyone to go with. Why? Are you asking me out?" she said sheepishly.

Jerry smiled at her. Morgan also noted that he had a nice smile and beautiful greenish eyes. "Yes, I am asking you out. Are you free tomorrow night? How about a movie? I'm not sure what's playing, but I can check the listing. I'm up for watching anything, but please, no chick flick." He flashed her another smile, and Morgan was captivated.

"Okay." She returned the smile. "No chick flick."

They both exchanged numbers and spoke for another hour at the bar. Jerry walked her to her car and watched as she drove off. He got into the driver's seat of his car and turned the key in the ignition three times before the engine started. His car was somewhat of an embarrassment, and he wondered what Morgan would think when he picked her up tomorrow. He drove back to his apartment and thought about her on the entire way back.

Jerry slept in until 11 am the next morning. It was a beautiful Saturday morning, and he made his way to the gym. He focused on his back and upper body and then did fifteen minutes of cardio on the treadmill. The cool shower at the gym was refreshing and energizing. He ran a few errands, studied for a couple of hours, and then got ready for his date. The whole concept of dating was foreign to him. It actually was exciting but a little nerve-racking at the same time. What to wear was the first question. His options were limited given the scarcity of his wardrobe. He decided on a pair of faded jeans and a white t-shirt. He debated for a few minutes between black loafers and sneakers. Then he decided to dress his attire up a little bit by going with the black loafers.

He sprayed some cologne around his neck and his wrists, and then he sprayed it across his white t-shirt. The scent of the cologne created a thick layer around him, and he started to cough. He knew he had sprayed too much cologne on his body, and he did not want to suffocate his date. He took a face towel and dampened it. Then he wiped his neck and his wrists. The scent of the cologne was still overpowering, and he considered jumping back in the shower. He looked at his watch, and it was 6:42 pm. He had to leave in the next three minutes to pick up his date so they could make it on time for the movie. The intense fragrance of his cologne was coming from his t-shirt, and it flowed directly into his nostrils. He took off the white t-shirt and threw on a black t-shirt.

Jerry grabbed his jacket and his keys, and he made his way abruptly to his car. He was surprised that his car started with the first turn of the key in the ignition. He hoped that the engine would start again on the first turn during his date. He was already embarrassed that he drove a jalopy, and the engine not starting would only add to the embarrassment.

He was familiar with the apartment complex that Morgan lived in as it was the same complex that Jian, from his finance class, resided in. Jerry made his way though some side roads. Then he came upon Green Acres apartments. It was a rather large apartment complex with individual buildings. Jerry weaved his way through the complex until he approached Building 3. He parked his car and walked towards apartment 301, which was an end unit. He knocked on the door, and within a few seconds, Morgan answered the door. Morgan was a vision of beauty in a light pink sweater and a pair of form-fitting jeans. Her shiny heeled black boots stopped just below her knees. She greeted him with a warm smile that lit up her face.

"You look beautiful," Jerry commented.

"Thank you." Morgan blushed. "You're not so bad yourself."

Jerry led Morgan to his dilapidated car, and he apologized to her for its condition. Morgan stated with a grin, "As long as it gets us to our destination and back. That's all I'm concerned about."

"Well, it hasn't failed me yet," Jerry responded. He opened up the passenger door, and Morgan situated herself in the passenger seat.

"You're quite the gentleman," Morgan said with a smile. Jerry made his way to the driver's side, got in the car, and closed the door. He placed the key in the ignition, and he prayed that the car would start. Thankfully, the engine started with the first turn of the key, and he breathed a sigh of relief. He steered his car in the direction of downtown Shreveport.

"Did I tell you how beautiful you look?" Jerry briefly looked in Morgan's direction before placing his eyes back on the road.

"Yes, you did." Morgan giggled.

"You have the cutest laugh."

"Stop. You are making me blush."

"Am I coming on too strong? If so, I'm sorry."

"No. You're not coming on too strong."

"Good," Jerry replied. He looked again briefly in her direction and smiled, which caused Morgan's heart to skip a beat.

Jerry was a very attractive man, and she felt as if she could get lost in his green eyes. The conversation shifted, and they discussed their goals and aspirations. Morgan was enjoying the conversation, and she couldn't help but think that Jerry might be the one. He seemed like the complete package. He had good looks, he was intelligent, and he was motivated and ambitious. What more could a girl ask for?

Jerry pulled his car into the movie parking lot. He had allowed Morgan to pick the movie, and she had decided on an action film. Jerry paid for her entry into the theater, and he bought both of them a hotdog and medium-sized Cokes. They made their way into the screening room and sat in the last row. They both enjoyed the film, which was filled with excitement and twist and turns. The ending was unexpected, and they talked about the film during the entire drive back to Morgan's apartment. They sat in the parking lot for almost half an hour, talking, and then Jerry walked her to the door of her apartment.

"I had a great time," Jerry stated.

"Me too," Morgan replied with a smile. They looked at each other for a few seconds with no words, and Morgan braced herself for a kiss. His eyes were mesmerizing, and his smile was captivating.

"Well, we have to do this again," Jerry said, breaking the silence. "I hope you have a good night."

Morgan was a little disappointed that he had not leaned in for a kiss, but she was also appreciative, as it confirmed her notion that Jerry was a gentleman. She felt herself falling in love with him during that brief space of time. She said goodnight and closed the door.

CHAPTER 16

LIFE WAS BACK ON TRACK FOR JERRY, AND HE WAS OPTIMISTIC ABOUT THE FUTURE. HE was performing very well in his classes, and his relationship with Morgan was progressing. For the first time in his life, he actually felt happy. He felt that he'd been given a second chance in life and that his current state was only a preview of more to come. He started to research MBA programs throughout the Northeast, with his main focus on New York City. One day, he planned to move to the Big Apple; a global city that was one of the financial powers of the world. He lay in his bed and daydreamed about his future life in Manhattan. He pictured himself in a sharp black suit looking out of the window of his condo as he gazed at the yellow cabs passing by. Jerry visualized the people walking in a hurried manner, which was based on the images he'd observed on television. He wanted to experience the fast pace of life instead of the snail pace of the South. He pictured himself driving an expensive car to his job on Wall Street.

Jerry snapped out of his daydream and looked at his watch. It was almost time to leave for work. He went into the kitchen to make a sandwich, but after removing a slice of bread from its packaging, he realized the bread had become moldy. He threw the remaining slices in the package away. He decided to grab a bite to eat in the cafeteria at his job. Jerry took a short shower, got dressed, and went on his way to work. He thought to himself that the jalopy would soon be a memory and he would one day be cruising in a European luxury car.

Jerry had been hired almost three months ago as a hospital patient transporter. He worked this job about two nights a week to supplement his financial aid. The extra money came in handy, especially now that he had a girlfriend. The occasional expenses for dinner dates and movie tickets added up.

Jerry made his way into the hospital cafeteria. He generally tried to avoid the food in the cafeteria, but he had no other choice at the moment. It was dinner time, and his stomach was growling. He stood in line, waiting to be served.

"I wonder what the mystery meat for today is," a voice said from behind him. Jerry turned around, and there was a redhead standing behind him. She appeared to be in her forties.

"Who knows?" Jerry replied with a shrug. "It looks like some type of beef. Maybe meatloaf. Your guess is as good as mine."

"I think the other option is some type of shrimp pasta," the redhead noted as she pointed in the direction of the food.

"I don't know how I feel about eating shrimp in a hospital. I think I'll pass on that."

"Next person in line!" the cafeteria lady said in a raised voice. The cafeteria lady had a hair net over her head, and her face was expressionless. Jerry was now at the front of the line.

"I'll have this," Jerry stated while pointing to the mystery meat. "I'll also take some broccoli and carrots." He was handed the plate of food, and he offered a thank you that the cafeteria lady did not acknowledge.

"Next person in line!"

Jerry grabbed a bottle of Coke and paid for his meal. He sat at a table in the corner of the cafeteria and began to eat his dinner. The mystery meat was actually not that bad. It certainly tasted better than it looked.

"Do you mind if I join you?" asked the red-headed woman in line, who had made her way over to Jerry's table.

Yes, I mind, Jerry thought to himself. He really wanted those words to come out of his mouth. There were many empty tables in the cafeteria, but yet she felt the need to invade his personal space. "No, not at all," he replied. He did not know if his response sounded genuine, but it seemed good enough for the red-headed lady as she pulled out the chair opposite of him and sat down.

"I'm Elizabeth Henson, but most people call me Liz or Lizzy. I'm one of the clinical pharmacists. I love drugs. The legal kind, of course." Elizabeth Henson laughed at her own joke. She then cleared her throat. "And you are?"

"I'm Jerry. Jerry Frye."

"So, what do you do, Mr. Jerry Frye? Do you work in the hospital?"

"Well, uh. I'm a patient transporter, but I only do it part time. I'm actually a college student."

"Wonderful! So, what are you studying?" Lizzy placed a shrimp in her mouth and gave Jerry an inquisitive look. She had curious blue eyes and very thin lips. Her red hair was combed into a side ponytail, and Jerry thought to himself that the hairstyle was rather young appearing for her age.

"I'm in business school," Jerry replied. "I'm getting ready to take the GRE, and I'm looking into MBA programs."

Lizzy appeared intrigued. "Very nice. I wish you all the best." She popped another shrimp into her mouth.

"Thank you," Jerry replied with a smile.

"So, how old are you?" Lizzy asked, switching subjects.

Jerry was slightly taken aback by the shift in the conversation. "Um...I'm twenty-one."

"So you're legal," Lizzy responded instantaneously.

"I guess," Jerry said cautiously. "Legal for what?" He was starting to feel awkward, and Lizzy sensed it.

"I'm just kidding. Never mind," Lizzy responded with laughter. "Forget I said that." There were a few moments of silence, and Lizzy blurted out, "So, are you dating? Are you engaged? What's your status? I'm sure you can see that I'm a very nosy person."

"I'm happily dating someone," Jerry shared, which he hoped would back Lizzy off a bit.

"What's her name?"

"Her name is Morgan."

"Morgan," Lizzy said slowly. "That's a beautiful name. I'm sure she's a beautiful girl."

"She's very beautiful." Jerry could not suppress his smile.

"I was once married," Lizzy shared. "My husband left me for the babysitter. She was only nineteen." The conversation had become even more awkward for Jerry. Lizzy continued, "She seemed like a nice girl, and I trusted her. Benny loved her. Benny is my eight-year-old son, not my husband. I mean, ex-husband. One night, I came home early, and there they were. I'm sure I don't need to go into detail, and you can read between the lines." Jerry nodded to confirm his understanding. He definitely did not want Lizzy to explain any further. "Thankfully, Benny was already in bed."

There was a long pause as Lizzy appeared to reflect on the hurt of her past. Jerry did not know what to say even though he felt that he should say something. "Well, I hope he's happy," Lizzy said with a sarcastic tone. Her mood appeared to have switched with the snap of a finger. "Well, if he can have a young partner, then so can I, right?" Lizzy's face lit up, and her mouth formed a wide grin. There was a piece of spinach from the shrimp pasta that was lodged between her teeth.

"I guess," Jerry responded hesitantly. He looked at his watch and stood up from his chair. "I have to take off. My shift starts in a couple of minutes." Jerry grabbed his tray and said goodbye. He wished he had exited the conversation earlier.

Jerry worked his shift up until midnight and went home. He hoped that he did not have another encounter with Elizabeth Henson. He got ready for bed. His first class was at ten in the morning.

Jerry and Morgan had been dating for almost four months now, and he felt like it was time to take the next step. He thought that most people might think he was crazy for taking such a huge leap, but he did not care. He was in love, and he wanted to marry her. Morgan made him happy. She made him feel wanted and appreciated, and the way she looked at him was priceless. It was obvious that she was in love with him too.

Jerry went to the jewelry store to pick out an engagement ring. He had a very low budget, but he hoped that he would find something beautiful in his price range. He peered through the glass counters and gazed at the exquisite jewelry. The diamonds sparkled underneath, and some were almost blinding. He wished he could select and purchase one of the fine pieces, but all of the jewelry he had seen so far had drastically exceeded his price range. He told the salesperson his price range, and it was suggested to him that he try the consignment store a few blocks away.

Jerry made his way to Alim's Consignment Shop. The slogan read "IF WE APPROVE IT, IT'S WORTH IT." Before he could fully enter the door, he heard a loud voice from across the room say, "Can I help you?" The words had come out of the mouth of a tall, lanky man. He appeared to be of Middle Eastern heritage. His long beard fell upon his chest.

"Do you carry engagement rings?" Jerry inquired.

"Yes, sir, we do," the man replied in a heavy foreign accent. "You name it, we have it."

"Great!" Jerry responded in an elated voice.

"So, what exactly are you looking for, my friend? Let me show you what we have," the man said with enthusiasm as he rolled some of his words. Jerry followed behind him. "Look at this beauty. This will definitely put a smile on your lady's face. I'll give her to you for eight hundred dollars. That's less than half of what's she's worth. What do you say, my friend?"

"The ring is beautiful, but it is out of my price range. Do you have anything less expensive?" Jerry asked.

"I've only began to scratch the surface. I have many options for you, so don't worry. By the way, I'm Alim, the owner of this wonderful establishment."

"It's nice to meet you," Jerry replied.

"What do you think of this beauty? She's not as beautiful as the one I just showed you, but she's still a beauty in her own right. I'll give her to you for five hundred dollars. So, what do you say, my friend?"

"It is nice, but do you have anything less expensive?" Jerry asked.

"Well, I do, but she will only be cute, not beautiful. It may put only half a smile on your lady's face." Alim proceeded to show Jerry another ring. "What do you think about her. Isn't she cute? I'll give her to you for three hundred dollars, but that's as low as I could go."

Jerry pondered for a moment. It was a nice ring with a small round cut diamond. It was not as nice as the first two rings, but it was still nice. "What else do you have? Anything a little less expensive?"

"Do you even want to put a smile on your lady's face, my friend?" Alim showed Jerry two more rings. They might as well have come from a Cracker Jack box. Jerry decided to go with the three-hundred-dollar ring.

"Well done, my friend. It may not put a full smile on her face, but you will definitely get half a smile." Alim rang Jerry up and added the taxes. Jerry had not factored in the tax, but he proceeded to make the purchase.

Jerry was excited about his purchase. It was Saturday, and he and Morgan had a dinner date at seven. He figured he would pop the question at dinner. He could hardly wait as he anticipated Morgan's excitement. He wore a brand new pair of khaki pants and a white button-down shirt with brown loafers. He sprayed his cologne on lightly. As he drove to pick Morgan up, he mulled over different scenarios in which to pop the question. He envisioned her excitement as he placed the ring on her finger. The possibility that she would turn down his proposal was out of the question. He made a detour to the grocery store and picked up a set of red roses. He then made his way to Morgan's apartment complex and parked his car in the lot.

After a couple of knocks, Morgan opened the door. She was wearing a flared red dress with black heels, and she looked absolutely stunning. They embraced with a kiss, and Jerry thought the smell of her perfume was delightful. Morgan had transferred some of her lipstick onto his lips, and she wiped his lips with her thumb. Jerry gave her the bouquet of roses, and she was elated. She insisted on placing them in a vase with water before they headed out.

"Where are we going?" Morgan asked as they drove away in his car.

"It's a surprise," Jerry responded and smiled.

"Okay. I like surprises," Morgan replied and returned a smile. "So, what all did you do today?"

"Um. Well, I pretty much studied," Jerry answered, which was a lie. "What did you do today?"

"I cleaned all day and did laundry. I'm glad to be out of the apartment."

After about fifteen minutes of driving, Jerry pulled his car into one of the parking spaces at King's Steakhouse. He'd heard a lot of good things about the restaurant, and they were known for their steaks, as implied in the name. The aroma of grilled steak penetrated the air. Jerry walked around to the passenger side of the car and opened the door for Morgan. They were right on time for their seven o'clock reservation.

They were seated at a corner table, and they were told that their waiter would be with them shortly. The lights in the restaurant were dim, which added to the romantic ambience. A male waiter introduced himself as Zachary, and he presented them with the menu. The waiter then went on to narrate the special of the day, which sounded extremely appetizing.

Jerry ordered the least expensive cut of steak and a side salad. He wanted to reduce the cost on his end, and he wanted Morgan to have the opportunity to order what she wanted. Morgan ordered the filet mignon, prepared medium, with a side of garlic mashed potatoes and a house salad. He asked Morgan whether she wanted a glass of wine, but she declined and opted for a Diet Coke. Jerry could not say he was not relieved, as he was already adding up the cost of the meal in his head. Dinner was delicious, and King's Steakhouse lived up to its reputation. They both enjoyed a slice of chocolate cake for dessert.

"I enjoyed my meal, Jerry. Thank you for dinner."

"You're welcome," Jerry replied, and he paused for a moment. "Morgan, I know we've only been together for maybe four months, but I know what I want, and that's you." He paused again for a few seconds. Then he continued, "I love you, and I want to spend the rest of my life with you." Morgan looked at him, and she was speechless. Jerry reached into his pocket and pulled out a small black ring box. He opened it, and the ring was in view. "Morgan Walters, will you marry me?" Jerry asked.

Morgan placed both hands over her mouth in disbelief. She relaxed her hands and exclaimed, "Are you serious? Oh my gosh! Are you really serious?"

"Yes, I'm serious," Jerry assured her.

"Yes, I'll marry you! Yes, I'll marry you!" Morgan became emotional, and she tried to compose herself.

"One day, I will get you a nicer ring. I promise."

"It's beautiful. I love it," Morgan replied. Jerry thought about Alim at the consignment store. He'd gotten way more than half a smile.

CHAPTER 17

JERRY AND MORGAN WERE OFFICIALLY MARRIED AT THE COURTHOUSE DOWNTOWN. Morgan's parents were less than pleased at the news. They had only recently heard of Jerry, and they thought that Morgan had rushed into her decision blindly without giving it sufficient thought. They were concerned that their daughter had not given herself enough time to get to know this Jerry Frye. It was also disappointing that they hadn't been able to witness their daughter's vows. The selfish act, as her parents called it, had created tension between Morgan and her father. There were words exchanged in anger that they both did not mean. Her mother, though hurt and disappointed, tried to intervene and make peace between Morgan and her father, though her efforts were made in vain. Morgan just wanted her parents to accept her decision to marry Jerry and to embrace the fact that she was happy.

Jerry moved into Morgan's one-bedroom apartment, as it was far nicer than the apartment that he resided in. He was excited about moving in with Morgan, but at the same time, it was a little overwhelming. He'd gone from being single to being married in a short space of time. They decided to keep Morgan's furniture, as it was also nicer in comparison to the furniture that he owned. There was no space for Jerry's furniture, so he sold it to a student on campus.

Morgan had an actual job, and she received great benefits and insurance plans. She added Jerry to her insurance plans and made him the sole beneficiary of her life insurance policy.

Jerry was looking forward to completing his final semester in college. He was preparing to take the GRE in less than two months. He knew that his hard work would eventually pay off.

He made his way into the hospital for his shift as a patient transporter. It was a busy night in the hospital, and the work kept him on his feet for most of his shift. The elevator ascended from the lower level, and the door opened on the first floor. Lizzy Henson came into full view, and she was ecstatic to see him. There was no one else in the elevator, and Jerry was hesitant to get on board. Reluctantly, he walked into the elevator and watched the door close.

"So how's that girlfriend of yours? Are you still going strong?" Lizzy inquired. She still wore that ridiculous side ponytail, and Jerry desperately wanted to tell her to act her age.

"That girlfriend of mine is now my wife," Jerry responded.

"Your wife? That was fast." Lizzy seemed shocked at the revelation. The door of the elevator opened, and Jerry was quick to get out. "Well, don't be a stranger. If you ever need to talk, the pharmacy is on the lower level." Jerry waved goodbye, but he did not respond to her invitation.

Jerry finished his shift, and by the time he got home, Morgan was already sleeping. She looked like an angel as she slept.

The first three weeks of marriage went relatively well except for the challenge of getting used to each other's habits. It annoyed Morgan when Jerry created a clothing pile, which he added to almost on a daily basis. Jerry's defense was that the clothes were not dirty enough to be washed but they were also not clean enough to be folded into drawers or hung in the closet. It was the pile that could be worn again. It also irritated Morgan when Jerry drank out of containers in the refrigerator or when he left dishes in the sink. Jerry was irritated that Morgan monopolized the bathroom. She took long showers, and her beauty products were piled onto the bathroom counter. A curling iron had found its home on the bathroom counter. Jerry did not feel as if he had any ownership of the bathroom. He felt like a guest when he went to relieve himself or take a shower. It was especially irritating when he had to get ready for classes and he had to compete with Morgan for the bathroom.

Their first major explosive argument came one Saturday after Morgan informed Jerry that it was her colleague's birthday and she wanted to hang out with her workmates. Jerry was scheduled to work a shift at the hospital that night. He was not receptive to the idea, and he told her that she could hang out with her colleagues another time when he would be able to accompany her. The argument escalated to the point that they were screaming at each other. Their raised voices drowned out each other's words, and they were not getting anywhere. Their communication had broken down completely, and their angry words had merged together, creating a clamorous, deafening sound. Morgan could not understand why he had a problem with her hanging out with her colleagues, and Jerry could not understand why she felt the need to hang out with her colleagues, especially without him. Why would she want to have an enjoyable time without him? She told Jerry that she still wanted to go out, and he made it clear to her that he forbade it. His response to Morgan was, "If you love me, you would respect my wishes." The conversation ended with Morgan in tears. She lay face down on the bed and sobbed uncontrollably. Jerry got himself ready for work, and he left Morgan still crying on the bed.

Jerry came back late from work, and Morgan was sleeping. He gently kissed her cheek and got ready for bed.

Their relationship was an up-and-down roller coaster. When they were on top, it was a wonderful feeling, but their relationship came quickly crashing down with forceful speed. Instead of being an intense thrill like that of a roller coaster, the drop was a dreadful, frightful, insufferable experience. Jerry was always quick to point out Morgan's faults, and he often blamed her for causing the arguments. Morgan was often left in tears, and they both were filled with anger and frustration.

After the intense emotions subsided, Jerry often bought Morgan flowers. He would apologize and beg for her forgiveness. The frustration and anger would leave Morgan's body like an exhaled breath, and the relationship would appear to be great again. They were on top of the tracks of the roller coaster again, and they were awaiting that imminent fall.

One day, Morgan lamented to Jerry that she had not spoken to her father since the revelation of the marriage. She spoke to her mother occasionally, but the relationship with her family was just not the same. Jerry told her that he was her family and he would always be there for her. He told her that all they needed was each other and they did not need anyone else. Morgan hugged him, but she was saddened at the same time.

One day, Morgan came home almost four hours late from work. She'd had a lot of paperwork to catch up on, and the work had taken longer than she'd anticipated. Jerry was fuming as she entered the door. His face was almost frightening, and Morgan was hesitant to walk further through the door. She closed the door behind her, and he demanded to know where she'd been for the last four hours. She explained to him that she'd been at work, catching up on some paperwork, but Jerry did not seem to buy it. He accused her of having an affair, which she adamantly denied. Despite multiple attempts to convince him that she was not having an affair, Jerry's belief was firm and unshakable. She continued to argue her case and was interrupted with a slap across her face from Jerry's hand. It was the first time that he had hit her. He called her horrendous names, and the tears streamed down her face.

"I can't do this anymore," Morgan said in a whispered voice. She felt helpless and trapped.

"You can't do what anymore?" he asked. His eyes were fixated on her.

"I can't do this anymore. I can't live like this. I don't know who I am anymore. Our relationship has many more downs than ups. There are more tears than smiles, and there's more sadness than happiness." Morgan sat on the couch and buried her head in her lap. She continued to cry, and her body shook from the sobbing and weeping.

"I'm sorry, Morgan. I love you. I never meant to hurt you. I promise I will never hurt you again," Jerry pleaded.

Morgan sat up, and she removed her hands from over her eyes. There was hurt and pain behind her eyes. "I'm sorry, Jerry. I want a divorce."

Those words were like a sharp knife cutting through his chest. He could not accept her words as reality. He felt rejected, and it left him with a sense of inadequacy and incompleteness. He was not going to allow her to leave him.

"Morgan, please believe me when I tell you that I'm truly sorry. I love you, and I've never loved anyone the way I love you. I can't live without you, Morgan. I would rather be dead than not have you."

Morgan looked at him, and she seemed to be in a state of confusion. It was almost as if she was playing tug of war with her heart and her mind. She loved Jerry, but she knew the relationship was unhealthy. Jerry took a tissue from the side table, and he wiped away her tears. "Please, Morgan. Please give me one more chance. I promise I will change. I promise that I will never hurt you again."

Morgan looked deeply into his eyes. He seemed remorseful for his actions. She thought to herself that he had no one else besides her. He'd lost his parents, who'd died in that tragic car crash. Morgan had never met his friends, and she was unsure whether he actually had any friends. She wanted to believe his apology and his promises, but she was unsure whether that would be the right decision. She chose to believe him, and she embraced him. "I love you too."

Jerry was relieved. He kissed her gently on the forehead, and again, he expressed his love for her. Morgan was mentally and emotionally exhausted. She took a long shower and retired early to bed. Jerry had picked up an extra shift at the hospital from midnight to eight in the morning. This was the first time he'd picked up that shift, but he figured that he had all day Saturday to catch up on sleep.

He lay on the couch until it was time for him to get ready for work. He reflected on the past couple of hours, which created a sense of anxiety and uneasiness. They'd had many bad arguments, but this argument had far exceeded them all. Morgan had never indicated before that she was ready to leave the relationship. It was evident that she had reached her breaking point and that the relationship could disintegrate at any moment. Jerry had been able to stabilize it for the time being, but how did he know she would not try to leave him again? This thought created fear in his mind, and he needed to ensure that this would never happen. He would rather she be dead than leave him.

Jerry turned on his computer, and he started to do some searches on the web. He searched for chemical agents that were fatal but virtually undetectable. He came upon the chemical succinylcholine, and he did more advanced research. He learned that succinylcholine was a chemical used to induce muscle relaxation, including the muscles of respiration, and it was a short-term paralytic agent. It was typically used to help with tracheal intubation. He learned that it was fast in onset and short-acting as the enzyme pseudocholinesterase broke succinylcholine down, making it almost impossible to detect, and its metabolites were naturally occurring molecules. This seemed like the perfect agent, but how would he get a hold of succinylcholine? He'd never thought this desire would ever cross his mind, but he hoped that Lizzy Henson was working tonight.

The shift was light, and he had a lot of idle time. He kept his eyes peeled for Lizzy Henson, but she was nowhere in sight. Sometimes she would be on the floors of the hospital, carrying out her duties. He decided to go to the pharmacy on the lower level of the hospital. He hoped that she was the clinical pharmacist on for the night. He neared the pharmacy, and to his relief, Lizzy was in sight. He waved enthusiastically to her, and she reacted with a wave. He never thought he would be happy to see Lizzy Henson.

"So, what brings you down to the dungeon of the hospital?" Lizzy inquired.

"You invited me. Don't you remember? Or did you not mean it?" Jerry responded with a smile. "You changed your hair, I see. You now have your ponytail on the other side."

"Wow. I can't believe you noticed. So, how are you? How's marriage life treating you?"

"Good. I can't complain," Jerry responded. "But enough about me. How are you doing? How's your love life going? Have you found that young partner yet?"

Lizzy laughed. "No. Not yet. I haven't given up, though. One day, my young Prince Charming will come riding up on a white horse. Or walking towards the pharmacy of the basement of the hospital." Lizzy laughed again. "I'm just kidding. I'm just kidding."

Jerry smiled at her. "So, give me a tour of the pharmacy. Are you the only one down here?"

"For now. My tech has taken a break. She should be back in about fifteen minutes. But I'll be happy to show you our wonderful pharmacy." Lizzy opened the door into the pharmacy and allowed Jerry entry. "So, what do you want to see? Basically, we have drugs, drugs, and even more drugs. We have a drug for this and a drug for that. Basically, we have drugs for everything."

"What about the really cool drugs? Like the ones they use when there's a code blue called in the hospital." Jerry had an intrigued look on his face. Lizzy showed him the code cart. "So, teach me about some of these drugs. What are they used for? Wait. I hope

I'm not taking up too much of your time. I know you're probably very busy."

"I can always make time for you, Jerry." She winked. "Besides, the night is not too busy." Lizzy went through some of the different medications in the code cart.

"So, when the doctor puts that tube down the patient's throat, what medications are used? I'm sure they just don't stick the tube down."

Lizzy was delighted at Jerry's fascination with her job. "You mean when the patient is intubated?" Lizzy gave him a smile.

"Yes. When the patient is intubated." Jerry gave her a smile back.

Lizzy showed him the drugs used, and Jerry's heart started to beat faster when he heard the name "succinylcholine." The phone rang, and Lizzy placed the small bottle of succinylcholine back into the cart.

"This is Lizzy," she stated through the telephone receiver. While Lizzy was distracted on the telephone, Jerry placed the bottle of succinylcholine in his pocket. He also placed a syringe and a needle into his pocket. A few seconds later, Lizzy got off of the phone. "So, where were we?" she asked.

"You were educating me about the cool drugs. You are a very smart woman." Lizzy started to blush. "But I have already taken up enough of your time. I should get back to work myself." Jerry said goodbye, and he made his way to the elevator.

Jerry got back to the apartment a little after eight in the morning. He opened the door to the bedroom, and Morgan was still lying in bed asleep. He closed the door slowly and made his way into the kitchen. He thought about their relationship and how much he loved her. He questioned whether she truly loved him. If she loved him, she would never have threatened to leave him. Did she want to leave him for another guy? He was not going to let that happen. She would be dead before he ever let that happen. He took the syringe and needle and the bottle of succinylcholine out of his pocket. He stared at the items for a few moments. He blamed Morgan for the evil act that he was about to carry out. He blamed her for trying to break them apart. Jerry removed the wrapping of the syringe and the needle, and he screwed the needle on. He then removed the cap from the bottle of the succinylcholine. He drew out some of the drug into the syringe and then replaced the cap on the needle. He placed the syringe in his pocket and opened the door to the bedroom.

Morgan opened her eyes and sat up in the bed. She was wearing shorts and a t-shirt. "You're home. Good morning."

"Good morning," Jerry responded and he sat on the side of the bed next to her. "How was your night? Did you sleep okay?"

"I slept okay given the circumstances of yesterday. How was your night?"

"It was okay," Jerry answered. "Look, Morgan, I want to apologize again for last night."

"You've already apologized, and I've accepted your apology." Morgan leaned forward and gave him a hug.

"I know, but I have to get this off of my chest. Just because someone does bad things, it does not make them a bad person. I'm deeply sorry for all of the bad things I've done, but I'm not a bad person. Do you believe that?"

"I do believe that. No one is perfect, Jerry."

"I just want you to know that I love you. I love you too much. The thought of you ever leaving me is unbearable. I could never allow you to leave me, Morgan. I will never allow that." Jerry leaned in to give her a hug again, and she laid her head on his shoulder. He took his right hand, and he placed it in his pocket. He took the syringe out and flipped off the cap with his thumb.

"What are you doing?" Morgan said in a soft voice as her head continued to lie on his shoulder. She was oblivious to Jerry's actions.

"Nothing, my love." He took his left hand and rubbed it up and down over her left thigh. Morgan thought it was a sweet gesture.

"Again, I'm sorry, my love. I'm not a bad person." He then took the syringe and jabbed the needle into her left thigh. Then he pushed the drug into her system.

The effects of the drug were immediate. He pulled both of her legs toward the foot of the bed so that she was now lying flat on her back. Morgan was not breathing, and her eyes were open. Within moments, it was apparent that Morgan was dead. He picked her up and laid her on her back onto the floor. He carefully hid the drug and all of the evidence, and he planned on getting rid of the evidence at the earliest opportunity. Jerry picked up the phone and called 911.

"Nine one one. What's your emergency?" a male voice said on the other end of the line.

Jerry responded in a frantic voice, "I just got home from work, and I found my wife seizing. I have her on the floor, and it does not look like she's breathing. Please send someone now. Please!"

The 911 operator took Jerry's home address, and he sent a dispatch out to the residence. "Does she have a pulse?"

"I did not detect a pulse, and I've been doing CPR. She's not responding!" Jerry wailed into the phone. "Where is the ambulance?"

"The ambulance and the police are on their way," the operator assured him.

Within moments, the sirens could be heard approaching, and Jerry ran to open the door. He motioned to them to hurry up. "My wife's not breathing. Please hurry!" Jerry ran back into the bedroom and started compressions on Morgan's chest. He was crying loudly, "Morgan, please don't leave me! Open your eyes, Morgan! Please don't leave me!"

The paramedics took over. Morgan did not have a pulse, and she was not breathing. She was hooked up to the monitor. "We have something," one of the paramedics reported. "She's in V-tach!" The paramedic shocked her, and ACLS was underway. She was intubated in the field, and IV access was obtained.

Jerry watched on in horror. The thought that they may be able to revive her scared him. Surely if they were successful, she had to be brain dead given the amount of time she'd been down. The paramedics placed her in the ambulance, and Jerry was denied the opportunity to ride along. He drove his car behind the ambulance.

Morgan was rushed into the emergency room, and she was placed into a room. The emergency room physician took over. After several more minutes, their efforts were deemed futile, and Morgan was pronounced dead. The physician, whose name was Dr. Tyler, walked out into the waiting room, and he gave Jerry the bad news and offered his condolences. Jerry screamed out, and he began to cry. Dr. Tyler gave him a couple of minutes, and he placed his hand on Jerry's shoulder.

"Can you tell me what happened?" Dr. Tyler asked.

In a choked voice, Jerry replied, "I came home from work a little after eight this morning. I work here at this hospital as a patient transporter. When I got home, I called out to my wife, and she was not responding. I walked into the bedroom, and it looked like she was having a seizure on the bed. Her body was shaking." Jerry demonstrated to the doctor the seizure-like activity that he'd witnessed. "She just would not respond. I picked her up from the bed, and I laid her on her back onto the floor. She wasn't shaking anymore, and she did not look like she was breathing. I checked her pulse, but I could not detect one. That is when I called 911. I tried to do CPR on her. When the paramedics came, they took over."

"Does she have a history of seizures?" the doctor asked.

"Not that I am aware of," Jerry responded.

"Does she have any medical problems? Does she take any medications?"

"I don't think she has any medical problems, and she does not take any medications. The only pills that I see her take are vitamins."

"Does she smoke? Does she drink alcohol or use drugs?"

"She does not smoke. She rarely drinks alcohol. I mean rarely. And no, she does not use drugs," Jerry answered.

"Do you know if she has a family history of any heart problems or if any diseases run in her family?"

"I actually do not know. I don't know her family history."

"Well, Jerry. I really can't tell you why she went into cardiac arrest," the doctor stated. "We have sent some lab work out and a drug screen. I am awaiting the results. It is very odd that a healthy young woman would go into cardiac arrest. The question is whether she had an underlying heart condition. I would definitely advise you to move forward with an autopsy. It might reveal the answers as to why your wife went into cardiac arrest. It might also help me when I have to fill out the death certificate."

The room that Morgan had been pronounced dead in was cleaned, and Jerry was allowed entry into the room. He approached Morgan's dead body, laid his head onto her chest, and cried. The nurse came in with paperwork for him to sign. She also wanted to know if he wanted to proceed with an autopsy. Jerry had given it thought while he was in the waiting room. The succinylcholine that he'd injected Morgan with would be undetectable. There was no way that the cause of her death would be identified. He also did not want to look suspicious by declining an autopsy, especially since it had been recommended by the ER physician. He was listed as a sole beneficiary on Morgan's life insurance. It was standard for the insurance company to investigate the cause of death, and an autopsy would satisfy the insurance company. Jerry made the decision to proceed with the autopsy.

CHAPTER 18

MORGAN'S FAMILY WANTED TO BRING THE BODY HOME TO PHOENIX AND GIVE HER A proper burial. Her father was convinced that Jerry was responsible for his daughter's death in some way, but he had no way to prove it. The autopsy results came back inconclusive, and the manner of death was undetermined. The death certificate stated cardiac arrest as the cause of death, with no secondary cause.

Jerry felt that he had gotten away with murder, but he was not free from the prison that he was living in. The blood of three people had stained his hands, and he could not wipe it off. The panic attacks returned, and they were worse than before. He could not concentrate on his studies, and the anxiety and panic attacks took over his life. The nights were met with terror, and insomnia visited him every night.

It was the night before the GRE, and he could not sleep a wink. He took some Benadryl, but he was still wide awake. He drank some more of the Benadryl, and he consumed more than the recommended dose. He awoke in a drowsy state, and he looked at his watch. He tried to focus on the hands of the clock. The time came into view, and Jerry realized that he had less than fifteen minutes to get to the testing center. He must have slept through his alarm clock.

Jerry got up in a frenzy and threw on a wrinkled t-shirt and a pair of jeans. He barely had time to brush his teeth and wash his face. He jumped into his dilapidated car and turned the key in the ignition, which did not start until the third attempt. He sped out of the apartment complex and headed westward, in the direction of the testing center. He was almost out of breath as he ran to the room where the testing was held. The facilitator had already started to give out the instructions. Jerry signed in, and another facilitator led him to his seat.

Jerry tried to focus on the words on the paper. The sentences on the paper seemed to all come together, and the words were incomprehensible. He tried desperately to concentrate, but he was not successful. At the completion of the exam, Jerry knew that he had failed. He had failed miserably, and he did not need to wait for the scores to confirm it.

His hopes of getting into an MBA program had gone out of the window. His dreams of becoming a successful businessman on Wall Street would never come to fruition. His life was falling apart in front of his eyes. He could at least try to get his degree and graduate. He had not done well on his last mid-term exams. In fact, he'd failed a couple of them miserably. His final exams were approaching, and it was imperative that he did well to avoid failing any of his classes.

Jerry went to work that evening, and he ran into Lizzy Henson. Lizzy expressed her condolences, and she offered her support, but her words were met with indignation. Jerry did not want to talk about Morgan, and he wanted to be left alone.

The following day, Jerry ran into Matthew Van Long at the grocery store. Matthew was a student in Jerry's statistics and calculus classes. His father was a judge back in Texas, and Matthew liked to brag that the law was on his side. He invited Jerry to a party that he was throwing at his place. Jerry declined the invitation, but Matthew just would not take no for an answer. Jerry finally gave in to his request. It was a Saturday, and he needed to get his mind off of the difficulties he was facing.

Jerry pulled into Mathew's place a little after 9 pm. He lived in a townhouse on a very nice side of town. The living room was packed with college students, and the alcohol was flowing freely. Jerry recognized some faces, and he made small talk with a couple of the guys in the corner of the room.

A little after 11 pm, Jerry was getting ready to leave. He found his host to thank him for the invite, but Matthew tried to persuade him to stay.

"The party's just getting started. You can't leave now," Matthew urged.

"I had a great time, but I'm going to head out. Thanks for inviting me."

"Before you leave, let me show you something." Matthew led Jerry upstairs into one of the bedrooms. "Not just anyone is allowed in this room, so consider yourself lucky." The bedroom was already occupied by five guys and one girl. "This is going to make you feel really good," Matthew stated. There was a table in the room, and two of the guys were snorting this white substance. Jerry knew exactly what that white stuff was, and he did not want anything to do with it. "Come on, Jerry. Give it a try. It will take all of your fears away, and it will make you feel on top of the world."

"Yeah, man. It's the best feeling in the world," one of the other guys in the room added.

Jerry thought to himself that one snort would not hurt. He would give anything to feel on top of the world, even if it was only for a few minutes. The guys and the sole girl in the room egged him on, and he fell into the temptation. One of the guys demonstrated how it was done, and Jerry followed the instructions. He snorted a line into his nostril, and he felt an instant rush to his brain. It was a feeling of energy that he'd never experienced before, and this was followed by an intense sense of happiness. From that moment, he knew he had fallen prey to the devil of this white substance. It was a feeling he would never want to end. He drank alcohol with his new set of friends in the forbidden room upstairs.

Finally, it was after 3 am, and most of the partygoers had already left. There were a handful of stragglers who were passed out in a drunken state. Jerry made the terrible judgement to drive home, and it was a miracle that he got back to his apartment in one piece.

He staggered up the stairs and fumbled with the lock for a few seconds before gaining entry into his apartment. He was too exhausted to change out of his clothes, and he collapsed onto the bed. He felt miserable and run down, and his body ached all over. He felt locked into a depressed state, and he felt restless at the same time. It was a horrible feeling that Matthew had warned him about. He needed to get another hit to experience that intense high again.

Jerry filled out the claim for the life insurance policy and sent in a certified copy of Morgan's death certificate. He was the sole beneficiary to Morgan's $500,000 life insurance policy. He'd actually been surprised when Morgan had suggested it. She'd also requested that he too get a life insurance policy, though he'd never gotten around to it. Morgan had been thinking long term, and she'd thought a life insurance policy would be beneficial, especially when they had kids.

The days passed, and Jerry had fallen into a deep depression. He had failed his final exams, with the exception of one C in economics. He was surprised that he'd actually made a C, as he'd been almost certain that he had failed the exam. Jerry was unable to graduate, and he was expected to repeat the classes that he had failed. That light that he'd seen at the end of the tunnel a few months ago had extinguished. There was not even a flicker.

It took almost sixty days before he was awarded the payment from the life insurance company, and when it came, he had more money than he knew how to spend. The light at the end of the tunnel was visible again. The first thing he needed was a hit to get him out of the rut and make him feel confident and unstoppable.

He contacted Matthew Van Long, who put him in contact with his dealer. The highs were amazing highs, but the lows were extreme lows, and he constantly craved that high feeling. He had developed a dangerous and expensive habit.

One night, he was engaged in a conversation with his dealer, which was out of the norm. Usually, they would carry out their business dealings and part ways. His dealer, who went by the name Buck, confided with Jerry how he'd become a dealer. Jerry, in turn, shared his story of how he'd become hooked on the white stuff. Jerry stated vaguely that he had done vile and horrendous things in life that he was not proud of and that these terrible acts had been haunting him day and night. He had failed his classes and his GRE exam, and all of his dreams were shattered. Jerry shared with Buck his wishes of starting fresh on a clean slate, though he knew it was not possible. Buck revealed to Jerry that he knew the exact person who could help him, though it would cost him. Jerry was skeptical whether anyone could help him.

Buck proceeded to tell him of his boss, who was a former CIA agent. His boss went by the name Regulator, and no one under him knew his real name. Buck stated that his boss could fix anything or make anything go away for the right price. Buck had Jerry's full attention, and Jerry wanted to know more. He wanted to meet Regulator, even though the thought of meeting someone by that name sent chills down his spine. Buck said that he could arrange for a meeting and that he would inform Jerry of the time and the place.

The next day, Jerry received a call from Buck, who instructed him to meet at Lou's Diner at 2 pm sharp and gave him the directions. He was advised where to sit, and he was given step-by-step instructions. Jerry looked at his watch, and it was 1:36 pm. He was slightly irritated that he had not been given advanced notice. He turned off the television, made his way to his car, and headed in the direction of Lou's.

Jerry pulled into the lot of the diner, and he looked at his watch. It was 1:53 pm. He walked through the door and was greeted by a waitress, who informed him that he could sit anywhere of his choosing. Jerry sat in a corner booth and ordered a cup of decaffeinated coffee. At 2 pm sharp, a man appeared to have materialized, and he stood above Jerry at his booth. The man then sat in the booth opposite of him. The stranger was a white man who appeared to be in his early to mid-sixties. His hair was mainly gray, with some dark strands, and he had a beard that was completely gray. His dark eyes were small but piercing, and he did not appear to blink.

"Jerry Frye, what can I do for you?" the stranger asked in an emotionless voice.

"Are you Regulator?" Jerry asked. He was terrified by the presence of this stranger, who was stone-faced and seemed devoid of emotion.

"Were you expecting someone else?" the stranger replied sarcastically. "So, what can I do for you? My time is extremely important, and I value every minute of it."

Jerry was taken aback by the man's response, and he felt that he was on the clock. He did not want to upset this man who referred to himself as Regulator. The waitress made her way over to their table, and the stranger ordered a cup of coffee. "Well, Buck said that you could help me. He said that you could help me put my past behind me and give me a fresh start."

"So, you want a new identity?" the stranger continued. His eyes remained fixated on Jerry.

"What do you mean, a new identity?" Jerry asked, confused.

"You want me to remove all traces of Jerry Frye and give you a new identity. New name and documents, a new life, and a fresh start as you call it. I can give you a birth certificate, driver's license, a college degree, and an MBA degree from the university of your choice."

Jerry's eyes became wide in shock and bewilderment. "You can do that?" he responded in disbelief.

"For $250,000, I can," the man replied.

Jerry was speechless as he watched the stranger staring at him. The price tag was enormous, but it was a small price to pay for a new life. He had already blown through several thousand dollars for that white stuff. If he paid Regulator $250,000, he would still have enough to live on when he started his new life.

"I don't have all day, Mr. Frye. Do you want my help or not?"

"I do want your help," Jerry answered, and he felt confident with his decision. "So, how does this work? Do I get my new life, and then I pay you?"

"That is not how it works. You pay me, and I will give you a new life," the stranger responded authoritatively.

"What about half down and the other half after I get my new life?"

The stranger looked at him with his chilling eyes. "You give me all of the money, not a penny short, and then I will give you your new life."

Jerry was shocked, and he started to question his decision. He had an uneasy, nauseating feeling, and he felt as if the coffee would erupt from his stomach. In a stuttered voice, Jerry asked, "How do I know that I can trust you after I give you my money? How do I know your plan will work?"

The stranger did not divert his eyes, and he watched Jerry very closely. Jerry felt his body start to tremble, and he tried desperately to appear calm and not to indicate to Regulator that he was shaken to his core. "I am a businessman, and my word is solid. You give me the money, and I will give you a new life. If you don't want my help, then don't waste my time. I have other pressing business to attend to." The stranger started to get up, and Jerry had a change of mind.

"Wait!" Jerry said quickly.

The stranger stopped midway. "Don't waste my time, Mr. Frye," Regulator cautioned, and he sat back down. "Do we have a deal?"

Jerry took a deep breath. "Yes, we have a deal." The words were out of his mouth, and he knew he could not take them back. "So, how do I get you the money? How do you get me a new life, and where will I live? I want to live in New York City, and I want to work on Wall Street." Jerry also blurted out the college and MBA program of his choice. It had to be an MBA from an Ivy League university.

"I will be in touch with you in forty-eight hours. I will tell you how to wire me the money, and you will be instructed what to do. You will start a new life in New York City." The stranger stood up, left some money on the table, which was more than what was needed for his cup of coffee, and walked out of the door of the diner. Jerry was uncertain whether the last fifteen minutes of his life had been real. Had he actually made a $250,000 deal with a stranger named Regulator to start a new life with a new identity? He pinched himself. It definitely was real.

———————

Two days later, Regulator called Jerry on an untraceable number and instructed him on how he was to wire the money. He received clear, step-by-step instructions, and he was warned not to deviate from the plan, or there could be dire consequences. He was told to go to the bank and ask for Andrew. He was not to let anyone else help him with the wire transaction. Jerry was on edge during the entire conversation. He started to feel sick again, and a wave of nausea rushed over him. Everything seemed surreal. Regulator's voice was stern and direct, and there were no unnecessary words used. He told Jerry that he would await the money, which he expected to be wired that day, and then he abruptly hung up the phone.

Jerry's heart was pounding, and he felt as though his heart would beat out of his chest. He sat down on the bed to collect his thoughts and to regain his composure. What other web had he woven himself into? He seemed to dig himself into a deeper hole at every opportunity. He then reminded himself that this deal with Regulator was to dig himself out of the hole that he'd previously created and to cover it up for good. This deal he had agreed to was to bring him above ground, where he could move around uninhibited with the sun shining on his face.

Regulator expected the money in his account by 3 pm sharp. Jerry's heart continued to beat fast as he made his way down to the bank. There was no turning back at this point. In fact, there'd been no turning back after he'd made that agreement with Regulator in the diner. He pulled into the parking space outside of the bank. He sat in his car for a few moments and took slow, deep breaths. He got out of his car and made his way into the bank. He was greeted upon entry by a young woman who appeared to be in her early thirties, and he was offered assistance. Jerry asked to speak with Andrew. The young woman asked him his name, and she told Jerry that she would inform Andrew of his presence.

A couple of minutes later, a white male in a black suit and a blue tie approached him. He was about five foot ten, with black hair and a clean-shaven face. He introduced himself as Andrew, and he led Jerry into his office. He closed the door behind them, and he offered Jerry a seat.

"I've been expecting you," Andrew stated as he sat in his leather chair. Jerry did not know how to respond, and he sat in the seat without a response. "We have some important business to take care of that is strictly confidential, and I trust that you will maintain good discretion in this matter."

"Yes," Jerry responded.

Andrew took Jerry's bank information and pertinent personal information. He typed away on the keyboard, and after several minutes, he indicated that the money had successfully been wired.

"It's done. Anything else I can help you with at this time?" Andrew asked, though he expected the answer to be no.

"No. That would be all."

Andrew stood up, and Jerry followed suit. He extended his hand out to Jerry for a handshake. "It was a pleasure doing business with you," Andrew stated.

Jerry could not say the same. "Thanks." He left Andrew's office and walked out of the bank.

The money was gone out of his account, and the sick feeling in his stomach returned. He realized that he had no way to contact Regulator, and the only thing he had was the hope that the call would be returned. An hour elapsed, and he had not received a call. He chastised himself for being so naive and stupid. His life seemed like it could not get any worse, but every day proved that to be untrue. How could he have let someone swindle him out of $250,000?

He anxiously waited in his apartment, and moments later, his cell phone rang. That familiar stern and emotionless voice was on the other end of the line. "You have seventy-two hours to move out of your apartment. Take the flight to New York City JFK airport on Monday morning leaving at 6:50 am." Regulator proceeded to tell Jerry the airline and flight number. He cautioned Jerry that there were only three seats left on the flight and that he needed to book his ticket right away. "There will be a man holding a sign with your name. He will take you to your predetermined destination," the voice stated. Jerry did not get a word in before the communication was terminated.

Jerry held his cellphone to his ear and repeated the word "hello" four times, but he knew Regulator was gone. What kind of game was this? What was the plan when he arrived, and where was this stranger going to take him? Where was he going to stay? Would he have a new identity when he moved to New York? All of these unanswered questions swirled around in his mind.

Jerry booked the flight to JFK airport as instructed. He pulled out two suitcases from under the bed, and he started packing. There were items that he would not need that he decided to bring to the thrift store. What was he going to do with the furniture? He could just give it away. He would have to figure it out soon. He also needed to terminate his rent agreement, which stated that a thirty-day notice was required. He would just have to pay the rent for an additional month. He already had cash in his wallet and his ID and credit card.

Jerry took a taxi to the airport early Monday morning. He checked in and waited at the gate. The entire experience was new to him, and this would be his first time flying in an airplane. He boarded the airplane, and he found his way to seat 16A, which was a window seat. His nerves were on edge as he waited for the airplane to take off. The thought of being thousands of feet above ground made him nervous, and he hoped that his panic attacks would not return. The airplane accelerated down the tarmac, and Jerry felt his body tilt back as the airplane lifted off of the ground. Jerry noticed that he was holding on tightly to the arms of his seat, and he released his grip. He peered out of the window, and it looked as if he was above the heavens as the airplane soared over the clouds. The fear turned into an exhilarating experience as he took in the moment. He was flying high, and he was on his way to New York City. He experienced periods where he just did not feel that the moment was real. His emotions seesawed from that of excitement to that of apprehension. He was excited to experience the city of his dreams, but he was also suspicious and uneasy of what awaited him.

The airplane landed on schedule. Jerry collected his suitcases on the baggage carousel, and he went through the automatic sliding doors. There was a line of people awaiting passenger arrivals, and some of them had signs. As expected, there was a man holding a sign that had the name Jerry Frye written on it. He approached the man, who was of East Asian heritage, and he introduced himself. The man did not offer an introduction in return.

"Follow me," the stranger ordered. Jerry did as he was told and followed closely behind. He was led to a parking lot, and his suitcases were placed in the back of a black Suburban. The man, who obviously worked for Regulator, opened the back passenger door, and Jerry slipped in the back row. The man then walked around and got into the driver's seat. He paid the parking fee and followed the directions that led him out of the airport.

Jerry leaned forward as he sat in the back seat, and he peered through the windshield. He wondered where the stranger was taking him. "Where are we going?" Jerry asked.

The man kept his eyes on the road and ignored the question. Jerry sat back in the seat. He knew it was futile to ask any more questions. He looked outside the window and observed the scenery. He watched the brown buildings and the green signs as they made their way onto Interstate 678 N. It started to drizzle, which gave his surroundings a bleak and dreary look. The black Suburban made its way onto Interstate 495 W Long Island Expressway, towards the Midtown Tunnel. They drove through a toll booth and entered the Queens Midtown Tunnel towards Manhattan. They exited the tunnel, and took the exit towards downtown.

They had been driving for over forty minutes. He gazed through the window, and he looked up at the towering buildings that penetrated the sky. It was a marvelous sight, and he felt as though he had entered another world. There were a multitude of yellow cabs that drove by, and the sidewalks were bustling with people. It was a stark contrast to what he was used to, but he could certainly get used to it, and he welcomed his new environment with open arms. The Suburban pulled up to a red light, and he observed the thick flow of pedestrians crossing the street. Some wore suits and business attire as they made their way with urgency across the street. There were some who were obviously tourists, as they held their cameras and appeared to be in awe of the city. The city was certainly diverse. As the Suburban waited at the light, Jerry was greeted with a mouthwatering aroma that appeared to be originating from across the street. There was a street vendor who was surrounded by a handful of people waiting to be served.

The light turned green, and the Suburban accelerated. The stranger made a few turns down streets lined with tall buildings. The Suburban then turned into a garage, and the stranger drove up to the fifth level of the building. He parked the Suburban into one of the spaces.

"Leave your suitcases in the vehicle and follow me," the stranger instructed. Jerry did as he was told and followed behind. The man swiped an ID badge, and they gained entry into the building. They walked down a deserted hallway, and the stranger swiped his badge to gain entry through another door. Jerry followed the man to the end of another deserted hall. The stranger knocked on the door, and a stern voice on the other side of the door ordered the knocker to enter. The door opened, and Regulator was in view. He was seated on a brown leather chair behind a desk. The walls of the room were white, and there was nothing hanging or mounted. The room was rather plain and quite uninteresting. The only thing on the desk was a manila envelope and a large manila folder.

"That will be all for now," Regulator stated while looking in the direction of his worker. The man exited the room and closed the door in obedience. "Have a seat, Mr. Frye." Jerry sat in the seat opposite Regulator, and he tried to appear calm. "Welcome to New York City, and I hope that it is everything that you've dreamed of," Regulator stated with a smile. The comment and the smile took Jerry by surprise. The smile softened Regulator's face, and it made him seem personable and relatable. The moment was short-lived as the smile was quickly wiped off of his face and his expression became intent and serious. "Now, let's get down to business." Regulator pushed the manila envelope towards Jerry and invited him to open it. Jerry took out a stack of papers that were held together by a large paper clip.

"Your name is now Anthony Dominic West," Regulator continued. "The real Anthony West was killed in France when the train that he was taking to Florence derailed due to excessive speed and crashed, killing fifty-two passengers on board. Anthony was studying abroad in Paris. He is of mixed race. His father, whose name was George Harrison West, was a black man, and he was born in Philadelphia. I use the word 'was,' as Anthony's father died when he was seventeen years old from a massive heart attack. His mother, whose name is Sarah West, is a white woman who was born in Livingston, New Jersey. Her maiden name was Madison. Anthony's parents met in New Jersey while attending college. Anthony West was born and raised in Livingston, New Jersey, and he lived a few months in Manhattan before deciding to take another life path, which influenced his move to Paris. His mother currently resides in a nursing home ten miles outside of Livingston, and she suffers from progressive relapsing multiple sclerosis. Anthony was an only child. After Anthony's unfortunate and premature death, there was no death certificate issued in the United States. His insurance company, bank, and the credit bureaus are not knowledgeable about his death. I have been able to access Anthony's personal and private information, and you will now have access to his credit and finances. This is your new social security number." Regulator pointed out the number, and Jerry looked through the pages in disbelief.

"This is your new date of birth. Anthony West was two years older than you. Therefore, you have been aged by two years. With all of the information that I have provided you in this envelope, you should have no problems obtaining a driver's license under your new name and requesting a copy of your new birth certificate. Lastly, my employee was able to successfully tap into the system of the university that you requested. You graduated summa cum laude with your business degree in finance, and you successfully completed your MBA." Regulator opened up the folder on the desk to reveal two degree certificates with the name Anthony Dominic West. "It looks authentic, doesn't it?" Regulator asked, which Jerry knew was a rhetorical question.

Jerry sat in the chair, speechless, as he paged though the documents. There were no words to express his feelings at the moment. He was experiencing a variety of emotions that were mixed together and did not clearly make any sense. It was a mixture of surprise, bewilderment, and disbelief, but also a feeling of elation, triumph, and hope.

"Is everything to your satisfaction?" Regulator asked.

"I cannot thank you enough," Jerry responded with a wide grin.

Regulator stood up, and Jerry stood up also. Regulator extended his hand towards Jerry for a handshake. "It was a pleasure doing business with you, Anthony West."

The name Anthony West was something that he had to get used to. "It was a pleasure doing business with you also," Jerry responded with a smile.

"Peter will come back in to escort you to the vehicle with your luggage, and he will bring you to a hotel. You can now begin your new life in New York City."

Peter, Jerry thought to himself. *So that's his name.*

CHAPTER 19

TWO MONTHS HAD PASSED SINCE HIS MEETING WITH REGULATOR, AND ANTHONY HAD started to settle into his new life. He interviewed for positions on Wall Street, and he was hired almost instantly as an investment banking associate after his CV revealed that he'd graduated with an MBA degree from a top business university. Anthony was ecstatic, and the first thing he did after receiving the exciting news of his new job was to go out shopping. He bought five suits of high quality. Three were black, one was gray, and one was brown. He also bought ten ties, three pairs of dress shoes, and dress socks.

He settled into a one-bedroom apartment in the Upper East Side, which was very pricy. *Who cares?* Anthony thought. He still had money from the life insurance settlement, and he now had a job on Wall Street. He tried on one of his black suits again, and he looked out of the window of his apartment. He watched the yellow cabs drive by, and he watched the people walking in a hurried manner across the street. It was everything that he'd wanted and hoped it would be. He took a deep breath, and he filled his lungs with air before exhaling the breath. He was living his dream.

Anthony woke up Monday morning at 6:30 am to the sound of his alarm clock. It was his first day at his new job on Wall Street. He was very excited but a little nervous at the same time. The first day was only orientation, and the next four weeks were training, so he tried not to stress himself out. He took a warm shower, brushed his teeth, got dressed for work, and drank a cup of coffee. He made his way out of his apartment building and headed to the subway station. Anthony descended the steps into the dim station and used his ticket to go through the turnstile. The station was busy and crowded. As he maneuvered his way towards the area of the train tracks, he detected a faint smell of urine. He could hear the train approaching in the distance, and it was in view after several seconds. The train came to a stop, and the doors opened. The scene was disorderly as passengers tried to enter and exit the train at the same time.

Jerry got on the train at the last moment, just as the doors were about to close. The train was crowded, and he was one of many passengers who had to stand up, as all of the seats were taken. He observed the people traveling with him, and he wondered where they were going. There were several passengers wearing suits, and it was apparent that they were going to work. A handful of the passengers were reading newspapers or some other type of reading material. There were several who were sharing laughs and talks with their riding companions, or possibly strangers. There were some passengers who appeared as though they did not want to be bothered. Some were wearing headphones, and some had their eyes closed and could have possibly fallen asleep. The train stopped at Anthony's station, and he got off. He followed the signs, and he walked up the steps and exited the station.

The sidewalks were bustling with people. He made his way onto Wall Street. He took a slow deep breath, and he breathed in the smell of opportunity and success. Anthony walked into the building of the investment banking firm. An overwhelming feeling of importance and accomplishment filled his body as he looked up at the inner walls of the building. He was a part of the leading financial center of the nation and the world. He was now integrated into the fiber of an economically powerful institution that was at the center of massive influence and wealth. He observed the men and women walking throughout the building. They were impeccably dressed, and they walked around with an air of importance.

Anthony made the decision that he would be the best investment associate and prove his value, with the goal of being promoted to associate vice president and steadily moving up the ladder.

The investment banking program was very intense, and he was in a fierce working environment. He was surrounded by eager and hungry associates and analysts who all wanted to have an edge over the other. He was in a lion's den, and he could be eaten at any moment if he was not on guard. At the start of the program, Anthony learned quickly that he had to change some of his habits. He was not very organized, and that changed quickly. He realized that organization and efficiency would be a main key to his success. He kept a daily calendar, and he worked from a list in which he prioritized his duties and responsibilities each day. He learned the value of time, and he was always on the clock. After the training program, the associates were assigned to teams, where they worked under senior bankers.

Anthony was enjoying his position as an investment banking associate. It was the hardest job that he had ever done, but it was rewarding. His goal was to stand out and prove his value to the firm.

It was 12:30 pm at the job, and it was time for lunch. His stomach was growling, and he decided to try the deli across the street. The deli was small, with limited seating, and the room was crowded. He was able to grab a seat at a small table in the corner of the room immediately after the occupants left. He sank his teeth into a roast beef sandwich and sipped on a large Coke. Minutes later, a woman approached his small table, and she asked if she could join him. Anthony obliged her request.

"Thank you for allowing me to sit with you. This place is packed, and there are literally no seats," the woman stated. She was an attractive black lady of medium brown complexion and with chin-length hair cut into a bob.

"No problem," Anthony responded. "It was mere luck that I was able to snatch this table."

"I'm Valerie Brooks, by the way."

"I'm Anthony West."

"It's a pleasure to meet you, Anthony. Do you work here on Wall Street?"

"Yes, I do," Anthony answered. They both discovered that they worked at the same firm. It turned out that Valerie was a second-year associate at the firm. They spoke about their job and their future goals for over twenty minutes.

"So, Anthony, are you married or in a relationship?" Valerie inquired.

Anthony smiled and responded, "No, I'm not. I hope you're not asking me out with a ring on your finger."

"Oh, no. No, no," Valerie replied. Then she tried to clarify her question. "I have a very good friend, who happens to be single, that I would love for you to meet."

"Is that so?" Anthony smiled again. "Tell me about this friend of yours."

"Well, her name is Giselle Bellamy, and she is twenty-two. Very attractive. Model features, actually. Very intelligent. Great personality. I think you will find her very lovely and charming."

"If that's an accurate description, then I certainly can't say no. So, tell me, Valerie. If your friend is all of these great things, then why is she single?"

"Well, Anthony, I could ask you the same question about yourself. But to answer your question, she just has not met the right one yet."

"No, Valerie! I'm tired of you trying to set me up," Giselle Bellamy said, scolding her friend. "Why can't you take no for an answer?"

"This one is different. I promise," Valerie pleaded.

"That's what you said about the last one," Giselle blurted out.

"I did not know he was gay. How was I supposed to know that? He did not give me any indication that he was gay. But you have to admit, he was a great guy. He just preferred men over women."

"And the time before that?" Giselle reminded her friend.

"Okay. That's not my fault. I never met the guy. He was a friend of a friend, and he sounded very good on paper."

"That date still goes down as the worst date in history," Giselle reminisced. "The date was so unbearable that I told him I was going to the ladies' room, and I made a quick exit out of the restaurant."

Valerie started to laugh. Giselle finally saw the humor as she reflected on the experience, and she joined her friend in laughter.

"See, Giselle, we can look back and laugh at it, but this guy is different. There will be no looking back and cringing. I promise if you give this one a try, I will never play matchmaker again."

"Fine," Giselle responded as she waved her white flag. "Tell me about this guy."

Valerie was excited that her friend had opened up to this new prospect. "His name is Anthony West, and he is a new investment banker associate at my firm. He has looks to die for. I'm telling you, Giselle, if I wasn't happily married, I would give him a chance. But aside from looks, most importantly, he seems to have a great personality. Looks, brains, and personality. Jackpot! You're welcome, Giselle."

"I'm not thanking you yet, given your failed record in the matchmaking department."

"That actually hurts my feelings," Valerie replied with a frown. "You will live to regret that comment."

"I hope so. I hope you redeem yourself."

"I have a feeling I will redeem myself," Valerie responded with confidence. "In return, I expect that my slate will be wiped clean, and I will no longer be viewed as a terrible matchmaker."

"Done," Giselle replied with a laugh. The friends shook hands in agreement.

The following day, Valerie wasted no time in seeking Anthony out and giving him Giselle's number. She encouraged him not to waste time in calling, and he took her advice. He, however, decided to call the following day, as he did not want to appear too aggressive, but he did not want to wait too long and appear uninterested.

It was Saturday afternoon around 2 pm when Anthony decided to give Giselle a call. After the third ring, she picked up.

"Hello."

"Hello. Is this Giselle?" Anthony asked.

"Yes, it is."

"This is Anthony West. I work at the same firm with your friend Valerie."

"Yes. Hello. Valerie told me about you."

They spoke on the phone for almost an hour, and their conversation focused on the city and all of the exciting things to do and see in Manhattan. Their conversation shifted to food, and they gave each other recommendations on the best places to eat in the city. Giselle recommended an Italian eatery, which she ranked the number one place to eat a New York pizza. She raved about the pizza, and she described it as the best pizza she had eaten in her entire life. Anthony suggested that they meet up there for dinner that evening. They agreed to meet up at Migliore Pizza Italiana at 6 pm.

Giselle was very excited about her date. Anthony seemed very nice and charming, and he had a great sense of humor. Valerie may have redeemed herself, but it was too soon to tell. Giselle rummaged through her closet, and she finally decided on a black and white striped maxi dress. She accessorized her dress with silver stud earrings, a silver bracelet around the right wrist, and her watch that she always wore around her left wrist. She lightly sprayed her neck and wrist with her favorite perfume, which always generated compliments. She decided to wear her hair down, and she allowed her natural curls to fall loosely down her back. She threw on a pair of black sandals, grabbed her purse, and made her way out of her apartment building.

Giselle walked the short block to the subway station, and she waited on the train. She tried to envision what Anthony West looked like. Valerie had described him as having looks to die for, but her friend often had the tendency to exaggerate. She did not want to get her hopes up about the date due to an underlying fear that she might be disappointed.

Giselle got off at the third train stop, and she made her way up the stairs to the exit. She walked a block to Migliore Pizza Italiana. It was almost 6 pm, and she wondered if Anthony had made it to the restaurant. She walked into the lively restaurant, and told the hostess that she was meeting someone by the name of Anthony West. The hostess informed her that Mr. West was already seated at the table, and she ushered Giselle to the table.

Giselle approached the table, and Anthony got up and pulled out her seat. She was very impressed by this simple act. Her first thought about Anthony was that he was a gentleman. Her second thought was the acknowledgment that Valerie had not been kidding. Anthony West was a very attractive man. Looks to die for may have been an exaggeration, but he was certainly a very handsome man.

"It's very nice to meet you, Giselle," Anthony stated with a smile. Giselle instantly noticed his beautiful smile, which lit up his green eyes.

"It's nice to meet you too," Giselle responded with a smile. Anthony thought that she was beautiful, and there was an instant attraction.

"So this is the place that you raved about. I like the ambience. I'm looking forward to trying this New York pizza."

"You won't be disappointed. I guarantee that it will be the best pizza you've ever tried. Sometimes I literally crave a slice of this pizza."

Anthony smiled at Giselle, and he thought her excitement about the pizza was rather cute. The waitress introduced herself, and they ordered a large New York pizza, and they both ordered Cokes.

Anthony shared a story about an incident in the subway station on his way to the Italian eatery, and Giselle thought the story was hilarious. They both laughed, and they were enjoying each other's company. The waitress arrived with a large hot pizza, and she placed it on a rack in the center of the table. A delightful aroma emanated from the pizza, and Anthony could not wait to sample a slice. Giselle insisted that he take the first bite, and he sank his teeth into a slice, which slightly burned the roof of his mouth. Aside from the minor burn, the pizza was very delicious.

"So, what do you think?" Giselle waited in anticipation for a response.

"It's very good."

"Isn't this the best pizza you've ever tried?" Giselle asked, expecting her date to agree.

"Well, I wouldn't say that, but it is definitely up there. It is definitely very good."

Giselle seemed content with his response. They laughed and joked throughout their meal, and they seemed to have made a connection. "So, Giselle, tell me a little bit about yourself. We have been so engrossed in conversations about the city and places to eat. What do you do for a living? Are you in school, or are you working?"

"I recently completed my bachelor degree in forensics, and I'm working in the forensic department downtown. I hope to go back and specialize in forensic toxicology."

"Forensics. Wow. So you enjoy that kind of stuff?"

"I love it. I enjoy putting pieces of the puzzle together. It is very exciting to me," Giselle responded. "So, you're an investment banking associate. Are you enjoying your position at the firm?"

"It's a lot of work, and it's a competitive position, but I am enjoying it. I welcome the challenge, and I'm hoping one day to advance my position in the firm or maybe have my own investment firm one day. Who knows?"

Giselle admired Anthony's confidence as he continued to talk about his goals and aspirations. She was impressed with his drive and ambition. "So, where are you originally from, Anthony?"

Anthony had the details of his new identity down pat. "Well, I was born and raised in Livingston, New Jersey. My mother is from Livingston, and my father was from Philly. My parents met in college."

"Are your parents still in New Jersey?" Giselle asked.

"Well, my dad died when I was seventeen years old from a massive heart attack."

"Oh, I'm so sorry," Giselle quickly interjected.

"It's okay," Anthony assured her. "It was hard when it happened, but I've coped with it."

"What about your mother?"

"My mother has a severe form of multiple sclerosis, and she is in a nursing home outside of Livingston. I think that she has developed early stage dementia."

"I'm very sorry to hear that." Giselle did not know what else to say, and there was a period of silence.

Anthony broke the silence. "So where are you from? Tell me about your family."

"Well, I was born in Baton Rouge, Louisiana, but I spent most of my life in New Orleans. I spent a short period of time in Shreveport, Louisiana before moving to New York City." The mention of the city Shreveport left a sour taste in his mouth. He did not want to hear about Shreveport ever again. "Have you ever been to Louisiana?" Giselle asked.

"No, I've never been," he lied.

"Well, you have to visit New Orleans one day. My parents still live there. My father is a certified public accountant in the city, and my mother owns her own Cajun restaurant, which she named

Cecile's Kitchen. The restaurant was named after my great-grandmother Cecile." As Jerry listened, he realized that Cecile's Kitchen was the restaurant that he'd visited during his trip to New Orleans. The conversation was too close for comfort, and he wanted to change the subject. He really liked Giselle, and he wanted to see where the relationship would go.

"So, what do you like to do for fun?" Anthony asked with the hope of changing the conversation. Giselle spoke about her interests, and it turned out that they had similar hobbies and interests. They talked and laughed for another hour after they completed their meal. They walked to a gelato shop, and each ordered a scoop of chocolate gelato on a sugar cone. They walked the streets of the city, and delighted in each other's company.

Giselle looked at her watch, and it was after 10 pm. The time seemed to have flown by. Anthony walked Giselle to the subway station. He rode the train with her, and he walked her to her apartment.

"I had a great time this evening," Giselle gushed.

"I had a great time too," Anthony responded with a smile. "I hope we can do this again."

"Definitely. You have my number," Giselle said flirtatiously.

"I hope you have a good night. Sleep well." Anthony turned around and walked away. Giselle admired the fact that he had not tried to kiss her or come into her apartment. She thought he was the perfect gentleman, and she felt that she was in love. Valerie's slate was wiped clean. She'd hit the jackpot!

CHAPTER 20

"SO, HOW IS THE LOVE LIFE GOING?" VALERIE ASKED GISELLE WITH A BROAD SMILE ON her face as she cut up the red potatoes.

"It's going great. It will be three months tomorrow that Anthony and I have been dating." Valerie was very happy for her friend, and she felt a great sense of pride for her role in bringing the two together.

Giselle was having Valerie and her friend Kate over for dinner at her apartment. They usually got together once a month to cook dinner and have a girls' night. Kate Davenport was a friend of Giselle's from work, and she worked in the forensic DNA analysis division. Kate was an attractive woman with shoulder length blonde hair and light brown eyes. Kate was quite content with her social life. She had no plans on settling down soon, and she loved the idea of dating with no strings attached. Kate had just returned from a trip to Cancun with her "no strings attached" boyfriend, and she had a great tan to prove it.

"I don't understand this need to settle down in our twenties," Kate remarked. "We are only young once. I will think of settling down when I'm in my thirties. There are too many fish in the sea to only catch one fish. When you're tired of all the varieties of fish in the sea, then you settle down with one fish. By that time, you will know what fish you like because you know what's out there. Then you will really appreciate that fish," Kate stated as she cut up the tomatoes for the salad. Giselle was amused and laughed at her friend's analogy.

"Kate, that's the most ridiculous thing I've ever heard in my life," Valerie commented. "Do not listen to her, Giselle. Take it from me. I married my college sweetheart right out of college, and it was the best decision that I ever made. Donald is the most amazing man that I've ever met, and I plan to spend the rest of my life with him. I don't need to sample other fish in the sea to know that I caught the best."

Kate put her index finger in her mouth, and she indicated that she wanted to throw up. Giselle laughed at her friend, but Valerie did not see the humor.

Giselle placed the roast in the center of the table. Valerie placed the seasoned red potatoes and the salad on the table, and they all sat down to eat.

"Can we pray first," Valerie asked. "Thank you for this food that we are about to eat, and may it nourish and strengthen our bodies. Amen."

"Amen," the other two replied in unison.

"What I'm trying to say is this. Everyone is different, and we all want different things in life," Kate continued. "What do you want, Giselle? Do you think that he may be the one?"

"Well," Giselle responded and paused for a few seconds. "He definitely has potential to be the one."

"But," Kate stated as she took a bite of a piece of potato. "I sense there's a but."

"Don't get me wrong. He's a great guy, and I always have an amazing time with him. He's smart and funny, and he's very nice to look at. We can talk for hours on end, but he never likes to talk about his past. He never wants to talk about his family."

"You did say that his father died, and his mom is at a nursing home and she is not doing well. That would be difficult to talk about," Valerie commented.

"Yeah. I get that. But it's not just that. I know he's an only child. But that's really all I know. He never wants to talk about his life growing up. I know nothing about his life in New Jersey. Even when I talk about my life growing up in Louisiana, he just kinda goes quiet. He just does not seem interested."

"Well, it's not like you had this fascinating life. I would fall asleep too if I had to listen to your life story," Kate teased.

"Very funny, Kate," Giselle replied sarcastically. "I've led a very interesting life, thank you. Anyway, it's just weird, or maybe I'm just reading too much into it. But any other topic, we can go on for hours."

"Maybe he's just a forward thinker. Some people are like that, you know," Valerie stated as she tried to make sense of what Giselle was saying. "By the way, Giselle, this roast is amazing. Very flavorful. You have to give me the recipe."

"Thanks," Giselle replied. "But I guess you guys may be right. Maybe I'm just reading too much into it."

"Or maybe you're not," Kate thought out loud. "People show you what they want to show you. We all have skeletons in our closet, and who knows what's in his background. Supposed he's married. Do you remember that guy that Valerie tried to set you up with that we found out was married with a child and he owed a lot of child support?"

"Okay. Let's not live in the past," Valerie interjected. "I had no idea he was married, let alone had a child."

"I say we do a background check on this Anthony West," Kate suggested.

"Uh, I don't know," Giselle replied with hesitation in her voice.

"I know you don't want to do a background check on someone you care about, but if you're experiencing any uneasiness, then it might be the best thing to do." Kate tried to give Giselle some assurance. "Look at it this way. If nothing shows up, then you can move on with your relationship without a cloud overshadowing it. If something bad turns up, then you can break it off and spare yourself heartache. You're only three months into your relationship.

It's better to know now than to find out something really bad down the road when you're fully invested in the relationship."

Kate had stated her case, and she'd made a lot of sense. "You're right," Giselle responded. "Let's do a background check on him. With my previous luck in the dating department, I need to know that I'm not getting into something that I'm going to regret."

The friends finished off their dinner, and they placed the dishes in the sink. Giselle insisted that she would wash the dishes later, and she went to her bedroom to retrieve her laptop. She placed the laptop on the dinner table, and the friends pulled up a chair next to her, one on each side.

Giselle typed in the address of the site that Kate recommended. Kate had done a lot of background checks in the past, which was not surprising given her dating history. Kate had paid a yearly fee for full access to the site, and she logged in her information.

"All right. Here we go," Giselle stated as she took a deep breath. She typed in the name Anthony West in the designated field, and she typed in New York as the state. If the state of New York did not give her the information that she needed, the next step would be to type in New Jersey. Giselle had limited information to go by. She knew his middle name was Dominic, and she knew he was born November 3rd, and she knew his age. Based on that information, she could calculate the year of his birth. She knew he was born in Livingston, New Jersey. She knew his father was born in Philadelphia, and she was almost certain that his father's first name was George. She knew his mother was born in Livingston, and she remembered clearly that her name was Sarah. Based on that information and some further web searches, Kate was able to bring up a background check on Anthony West.

They all stared at the screen as the information loaded. Anthony West's record was now in view, and Giselle realized that she was holding her breath. Giselle's heart raced as she scrolled down the screen, and she looked at all of the information. At the completion of the search, she breathed a sigh of relief.

"See. Now you have nothing to worry about," Kate stated as she put an arm around Giselle. "There are no arrests or warrants. There are no liens or bankruptcies. There are no marriage or divorce records. There are no court records. It looks like he has a clean record. This is cause for celebration. Do you have any wine?"

"I have a bottle of red wine in the cabinet," Giselle replied. Kate opened up the bottle of wine, and she poured three glasses. Kate toasted Giselle to a long life of love and happiness. The friends clicked their wine glasses.

"Cheers!"

***

"Can you believe that ending?" Giselle said to Anthony with excitement as they exited the movie theater. "I had no idea the maid was the culprit. That ending was so unexpected."

"I suspected the maid was up to no good, but I did not suspect she was behind it all."

Giselle and Anthony discussed the movie the entire train ride back to her stop. As usual, Anthony always walked her back to her apartment after their date. He followed her inside of her apartment.

"Do you want a glass of wine?" Giselle asked.

"Sure. I can get it," Anthony replied. He went into the kitchen and reached for two long stem goblet wine glasses. He popped open the bottle of red wine and poured the alcohol about halfway into the two glasses. They sat on the couch, and he placed an arm over her shoulder. She nuzzled her head onto his chest and placed her legs up on the couch.

"So, how was your week?" Giselle asked.

"Hectic. Cash flow analysis. Executing financial transactions. Talking to corporations about mergers and acquisitions. That kind of stuff. What about you? How was your week?"

"This was a tough week. I'm on the case of a little girl whose parents are accused of murdering her. I'm going through some of the evidence." Giselle sat up and sipped her wine. Then she rested her head back on Anthony's chest. "This job can be really tough. Not the day-by-day job itself, but the emotional aspect. I try not to become too emotionally involved in the cases, but sometimes you can't help it."

"I understand," Anthony replied as he took a sip of wine from his glass. "But you can't let yourself get emotionally involved. It can drive you crazy. You have to learn to separate the duties of your job from your emotions."

"You're right. It can become a weight on your shoulders. I need to be able to separate the two. For example, there was a case that I was briefly involved in a few years ago that I've never been able to get out of my mind. I was an intern with the crime scene investigation unit in Shreveport, and it involved a college student who was raped and murdered in her apartment." Anthony's body immediately tensed up. "Are you okay?" Giselle asked as she sat up erect on the couch.

"Yes. I'm okay," Anthony stated as he cleared his throat. He felt as if beads of sweat were forming on his forehead.

"It was the most horrific scene that I've ever witnessed. I saw her lying lifeless on the floor, and it was the worst thing imaginable. Everyone said it was this student named Nathaniel Wellington and the case was closed. After all, his fingerprints and DNA were found at the scene of the crime. He committed suicide in the jail." Anthony listened to Giselle, and his body was very uneasy. Giselle continued, "Even though his fingerprints and DNA were at the crime scene, I'm just not so sure that he did it."

"Why do you say that?" Anthony asked as he tried to remain calm and collected.

"You're going to think that I'm crazy when I tell you this." Giselle paused for a moment. "So, I went to visit Nathaniel in the jail the day before he committed suicide. He told me that he thought he'd been framed, but he did not know who would try to frame him. I didn't believe him at first. It seemed like a farfetched defense. But as I spoke to him longer and I looked into his eyes, I started to believe him. His eyes told a different story, and they were windows into his soul. I just can't explain it. My boss at the time did not feel the same way that I did. What do you think?"

"Can we not talk about this and just enjoy the rest of the night."

"Okay. But just tell me what you think," Giselle pleaded.

"I think that this guy was manipulating you. That is what criminals do. They play on the emotions of others. They are master manipulators. So let the evidence speak for itself. It seems like he got what he deserved."

"You really think so?"

"Yes, I really do," Anthony replied. "So, can we now drop this?"

"Okay." After almost a minute pause, Giselle asked, "But could Nathaniel be different? Could he have not been a criminal, and could he have been framed?"

"That's enough, Giselle!" Anthony realized that his tone was raised. He noted that Giselle's body had become tense, and he softened his tone. "I'm sorry, love. I'm just not feeling well. I think it is all that buttery popcorn I ate at the movie. But to answer your question, I don't know Nathaniel, so I can't answer that question. But if his DNA and fingerprints were found in the apartment and he lived in the same building, chances are that he may have done it."

"How did you know that he lived in the same building?" Giselle inquired.

"You told me," Anthony reacted.

"No, I didn't." Giselle appeared perplexed.

"Oh. Well, maybe I assumed." Anthony did not know what else to say. "I love you, Giselle, and I believe in you. You are great at what you do, and your department is lucky to have you."

Anthony was not feeling well after that conversation. He hoped that Giselle had dismissed his comment about Nathaniel residing in the apartment building.

"Do you want some tea?" Giselle asked.

"No. I think I'm just going to head home and get ready for bed. It's just been an exhausting week."

"Okay. I'll walk you to the door." Giselle walked Anthony to the door, and he kissed her good night.

Giselle walked back into the living room area and sat on the couch. She gulped down the rest of the red wine. She felt very uneasy, but she just could not put a finger on it. There was just something about Anthony that was not sitting right with her. He did not have a criminal record or anything concerning on his background record. He was well educated, and he had a great job on Wall Street with room for advancement. Then, what was it about him that made her very uneasy?

Giselle grabbed the stems of the wine glasses from the center table, and she brought them to the kitchen. As she was about to place the glasses in the sink, she noted a clear fingerprint on the wine glass that belonged to Anthony. She knew the other wine glass was hers, as it had a red lipstick stain on the rim. She had only touched the stem of the glass, so the fingerprint had to belong to Anthony. She decided not to wash Anthony's glass, and she placed it in a clear food storage bag and sealed it.

Giselle then got ready for bed. She took a shower, and the warm water felt good on her body. She tied the towel around her and reached for the toothbrush in the toothbrush holder. As she brushed her teeth, she thought about the wine glass with his fingerprint. She did not know what it would prove, but she would bring the sealed item to her job, and she would run an analysis on the fingerprint. She expected that the results would reveal to her what she already knew. Nothing. Giselle thought to herself that her past dating experiences might have been making her paranoid. She also thought that her feelings were not fair to Anthony. He should not have to pay for her past experiences. She decided to wash his wine glass and place it back in the cabinet. Giselle went into the kitchen and retrieved the clear bag that was sealed with the wine glass. She thought for a moment, and her decision went back and forth. After a few minutes, she decided to bring the wine glass to the lab on Monday.

Giselle opened her eyes and stared at the alarm clock. The time was 5:01 am, which was an hour before her alarm clock was set to go off. She had not slept well that night, and she'd found herself tossing and turning. Her mind raced at full speed as one thought was replaced with another. She struggled with the idea of whether to proceed with the analysis or whether to abort her plans. Giselle placed herself in Anthony's position, and she thought how angry she would be if he obtained her fingerprints without her knowledge and conducted an analysis on the sample. The word "anger" was an understatement. She would be infuriated. In fact, she would never speak to him again. How could a relationship grow and flourish if it was bound by suspicion and skepticism? If this relationship was to evolve, she had to allow herself to trust him and not allow her fears to dictate the relationship. These thoughts weighed heavily upon her, and she decided not to run the tests. It was still dark outside. It probably would have been futile to try and go back to sleep.

The tiredness was still behind her eyes as she got out of bed and made her way into the kitchen. Giselle turned on the coffee machine, and after a couple of minutes, the coffee was ready, and it was piping hot. She was not much of a coffee drinker, but a hot cup of coffee was imperative to start the day. The aroma from the coffee and the warm liquid running though her system gave her an instant perk, and the tiredness seemed to vacate her body. She turned on the news and got herself ready for work.

Giselle exited her apartment, and as she was about to lock the door, a strange feeling descended upon her. That uneasy feeling had taken over her body again. The door knob was still in her hand as she contemplated her decision. Yes, she wanted to trust him, but that uneasy feeling inside of her could not be ignored or discarded. Giselle opened the door to her apartment, and she made her way into the kitchen. She opened up the cabinet and removed the plastic bag that contained the wine glass. The plastic bag was sealed, and she placed it in her large handbag. Giselle left her apartment and made her way to the train station.

Giselle boarded the train and grabbed a seat. She thought about Anthony the entire ride. Her mind was so absorbed with thoughts of him that she almost missed her stop. She got off the train and walked up the stairs to the exit. The light of dawn was present in the sky. Her job was two blocks away. She arrived at the latent lab almost an hour before her work officially started. Giselle was alone in the lab, and she stared at the glass in the plastic bag. Her specialty was identifying and evaluating fingerprints.

Giselle put her hands in a pair of small gloves, and she got to work. This was an opportune time, as her colleagues were not expected at work for another forty-five minutes. She sprinkled some black fingerprint powder onto a piece of paper. She then took a brush and placed it in the powder. After getting rid of the excess powder, she dusted the surface of the glass, which revealed several prints. There was a clear depiction of five fingerprints, one for each finger that had grasped the glass. There was also a part of a palm print noted. She lifted a fingerprint with clear adhesive tape, and ensured that there were no bubbles or creases in the tape. The tape, which contained the fingerprint, was then removed, and she placed it on a latent lift card. The process was repeated for the four other fingerprints, and the tape was also used to lift the piece of the palm print. Giselle condemned herself for what she was doing, but she could not resist moving forward with the analysis. The next step was to load the fingerprints in the Automated Fingerprint Identification System. As she waited, she thought to herself that her actions were ridiculous. What was she going to accomplish?

Giselle sat back and waited, and what materialized before her eyes was completely unexpected. She was in utter shock. She leaned forward and visually compared the fingerprints that were loaded to those that had come up as a match in the system. They were a perfect match. Her emotions were a mixture of confusion and horror. Who is Jerry Frye? This has to be a mistake! Giselle typed in more information, and she knew it was not mistake. A picture of Jerry Frye came up, and he was sixteen years old at the time. He had been confined to juvenile detention for theft and assault with a deadly weapon. The picture of Jerry Frye was undoubtedly a picture of Anthony West at a younger age.

Giselle stood up from her chair, and she almost lost her balance. Her body was in shock, and her legs had difficulty holding the weight of her body. Giselle immediately sat back down, or she would have collapsed onto the ground. Her heart was racing, and she was breathing heavily. A multitude of questions fired throughout her brain. Why and how had Jerry Frye changed his identity to Anthony West? Who was the real Anthony West? Who was the real Jerry Frye? What else was in Jerry Frye's past that he'd felt the need to change his identity? What had happened after he'd left the juvenile detention center? Where had his life taken him? Should she go to the police? She couldn't go to the police. His fingerprints had been obtained without cause and without his knowledge. She had, however, obtained information that should be investigated by the authorities. Giselle decided that she would first do the investigation herself. It was imperative that she find out what was in Jerry Frye's past.

Her mind was not focused at work. The only thing she could think about was the identity of Jerry Frye and his new identity in the form of Anthony West. Giselle called Kate after work and indicated that they needed to talk about an urgent matter. She met up with her friend at Kate's apartment after work.

"What's wrong?" Kate asked with concern in her voice. "Have a seat. Do you want some water?"

"No thanks," Giselle responded as she sat on the brown leather couch. Kate lived in a small apartment in Lower Manhattan. The décor of the apartment could easily be described as eclectic.

"What's the matter?" Kate stated as she sat next to Giselle on the couch. "Talk to me."

"First of all, you have to promise me that you're not going to say anything to anyone," Giselle cautioned as she looked her friend in the eyes.

"Giselle, you're scaring me."

"Kate, you have to promise me."

"Of course. I promise. I won't say anything."

Giselle took a deep breath and then continued. "It's Anthony. He's not who he says he is."

Kate had a confused look on her face. "What do you mean he's not who he says he is?"

"I mean he's not Anthony West. His real name is Jerry Frye."

"Wait. I'm confused," Kate responded with a clear look of bewilderment on her face. "What do you mean his real name is Jerry Frye?"

"I obtained his fingerprints from a glass when he was over last Friday. I ran them in the lab this morning."

"You did what!" Kate said in disbelief as she shifted her body on the couch. She was looking directly at Giselle. "Why would you do that?"

"There was something about him that just was not sitting well with me. I can't explain it. It was just a gut feeling. I thought to myself that I was just being paranoid. He seemed like an all-around great guy. We also ran that background check, and I thought it would remove any concerns, but it was just this feeling that I had that I just could not shake off. He came to my place Friday night after we took in a movie, and our interaction just seemed off. He did say that he was not feeling well, so I attributed it to that. But when he left, the unsettling feelings that I had returned. I was putting the wine glasses away when I noted a fingerprint on his glass. I knew it wasn't mine because my glass had a lipstick mark, and I'd only held the stem of his glass. It must be the forensic scientist in me, because my first instinct was to run the prints. I tried to talk myself out of it, and I actually did, but this morning, I could not resist the urge to run the prints."

"So, what happened when you ran the print?"

"Well, fortunately, there were latent fingerprints from all fingers and a part of a palm print. When I placed the prints in the database, there was a match. I visually compared them, and without a doubt, the fingerprints were a match."

Kate's eyes were wide open, and her jaw dropped as she waited for Giselle to divulge more information.

"The name that came up as a match for the fingerprints was Jerry Frye," Giselle continued. "So I did more research. The finger-prints were obtained when Jerry Frye was sentenced to a detention center for theft and assault with a deadly weapon. The picture of Jerry Frye was definitely Anthony West. A younger version, but it is definitely him."

"This does not make sense," Kate stated with a questioning look on her face. "Are you absolutely certain about all of this?"

"I am one hundred percent certain. It's very strange. I have to get to the bottom of this. I have to find out more about this Jerry Frye. I need to find out what is in his background that he is hiding and why he felt the need to change his identity."

"This sounds like it could be dangerous. Maybe you should just go to the police," Kate suggested.

Giselle's phone rang, and it was Anthony that was calling—or should she have said Jerry Frye? The beating of her heart intensified. She decided to ignore the call, and the phone went to voicemail. "What am I supposed to tell the police? I obtained fingerprints without consent or just cause, aside from my gut instinct, and I ran the fingerprints in the database. I can't do that. I can't go to the police."

Kate was very concerned. "Maybe you should just break it off with him. You could tell him it's not working out, or whatever you want to say. Maybe you should just get far away from him."

"I can't just ignore it. It will haunt me if I don't get to the bottom of this."

"Just be careful, Giselle. If there's anything you need me to do, just let me know. Call me anytime."

"Thanks." Giselle hugged her friend and left the apartment.

Giselle walked down the sidewalk and headed to the subway station. The sky was gray, and it looked like it was about to rain. Before descending the stairs to the subway, her phone rang. The name Anthony West appeared on the screen, and her body stiffened up. The phone continued to ring, and she made the decision not to answer the call.

Giselle walked down the steps and maneuvered through the crowd until she arrived at the platform. It was still rush hour, and the subway station was congested with people. There was a disheveled man sitting on the ground a few feet away from her, and she watched momentarily as he played the guitar. The man possessed some talent as he strummed the guitar and belted out the tune "One Love" by Bob Marley. There was a blue plastic cup in front of him, and a couple of dollars were seen peeking out above the rim.

She heard the sound of the train approaching, and it slowed down as it moved past her. The train appeared full, and there were many passengers that were standing. The train came to a stop, and the doors opened. Passengers exited the train, and some of the passengers coming on board tried to enter at the same time. Giselle was able to board the packed train, and she reached up and grabbed one of the pivoted handles. The train halted at the third stop, and she got off and then exited the subway station.

Her phone rang, and the name Anthony West appeared on the screen. She again ignored the call and allowed it to go to voicemail. Her phone indicated that a message had been left. She listened to the message, and Anthony appeared to be in a rather good mood. In a cheery tone of voice, he asked Giselle to call him back. It started to drizzle as she walked in the direction of her apartment. Giselle removed her black umbrella from her bag and shielded her body. The rain started to come down harder, and she impulsively increased her speed. She then made a left turn down the street that led to her apartment.

Giselle approached the main door to her apartment building, and she fumbled in her large bag for her keys, which had an access card to get into the main building. The rain was gushing down, and she was getting wet despite being under the umbrella.

"Hello, Giselle."

The familiar voice stopped her in her tracks. Giselle turned around, and Anthony was standing in front of her. He was wearing a black raincoat, and the rain was dripping off of the material. The image of him standing in front of her sent chills down her spine.

Giselle took a deep breath. "Anthony. You scared me," she stated as she tried to remain calm.

"I'm sorry. I didn't mean to scare you. I've been trying to reach you."

Giselle opened the main door, as she was getting soaked, and Anthony followed her into the building. She did not want this man in her apartment, and she desperately wanted him to leave. "I'm sorry. My phone must be on silent, and I forgot to put the ringer back on." Giselle stood in the foyer, and she watched Anthony remove and bundle up his wet coat.

"Can I come up for a few minutes?" he asked.

Giselle's reply was delayed. "I have a lot of work to do tonight, and I'm not feeling too well. I just want to finish some work up and head to bed early."

"You're not feeling well? What's the matter?" Anthony inquired.

"I'm having a headache. It feels like a migraine."

"I'm sorry, love. I'll only come up for a few minutes. Maybe I can make you a cup of hot tea. I can even whip you up something to eat. What do you have to cook?"

"That's okay. You don't have to do all of that. I'll give you a call tomorrow." She hoped that Anthony would take the hint and decide to leave.

"It's no problem at all. In fact, I insist," Anthony responded. Giselle was very hesitant, but she knew Anthony was not going to take no for an answer. He followed her into the elevator, and they made the ascent to the fourth floor of the building. Anthony followed closely behind as she walked the hallway that led to her door. Giselle wondered if Anthony knew that she knew his secret. Would he hurt her because she knew he was not who he said he was? There was no way that he could be on to her. She opened the door, and he followed her into the apartment.

"I'm sorry about Friday. I did not mean to leave so abruptly," Anthony apologized. "I think it was definitely the buttery popcorn. From now on, just plain popcorn." He smiled at her, and she forced a smile back. "Sit down, love," he continued. "What do you have in your fridge? I can make you something to eat."

"Anthony, you really don't have to do that."

"Do you want me to just order in? I can order a pizza. Or maybe Chinese food."

"No. I'm really not very hungry," she stated. Anthony sat on the couch, and he invited her to sit next to him. She really wanted him to just leave, but she was uncertain how to make this request. An option would be to just be blunt and demand that he leave, but she was unsure how he would react. He asked her again to sit next to him, and she obliged. Anthony placed his arm around her, and she felt her body tighten up. Giselle wondered if he'd noticed her reaction. She did not want this stranger touching her. She had no idea who the man sitting next to her was. Her phone started to ring inside of her bag.

"I thought you had your ringer on silent," Anthony stated as he looked at her.

"Ah. I guess it was not on silent. Maybe I was in the subway station when you were trying to call."

Anthony continued to look at her. "Okay," he responded. Giselle was unsure whether he believed her. "Are you going to answer it?"

Giselle walked over to her bag that was sitting on the kitchen counter. The phone stopped ringing by the time she got to it. After a few seconds, the phone started to ring again. It was Kate calling.

"Hello," Giselle answered. Kate expressed on the other end of the line that she was worried. She asked Giselle is she was okay and whether she was going to end the relationship. Giselle responded with one word answers. It was apparent to Kate that Giselle was not alone, and she asked if Anthony was present. Giselle responded, "Yes."

"Okay. I'll talk to you later," Kate said.

"Thanks for checking up on me," Giselle said through the receiver. Then she hung up the phone.

"Who was that?" Anthony inquired.

"Oh, it was my friend from work. She was just checking up on me since I was not feeling well."

"What's your friend's name?"

"Kate. Her name is Kate."

"So, are you going to sit back down?" Anthony motioned with his hand as he patted the cushion. Giselle reluctantly sat back down next to him. He placed his arm around her. He then leaned in to kiss her, and she inadvertently pulled away. "Is everything okay?" Anthony asked, surprised at her reaction.

"Oh, yes. I'm sorry. It's just that I'm not feeling well. I'm going to take a Tylenol. I just really want to head to bed."

"Okay. I'll leave," Anthony stated. Giselle was relieved that he'd opted to leave, and she offered to walk him to the door. He stood in the doorway and looked at her. "Are we okay?" he asked with uncertainty written on his face.

"Of course we're okay," Giselle replied with a smile as she tried to appear convincing.

Anthony gave her a gentle kiss on her lips. "Well, I hope you feel better. I'll talk to you tomorrow?"

"Yes," Giselle replied. Anthony walked away, and she closed the door. She turned the lock and then secured it with the door chain. She leaned her back against the door and breathed a big sigh of relief.

Giselle walked into her bedroom and retrieved her computer. The next order of business was to find out the identity of Jerry Frye. She sat with her computer at the dining table, and she logged onto the internet. It was still raining outside, but the rain appeared to have slowed down, and the drops hitting the windowpanes were not as intense. Giselle did a person search on the web. The information she'd obtained from the system at her job had revealed that Jerry Frye was from Greenville, Mississippi. His middle name was Timothy. He'd been sixteen years old at the time, and according to his date of birth in the system, his current age would be twenty-three.

Giselle continued her search, which revealed that he'd relocated to Louisiana from Mississippi. More specifically, he'd moved to Shreveport, Louisiana. She was able to bring up his address in Shreveport. The name of the street was awfully familiar. She searched the address, and to her surprise and astonishment, it was the apartment complex where Sofia Valadez had been murdered. Jerry had later moved to another apartment in Shreveport, which was the last address listed under his name.

Giselle was confused, and she questioned the meaning of the information she'd unearthed. Anthony West, who was actually Jerry Frye, had told her that he had never been to Louisiana. Why would he have lied about something like that? Could he have had something to do with Sofia's murder, or was this all a strange coincidence? She had to find out.

Giselle had to go into work the next day to take care of a few important items, and then she would take a few days off. An option would be to call in sick or maybe even take an emergency leave, though what would be the emergency? She could probably take a flight out to Shreveport Wednesday morning.

CHAPTER 21

THE FOLLOWING DAY, GISELLE LEFT WORK AT 5 PM SHARP. SHE HAD A 7:35 AM FLIGHT out to Shreveport the following day with a short layover in Dallas. Her phone rang as she was walking to the train station, which caused her to stop suddenly. The name Anthony West appeared on the screen. Her initial thought was to ignore the call, but she did not want him showing up at her apartment again because he could not get a hold of her.

"Hello," Giselle said as she answered the phone.

"Hi, love. How are you feeling?" Anthony asked in a cheery tone.

"I'm feeling better, thank you. I was actually going to call you, but you beat me to it. I'm heading out to New Orleans early tomorrow morning. My grandmother is not doing too well." Giselle thought to herself that she was not actually lying about her grandmother, though what she was referring to was not a recent event. Her grandmother's health had been declining over the past year. She, however, felt a little guilty for using her grandmother to create a lie.

"I'm so sorry. I can come over," Anthony offered.

"No," Giselle said abruptly. "I mean, it's okay. I'll be fine."

"How long will you be gone for?"

"I'm not sure at this time."

"I wish I could be there with you. It would be hard for me to take time off of work, but I can fly down Friday night. I want to be there to support you."

"Thank you. I really appreciate it, but you don't have to fly down. Just you offering your support means a lot to me."

"Well, can I see you before you leave?" Anthony asked. Giselle did not know how to respond, and there was silence on the phone. "Hello. Did I lose you?"

"Sorry. I think we had a bad connection," Giselle answered.

"I know you have to pack and get ready for your flight tomorrow. Maybe we can grab a bite to eat at Migliore Pizza Italiana. We can get your favorite pizza."

"Anthony, I don't know. I really should just go home."

"I would really like to see you before you leave. Just a quick bite. I promise. You have to eat. I'll leave you alone after that."

Giselle decided to give in. She would be in a public place with him. Then she could be left alone. "Okay. I can head there now."

"Great," Anthony responded in an elated voice. "I'll see you in about twenty minutes."

Giselle arrived at the eatery before Anthony, and she was seated at a booth. Shortly after sitting down, she saw Anthony enter the door. He spotted her and waved. He made his way over to the table, and he sat opposite her in the booth.

"Hi, love. I hope I didn't keep you waiting too long," Anthony stated.

"No. Not at all. I just arrived."

"Good. So, shall we order the New York pizza?"

"Sure."

The waitress came by, and Anthony ordered a large New York pizza. He ordered a Coke, and Giselle ordered a glass of water.

"You don't seem happy about the pizza. Is it your grandmother?" Anthony asked.

"Yeah. I'm just not hungry."

"Is that all it is?"

Giselle looked at him. "What do you mean?"

"I mean things have not been the same between us since last Friday. You don't call. I feel like you don't even want to be around me anymore. Am I wrong?" Anthony was looking directly at her, and she felt as though he could read her mind. "Am I wrong?" Anthony repeated himself.

"Of course you're wrong," Giselle stated, and she was unsure if she sounded believable. "I've just had a lot on my mind lately. Work. My grandmother. The day you came by, I was not feeling well."

"Uh-huh." Anthony continued to look at Giselle, which made her uncomfortable. The pizza arrived, and she was happy that the conversation had been interrupted. She took a slice of the pizza and placed it on her plate. She added some parmesan cheese and some crushed pepper to the slice of pizza. She looked up, and Anthony was still staring at her.

"Aren't you going to dig in?" Giselle asked.

Anthony took a slice of the pizza and placed it on his plate. "Are you sure you don't want me to meet you in New Orleans on Friday? I can leave directly from work."

"Anthony, I really appreciate it, but I don't think that's necessary. I will call you as soon as I arrive, and I will keep you up to date."

"Okay." Anthony took a bite of his slice of pizza. He changed the subject. "This really is good pizza. I can see why you love this place."

"Yep. It's my guilty pleasure," Giselle responded. She was happy that the conversation had changed to a lighthearted subject.

"I've been meaning to upgrade my phone," Anthony stated. "Do you like your phone?"

"I love it. I got this phone about four months ago."

"Can I see it?" Anthony asked. Giselle hesitated for a moment. She thought to herself that she did not have anything suspicious or incriminating on her phone. Anthony sensed her unwillingness. "I just want to take a look at its features," he continued. Giselle reluctantly handed him her phone. "Wow. This is a nice phone." Anthony played around with the phone for several minutes. Then he handed it back to Giselle. "I just might buy this phone. Maybe you can come with me to buy a new phone when you're back in town."

"Sure. I can do that."

The remainder of the dinner consisted of lighthearted conversation. Anthony paid the bill, and they got up to leave.

"Do you want me to walk you back to your apartment?" Anthony asked.

"It's still bright outside. I'll be fine. I'm just going to go home and pack and make it an early night."

"Okay. Well, get home safely." Anthony reached in to give Giselle a kiss, and her body immediately flinched. He pulled back in response to her reaction. She knew that he sensed something was wrong. He didn't say a word, and he walked out of the restaurant.

Giselle made her way to the subway station and prayed that she was not being followed. The subway station was swarming with people. She weaved her way through the crowd and arrived just on time as the train was pulling up. Giselle hopped on board the train and grabbed onto one of the handrails. She looked around, expecting to see Anthony on board the train, but there were no signs of him. She chastised herself for being paranoid. Why would Anthony be on the train?

Giselle emerged from underground and immediately observed her surroundings. The sidewalks were congested, and there was a rush of people crossing the street. The yellow taxi cabs were intertwined between a sea of cars. She looked in every direction, and Anthony was nowhere in sight. She walked briskly in the direction of her apartment. Then she made a left turn down her street. She looked back, and there was still no sign of Anthony. Giselle looked for her key in her large bag. There were too many things in her bag that created a hiding place for her keys. She felt something brush across her legs, which instantly made her jump. She turned around quickly and realized it was a black cat with piercing green eyes. The cat revealed its fangs, and then it disappeared behind the bushes. Giselle quickly entered her apartment building and closed the door.

Giselle arrived in Shreveport, Louisiana at 2:35 pm after a layover in Dallas. She'd never thought that she would see the city again. Her mind had been immersed with thoughts of Anthony West and Jerry Frye during the entire plane ride. Giselle had tried to devise a plan. She had no plan. The first step would be to pay a visit to her former boss, and hopefully, he could help her unearth the documents related to Sofia Valadez's rape and murder. Her phone rang while she was still in the airport, and it was Anthony West calling. Giselle grudgingly answered the phone, and she informed Anthony that she had arrived safely in New Orleans, which was a lie. The conversation was brief, lasting for less than five minutes.

Giselle rented an economy size car. She drove out of the airport rental garage and then made a right turn onto a main road. She drove in the direction of the hotel. The streets were familiar, and a lot of her surroundings had not changed. It felt as though she had never left. Giselle pulled into the lot of the low-budget hotel that she'd booked. She walked into the lobby and made her way to the front desk.

The attendant was a young brunette who appeared to be in her mid-thirties, and she was far from accommodating. Her badge indicated that her name was Louise. There was no salutation or welcoming words. She smacked on her gum, which was visible as she chewed.

"Can I help you?" Louise asked without looking up from the desk. She was filling out a white form.

"Yes. I'm checking in."

"Name?" Louise asked, still not looking up from the piece of paper.

"Giselle Bellamy."

Louise finally looked up from the sheet of paper. "I need your ID and credit card." Giselle presented the attendant with the requested cards, and Louise typed on the keys of the computer. "Okay. You're checked in."

Giselle was handed a card key, and she made her way to the elevator. The elevator creaked as it made its way up to the third floor. The corridors were dim, and the carpets appeared worn. There was paint peeling from the walls. She made her way to room 309 and placed the card key into the slot. She entered the room, and her first thought was that the room needed a thorough makeover. There was a stain on the carpet, and the walls desperately needed a fresh set of paint. The red comforter was worn, and it likely would not survive another cycle in the washer or dryer. Giselle turned on the dim light in the bathroom. There were rust stains around the sink and the toilet, and two of the tiles were cracked. She quickly used the bathroom before heading out. The hand towel was rough on her skin as she dried her hands. Giselle thought to herself that she'd gotten what she'd paid for. She considered paying the extra money and moving to a nicer hotel the following day.

Giselle drove to the criminal investigation department downtown. She had been acquainted with several people in the department, and she hoped that many of them were still there, more specifically, Michael Bricks. Mr. Bricks was the crime scene investigator whom she'd shadowed during her training in Shreveport. She'd worked under him at the crime scene involving the rape and murder of Sofia Valadez.

Giselle walked into the brick building, and her surroundings were very familiar. There was a police officer sitting in the far corner of the room, and he was reading a newspaper. The officer looked up at her as she made her way to the front desk. Giselle identified herself to the front desk lady and asked if Mr. Michael Bricks was available. The front desk lady, whose nametag read Marcia, asked Giselle whether she had an appointment, to which she replied no. Giselle informed her that she'd trained under Mr. Bricks.

Marcia picked up the phone and dialed a number. "I have Giselle Bellamy wanting to meet with you. She says that she trained under you," Marcia said through the receiver. After a few seconds,

Marcia hung up the phone. She informed Giselle that Mr. Bricks would be out shortly.

A couple of minutes elapsed, and then Mr. Bricks appeared through a door. "Giselle Bellamy. What a pleasant surprise," he stated with a wide grin.

"Hello, Mr. Bricks. How are you?" Mr. Bricks extended his right hand, and Giselle reciprocated, shaking his hand.

"I'm great. Come in." Mr. Bricks gestured with his hand. Giselle walked through the door, and she followed the familiar hall to his office. "Have a seat," Mr. Bricks offered. Giselle sat on the chair in front of his desk. "Coffee?" he asked.

"No thank you."

Mr. Bricks poured himself a cup of coffee. Then he sat behind his desk. "So, are you still in New York?"

"Yes. I am."

"So, how's the job? Is New York City everything that you hoped it would be?"

"Work is good. New York City is great. But I have to admit, sometimes I yearn for the slower pace. But how are you?"

"I'm doing great. I've been over the moon. Jenny and I welcomed a healthy baby girl three weeks ago. Her name is Abigail Grace. We call her Abby." Mr. Bricks was beaming as he spoke about his daughter.

"Wow. Congratulations. That is great," Giselle replied. Mr. Bricks pulled out his wallet and showed Giselle a picture of his baby girl. He could not contain his emotions, and he was smiling from ear to ear. "She is absolutely beautiful, Mr. Bricks."

"Thank you. She looks like her momma." Mr. Bricks placed the picture back in his wallet. "So, Giselle, what brings you back to Shreveport?"

"I don't even know where to start. I'm going to be straight with you, Mr. Bricks. I'm here because I feel there is more to the Sofia Valadez case." Giselle watched as Mr. Bricks's facial expression changed from calm to a confused look. His forehead creased, and he stroked his chin.

"Sofia Valadez. The college student who was raped and murdered?"

"Yes."

"So you say there's more to the case. What do you mean?"

"I think there might be someone else involved."

"Go on. I'm listening."

"There's a man I encountered in New York City who is not who he says he is. I discovered that he changed his entire identity. He took on a whole new persona. I did some research, and I found out that his real name is Jerry Frye. I did more research, and I found out that he was at a juvenile detention facility in Mississippi. Then he moved to Shreveport. He lived in the same building as Sofia Valadez when she was murdered."

"Okay. So what's your proof that he was involved? This guy committed a crime if he illegally changed his identity, but that's it. Everything else you're telling me is circumstantial," Mr. Bricks replied.

"This man never wants to talk about his past. He lied to me when he told me he'd never been to Louisiana. Why would someone lie about that? I did not think about this at the time, but it struck me hard on the flight here. I was talking about the case with him, and he seemed very uncomfortable. He blamed it on the food he ate, but now that I look back, that may have been a lie. I told him that I did not think Nathaniel Wellington was guilty. He told me that if his fingerprints and DNA were found in the apartment and he lived in the same building, chances are that he may have done it."

"That sounds like a reasonable assessment on his part," Mr. Bricks commented.

"But I never told him that Nathaniel lived in the same apartment."

"Giselle, again this is all circumstantial. There is no evidence here. He may have other reasons why he lied about never going to Louisiana. It is your perception that he was uncomfortable when you discussed the case with him. Not many people can handle listening to someone talk about a rape and murder case. And you may have mentioned to him that Nathaniel lived in the same building. Or maybe he assumed or somehow saw it on the news. Who knows."

"It's just a very strong feeling that I have. Something is just not right. It's my intuition," Giselle responded.

"Ms. Bellamy. I distinctly remember having this exact conversation with you. Our line of work is not based on intuition. It is based on facts. It's all about what you can prove, and so far, you have not presented me with any facts. I hope you're not working with your intuition in New York City. It would give me great displeasure to know that my impact on you led you to tackle each case using a hunch."

"No, Mr. Bricks. This case is completely different. I have never felt this way about any case before. I can't tell you why I feel this way, but I just do. Please allow me to review the files again."

"Giselle, I don't know. I think you should leave it alone and move on. You're going to drive yourself crazy."

"I'll drive myself crazy if you don't allow me to get to the bottom of this," Giselle pleaded.

"Just out of curiosity, what kind of relationship did you have with this guy?"

Giselle had been hoping that she would not be asked this question. "We dated briefly."

"Ah. I see." Mr. Bricks took a deep sigh. "What exactly are you looking for? The case has been thoroughly reviewed. The forensic team combed the apartment. The forensic pathologist did a thorough exam. The only incriminating evidence found were fingerprints and DNA that belonged to Nathaniel Wellington, and he is dead."

"Suppose Nathaniel was set up," Giselle thought out loud.

"That's a big suppose."

"Please, Mr. Bricks. Please allow me to review the case again." Giselle waited for a response for what seemed like a long time.

"And if you can't find the answers that you are looking for. Then what?"

"Then I'll just have to let it go."

Mr. Bricks looked at Giselle. Deep down, he knew that she was not going to let it go if she did not get the answers that she needed. "Okay. I'll get you access to the file."

"Thank you so much. I can't thank you enough," Giselle said with a sense of relief in her voice.

After about twenty minutes, she was led to a room. A thin, tall man by the name of Mark accompanied Giselle to review the file. He was very pale, and he had a prominent, hooked nose. She was unsure what Mark's role was in the department, and frankly, she did not care enough to ask. Giselle opened up the file, and she carefully reviewed it page by page. At the completion of the file, she went back to the beginning and reviewed it again. Giselle paged through the file for over two hours but could find nothing to shed more light on the case. She looked over at Mark, who was evidently bored. He yawned as he paged through a magazine.

Why did the detectives suspect Nathaniel Wellington? Giselle thought hard about this question. Nathaniel did not have a record. What led the detectives in his direction?

"Are you finished?" Mark asked in an annoyed tone of voice.

"Yes, I am. I need to speak again to Mr. Bricks."

Giselle was led back to Mr. Bricks's office. Mark knocked on the door, and a voice behind the door ordered the knocker to enter. Mr. Bricks was sitting behind his desk.

"Giselle, come in," Mr. Bricks stated with a smile. Mark closed the door and allowed the two some privacy. "So, did you find what you're looking for?"

Giselle took a seat. "Not exactly. But an important question came to mind."

"And what's that?"

"Why did the detectives suspect Nathaniel? He did not have a record, so his fingerprints and DNA were not in the system. Detectives Young and Sanchez were on the case. What led them in Nathaniel's direction?"

"I don't know the answer to that question, Ms. Bellamy. I do know that Detective Young has moved back to Alabama to be closer to his family, so he is no longer in that department."

"Could you please contact Detective Sanchez and ask him if he would be willing to talk to me? Please?" Giselle looked at Mr. Bricks, who was staring right back at her.

"Giselle, this is not a standard request. Why don't you—"

"Please, Mr. Bricks," Giselle interrupted. "This is my final request."

Mr. Bricks pondered for a moment. "All right. I'll give him a call." He dialed a number and waited for a few seconds. "Hello. This is Michael Bricks, crime scene investigator. May I speak to Roberto Sanchez," he said through the receiver. Mr. Bricks remained on hold a little longer. "Roberto. Michael Bricks here. How are you?" A pause followed. "I'm great. Couldn't be better," he continued. "Yes. Jenny and Abby are doing great." There was another pause. "Roberto, I'm going to need you to do me a favor. I have a former intern here with me as we speak. Her name is Giselle Bellamy. I'm sure you remember the Sofia Valadez case." Another pause ensued. "Yes. Well, Giselle here is very interested in the case, and she has a few questions. I was wondering if you would be able to answer some of her questions." There was another pause. "Well, she feels like there may be more to the case." Mr. Bricks listened through the receiver. "Uh huh. Uh-huh. Great. I'll send her down to the station." Mr. Bricks hung up the phone. "So, Mr. Sanchez is willing to meet with you if you can head over to the police department now. He was very absorbed in the case, and frankly, he took it to heart. He even attended Sofia's funeral in Laredo."

"Wow. That's great," Giselle said with excitement. She was happy to be meeting up with someone who was just as engrossed in the case. Giselle thanked Mr. Bricks for his time and assistance, and she exited the building.

Giselle drove over to the police station. The moment she got out of her car, her phone rang. It was Anthony West calling, and she answered the phone. He inquired about the health of her grandmother. She reported that her grandmother's health was about the same but that it was good to be back home with her family. Giselle indicated that she had to go but would call later. She hung up the phone and made her way into the police station through the glass doors.

Giselle walked into the lobby, which had a symbol on the floor that read "Shreveport Police Department." There were two glass windows ahead of her, and there was a man seated behind one of the windows and a woman seated behind the other. There was a wall separation between the two windows, and in front of the wall were two flag stands, one with the United States flag and one with a Louisiana flag. Giselle made her way up to the front counter that had the woman seated behind the glass. The woman moved the glass sideways and asked how she could help. Giselle reported to her that she was there to see Mr. Roberto Sanchez and that he expected her. The woman politely asked for a few seconds, and then she closed the glass window. She picked up the phone, and her conversation was barely audible. The woman reopened the glass window and informed Giselle that Mr. Sanchez would be with her momentarily. Giselle was asked to sign in, and she printed and signed her name on a sheet of paper and recorded her time of arrival. She then sat down on one of the chairs in the lobby.

About five minutes had elapsed when a man walked out of a door, and Giselle assumed it was Mr. Sanchez. The man was a

Hispanic male with a brown complexion, and he was about five foot ten and average build. He had straight black hair that was shaved low on the sides and had an almost spiky appearance on top. He was wearing a long-sleeved light blue dress shirt and gray slacks.

"Hello. Are you Giselle Bellamy?" the man asked.

"Yes, I am."

"Roberto Sanchez. Nice to meet you." He extended his hand, and Giselle shook his hand. "I heard that you wanted to discuss the Sofia Valadez case with me."

"Yes, I do. Mr. Sanchez, I want to thank you for taking the time out to meet with me. I know you're very busy."

"No problem at all. And call me Roberto. Please, follow me." Giselle followed Roberto through a door, which led to an open room that contained a lot of activity. There were several desks arranged throughout the room, with workers seated behind most of them. Some of the individuals were in dressy casual attire, and some wore police uniforms. There were several conversations being carried out throughout the room, including a handful of workers who were engaged in conversations over the phone. Roberto led Giselle to his desk and offered her a seat. "Do you want a cup of coffee?" he asked.

"No thank you."

Roberto took a seat behind his desk, and he placed both hands behind his head. "So, Giselle, Michael tells me that you think there may be more to the Sofia Valadez case. Enlighten me."

"Yes, I do. There is a man that I encountered in New York City that I strongly believe has a connection to the case."

"Who is this man, and why do you think he's involved?"

Giselle shared with Roberto the same information she'd shared with Mr. Bricks.

"Giselle, this is all speculative," Roberto stated. "I, for one, was deeply involved in the case. My partner at the time and I picked up Nathaniel Wellington, and there was guilt written all over his face. His guilt was confirmed when his DNA and fingerprints were found at the scene of the crime."

"That brings me to a very important question. Nathaniel Wellington did not have a criminal history, so his fingerprints and DNA would not have been in the system. What led you and your partner to suspect Nathaniel Wellington's involvement?"

"We got a tip-off from one of the tenants," Roberto responded. "We were told that Sofia was seen in Nathaniel's company outside of his apartment on the night that she was murdered. He was the last eyewitness report."

"Do you recall the eyewitness who made this claim?" Giselle asked.

"Yes, I do." Roberto picked up a file on his desk, and he searched through the pages. "Yes. His name is Jerry Frye." Giselle's jaw opened, and she was speechless. "Giselle, are you okay?"

"Oh my goodness. That's him," Giselle stated, still in shock. "That's the guy I was telling you about. He's involved, and I know it. This cannot all be a coincidence. I think that he may have set up Nathaniel Wellington. Nathaniel believed he was set up, and I believe him. I believe that Jerry Frye had something to do with it. I just need to prove it."

Roberto Sanchez was pensive, and it appeared as if he was pondering over Giselle's words. "What you're telling me is very suspicious. I share your concern, but I wish we had more evidence. What kind of relationship did Jerry Frye have with Sofia Valadez, and why would he want her dead?" Roberto thought to himself for a moment. "We need to find out more about Jerry Frye. Who knew him, and what can they share with us that can potentially shed light on the case?" Giselle was relieved that Roberto shared her sentiments about the case. "You said that this person changed his identity and he is the real Jerry Frye," Roberto continued. "Are you absolutely certain about this?"

"I am one hundred percent certain," Giselle stated. "The fingerprints were an exact match, and the picture was definitely him."

"We can get this guy for identity theft. I can request a warrant from the judge, which would get entered into the national database." Roberto looked at his watch. It was almost 6 pm. "Let's meet up here tomorrow at 8 am. In the meantime, I'm going to see what information I can gather. Give me your number, and I will call you if I get any more information." Giselle and Roberto exchanged numbers.

"Thanks again for your time. I'll see you tomorrow at 8 am. If I find out any information beforehand, I will give you a call." Giselle stood up from her chair, and Roberto followed. They exchanged goodbyes, and Giselle left the police station.

Giselle drove in the direction of the cheap hotel where she was staying. The thought of spending the night in that room was quite depressing. She'd already paid for the room for the night, but she decided to cancel the reservation for the other nights and check into a nicer hotel.

Giselle realized that she had not eaten all day aside from a turkey sandwich she'd had at Dallas Fort Worth International Airport. She pulled into Bessie's Pancake House, which was on the same street as her hotel. The pancake house had a reputation for authentic homestyle pancakes. Giselle pulled into the lot behind the restaurant, and she made her way inside. The restaurant was built like a log cabin, and it possessed a rustic décor. She was greeted at the entrance, and a waiter led her to a booth. A few seconds later, another waiter approached her booth and took her order. Giselle ordered a three-stack of pancakes with a strawberry topping, a side of bacon, and a Coke. She observed her surroundings, and only about one third of the tables were occupied by diners.

Her mind ran over her conversation with Roberto Sanchez. She was still in shock by the revelation that it had been Jerry Frye who had given the detectives the tip-off. Giselle strongly believed that

Jerry Frye had been involved in Sofia's murder, but she did not know how to prove it. She wondered if he'd had a relationship with Sofia, or if she'd just been an acquaintance, or if he'd even known her at all.

The waiter brought the food and placed it in front of her. She drizzled butter pecan syrup over the pancakes, and she took a bite. The pancakes were warm and fluffy, and the bacon was crispy, which was just the way she liked it. The pancake house was open twenty-four hours, and she was not in any rush to leave.

Her phone rang, and the name Anthony West appeared on the screen. She answered the call, and Anthony's voice was somber. He asked how she was doing, and he inquired about the health of her grandmother. She informed him that the status of her grandmother's health had not changed and that she was taking it one day at a time. They spoke for almost ten minutes, and Giselle could not help but feel that the conversation was extremely awkward. She thought to herself that her feelings may have stemmed from the fact that she was embroiled in a lie. Anthony, however, seemed disinterested in her responses, and his mind seemed to be far away. Giselle informed Anthony that she was eating dinner and she would call back at a later time. She hung up the phone, and a chill went down her spine. Her mind refocused on Sofia Valadez and Jerry Frye's suspected involvement.

Her phone rang again, and surprisingly, it was Roberto Sanchez calling. Giselle answered the phone, and they exchanged greetings. She was anxious to find out whether Roberto had obtained additional information. Roberto informed her that he had done some digging on Jerry Frye. He'd found out that Jerry Frye had been enrolled in college but had never graduated. He'd also found out that Jerry had worked at the community hospital downtown, though Roberto was uncertain about his employment position. Roberto had discovered that Jerry had been married to a woman by the name of Morgan Walters for only five months and that she'd died unexpectedly from a cardiac arrest. Jerry had been the sole beneficiary of Morgan's $500,000 life insurance policy. Shortly after, Jerry Frye had fallen off of the grid.

Giselle was shocked to learn of this revelation. She also questioned whether Jerry Frye might have had any involvement in his wife's death. Roberto planned to visit the college and Jerry's former workplace the following day, and Giselle agreed to join him. The plan was still to meet up at the police station at 8 am.

Giselle sat in the restaurant for another hour after completing her meal. Her thoughts were consumed with Jerry Frye. The information about Jerry's marriage and his wife's untimely death was shocking. The life insurance money that he'd been awarded made the entire situation even more suspicious.

It was dark outside, and Giselle finally decided to leave the restaurant. She walked around to the back of the restaurant, where her car was parked. The area was dimly lit, and there were not many cars in the lot. She approached the driver's side, and she searched for the car key in her bag. Giselle felt a pointy object pressed against the middle of her back, and she froze in fear.

"Hello, Giselle," a voice said from behind her. She instantly recognized the voice. "Turn around slowly, and if you scream or make the wrong move, you're dead." Giselle slowly turned around, and underneath the dim light, she recognized his face. "How's your grandmother?" Anthony said sarcastically in a chilling voice. Giselle was immobile and speechless. A sharp knife was pressed against her abdomen with just enough force to inflict some pain.

"How did you find me?" Giselle asked in a stuttering voice.

"Words of advice. Never give a person you don't trust your phone," Anthony replied with a sadistic grin. "I activated a tracking device on your phone at the restaurant." Anthony's eyes remained fixated on Giselle, and he saw the fear in her eyes. "Why were you at the police station?"

Giselle hesitated for a moment. "I knew someone at the police station when I worked here, and I just wanted to see how he was doing," Giselle answered. She knew she was not deceiving Anthony.

"You little liar. Do you take me for a fool?" Anthony replied with a slightly raised voice. He pressed the blade of the knife more forcibly into her abdomen, and if he had pressed any harder, the blade would have pierced her flesh.

"I'm a liar, Jerry Frye?" Giselle uttered. She knew at that moment that she had cast upon herself a death sentence, and she wished immediately that she could take the words back.

The shock was now evident on Jerry's face, though it was apparent that he was trying to hide his emotions and remain calm. He tugged her arm and led her to a car nearby. "Get in the car," he ordered sternly. The knife was now pressed against her side. Giselle obeyed his command, and she got in the front passenger seat of the car. He quickly jumped into the driver's side and drove the car out of the lot, onto the main road. "I'm warning you again, Giselle. You make a wrong move, and the blade of this knife will cut the flesh of your neck."

Giselle was stricken with fear. "Where are you taking me?" she managed to ask. Jerry stopped at a red light, and he completely ignored her question. The light turned green, and he accelerated the car forward. He made a right turn onto Farland road, and he pulled into the lot of the Hunny Bunny Motel. The motel was a rundown building that catered to a lot of immoral and corrupt activity. The motel was no stranger to drug dealing and prostitution. Giselle knew firsthand about the motel, as she'd been on a case that involved the murder of a prostitute who had been found dead outside of the building.

Jerry got out of the driver's seat, and he walked around to the passenger's side. He opened the back seat door behind Giselle, and he removed a black backpack. He opened the door of the passenger's side, and he pulled her forcefully out of the car. "Follow me. I'm sure I don't have to remind you to keep quiet or you're dead. Act calm, and I might just spare your life." Jerry pulled Giselle in the direction of the motel. The grip of his hand around her arm was very tight, and she was almost certain that he had caused some bruising. "Act cool," Jerry whispered as they entered the dilapidated building.

The lobby was rather small, and it had an old, musty smell. There was a middle-aged black man seated in the lobby. Giselle made eye contact with the man as she made her way with Jerry to the front desk. She hoped that the man saw the dread and terror on her face. There was a heavyset white male behind the front desk. He had tattoos covering his arms, and he had inking across his neck. There was a tattoo that read "Brandy" across the left side of his neck. He had a long strawberry blonde beard that was braided and tied with a rubber band at the end.

"Checking in?" the attendant asked.

"Yes. Me and my girl are checking in for one night," Jerry responded.

"I'm going to need your ID."

"I don't have my ID," Jerry lied.

"No ID, no check in. That's policy."

Jerry opened his wallet and removed five one-hundred-dollar bills, which was more than ten times the charge of a one-night stay. "Keep the change," Jerry replied. The attendant did not say another word. He took the money, and he handed Jerry a card key to a room.

"Let's go," Jerry whispered in Giselle's ear. Giselle locked eyes again with the stranger in the lobby, and with a timid expression on her face, she mouthed the word "help" without making a sound. Jerry and Giselle exited the lobby and walked up the stairs, which were located on the outside of the building. Jerry again gripped her arm, which had become quite painful. They stopped in front of room 208, which ironically, was the apartment number that Sofia had resided in.

They entered the room, which reeked with the smell of cigarette smoke. The carpet was old and worn, and it had multiple unidentifiable stains. There was a queen size bed in the room, covered with an old navy blue comforter. There were a few holes in the comforter that were likely the result of cigarette burns.

Jerry pulled the wooden chair from the small round table, and he placed it closer to the bed. He ordered Giselle to sit on the chair, and she followed his instructions. Jerry took a rope out of his backpack, and he ordered Giselle to place her hands behind the chair. Giselle was reluctant, and he revealed the knife again. "Don't be scared. I just want to talk to you." He appeared devoid of emotion and cold-hearted. He tied her hands behind the chair with a rope, and then he secured the rope tightly, causing a burn to her wrists. He then proceeded to tie her legs together at the ankles with a rope. Jerry sat on the bed, and he angled the chair towards him and then looked Giselle directly in her eyes. The tears were rolling down her cheeks, and he smiled.

"What do you think you know about Jerry Frye?" he asked with a callous tone.

"I don't know anything," Giselle replied with a quiver in her voice.

"Then why did you lie to me? Why were you at the police station, and what did you tell the police?"

"I didn't tell the police anything. I swear I was just there visiting a friend," Giselle pleaded.

"Liar!" Jerry stated in a raised voice as he stabbed the bed with the knife. "Why are you lying to me?" Jerry seemed very frustrated, and he appeared as if he could strike at any moment.

"Okay. Here's the truth. A lot of things just did not make sense to me. I found out that you were not who you said you were, and I just wanted to know the truth." Giselle looked at Jerry, and there was no compassion behind his eyes. She wondered if she would make it out of the room alive or if she was approaching the end. She did not want her last breath to be in a decrepit room of the Hunny Bunny motel.

"How did you know my real name is Jerry Frye? How did you find out?" Giselle stared at him, and she was terrified to share the truth. "How did you find out?" his tone escalated.

"I ran your fingerprints in the database, and it came up belonging to Jerry Frye."

"You did what!" Jerry stated in disbelief. He placed his right hand over his forehead as he tried to come to grips with what he'd just been told.

"Did you do it?" Giselle asked. Jerry removed his hand from his forehead, and he looked directly at her. "Did you rape and murder Sofia Valadez?"

Jerry's facial expression went from emotionless to sadistic as he grinned and tilted his head back. Jerry stood up, and he pulled out a role of duct tape that was in his backpack. He tore a piece of the tape and secured it over her mouth as she tried to move her head away. He then grabbed the knife that was lying on the bed, and he walked behind the chair. Jerry was fully out of Giselle's view. He bent his knees and buried his head on her left shoulder. Jerry then took the knife and gently touched her neck with the blade. "I guess you will never know." At that moment, a loud knock was heard at the door.

"This is the police! Open up!" The knocks became even more forceful and powerful. "Open up! Police!"

"Go away, or she's dead!" Jerry screamed out. "I'm not joking! I'll kill her!"

"You don't want to do this!" a voice said from outside the door. "Drop your weapon! No one has to get hurt!"

"Leave me alone!" Jerry shouted. "Go away!"

"Sir! We just want to talk to you! If you comply, no one will get hurt!" the officer stated in a loud voice. "Drop your weapon! If you don't comply, we will be forced to take action!"

Jerry was uncertain how many police officers were posted outside. He heard sirens wailing in the distance, and the sounds appeared to be getting closer. "Don't make me do this!" Jerry shouted. "The blood will be on your hands! I'm asking you again to go away!"

"You know we can't do that!" the voice said. "We don't want anyone to get hurt! We are asking you to drop your weapon and come outside with your hands up! If you follow these directions, we promise you that you would not get hurt!"

Jerry looked at Giselle, and there was extreme terror in her eyes. A tear dropped from her cheek onto her lap. "Look what you caused," Jerry said with a grimace. "This is all your fault. Why did you do this to me?" Jerry sat on the bed and looked into her eyes. "Why did you do this to us? We had such a good thing going. I fell in love with you, and I would have given you the world." Jerry was getting emotional, and he wiped his eyes. "Why couldn't you just love me? Why did you have to do this?" Jerry ripped the duct tape off of Giselle's mouth. "Answer me. Why did you do this to us?"

"I'm sorry, Jerry. I never meant to hurt you." Giselle's eyes were filled with tears. "Believe me when I say that I did not want all of this to happen. I fell in love with you, and I did not want any of this to be true."

"Come out with your hands up!" the voice said again.

"I'm sorry, Jerry," Giselle wept. "If you don't follow their instructions, they will hurt you. Please turn yourself in. I don't want to see you die."

"I'm already dead," Jerry stated. He knelt on the floor, and he laid his head in her lap. "I have nothing else to live for. I don't have any family or friends. No one in my life ever cared about me."

"Don't say that, Jerry. I know it may not seem so right now, but I care about you. Please forgive me for hurting you. I wish that I could undo all of this. I wish we could go back to the first time that we met at Migliore Pizza Italiana." Giselle looked at Jerry and smiled. "I had so much fun, and I could not wait for our second date. I thought you were smart and witty, not to mention very handsome.

I was so happy when you asked me to be your girlfriend." Jerry looked up at Giselle, and she smiled again at him. "I would love to give you a hug. Please untie me. I promise I won't do anything."

Jerry looked into Giselle's eyes. After a few moments, he made the decision to untie her. Giselle stood up, and she gave him a hug.

"We're asking you again to drop your weapon!" said the voice. "Come out with your hands up, and you will not get hurt!"

"Turn yourself in, Jerry," Giselle encouraged as she touched his hand. "It's the right thing to do."

Jerry considered Giselle's words. After a few moments, he shouted, "I'm unarmed, and I'm coming out with my hands up!" Jerry slowly opened the door, and he walked out with his hands up. There were at least seven officers in view who had their guns pointed at him. One of the officers patted him down and then shouted to his colleagues that the suspect was unarmed. The officer handcuffed Jerry's arms behind his back and led him to the back of a police car.

CHAPTER 22

"JERRY FRYE HAD HIS ARRAIGNMENT TODAY," ROBERTO SANCHEZ INFORMED GISELLE over the phone. It was a quarter past three in the afternoon, and Roberto was sitting at his desk in the police station. "Jerry was charged with identity theft, kidnapping, and attempted murder, and he pleaded no contest. He got himself an attorney. A pretty good one, actually. However, he was not granted bail, so that son of a gun is behind bars." Roberto answered a few more of Giselle's questions, and then the call ended.

About five minutes later, he received a call from the front desk stating that there was a woman who had some information about Jerry Frye. Roberto was curious about the identity of the woman, and he wondered what kind of information she had. Roberto told the front desk attendant that he would meet with the woman, and he walked out to the lobby. The woman was a red-headed lady who had her hair combed in a side ponytail.

"Hi. My name is Elizabeth Henson, but you can call me Lizzy."

"Roberto Sanchez. Call me Roberto." The two of them shook hands. "You have some information for me in regards to Jerry Frye?"

"I think so. I'm not sure how useful it will be," Lizzy responded.

"Well, I'm all ears. Follow me." Lizzy followed Roberto through a door, and he led her to his desk. The room was energetic, and there were phones ringing. "Have a seat, Lizzy. Do you want some coffee?"

"No thank you."

"What's your relationship to Jerry Frye?"

"I knew him as a coworker. Well, I am a clinical pharmacist, and Jerry Frye worked as a patient transporter. We worked at the same hospital. That's the extent to which I knew him."

"Okay. So what information do you have on Jerry Frye that you think may be useful?"

"I saw the news yesterday, and I was horrified to learn that Jerry had kidnapped a woman and tried to kill her. It was mind-blowing to me that he was able to change his identity when he left Shreveport and start a new life. I could not wrap my head around what was taking place. This was someone I knew and once worked with in close proximity."

"Uh-huh. So what transpired?" Roberto inquired.

"The last time I saw Jerry Frye, it was at work after his wife died. I tried to offer my condolences, and my words were met with annoyance and indignation. I understood that he was hurting, but his reaction was rather strange. He did not want to talk about his wife. I think her name was Morgan. But there was an incident that transpired before that encounter that has weighed heavily on my conscience."

Lizzy paused for a few seconds, and then she continued, "The night preceding his wife's death, we were on shift at the hospital. He came down to the basement where the pharmacy was located, and he seemed awfully interested in my job. He wanted a tour of the pharmacy, and he was particularly interested in the drugs used in emergency situations or running a code. I gladly showed him the medications that were kept in the code cart. The thing is, I had stocked the code cart before he came, and I knew how many vials of the drugs were in the cart. I recounted the vials later because I do that sometimes. I really think that I can be OCD sometimes. Well, anyway, I was short one vial of succinylcholine. I thought to myself that maybe I just made a mistake counting the first time, though I highly doubt it. When I heard about Jerry's wife's death, the thought of whether he poisoned her crossed my mind, but I tried to dismiss the thoughts. I did not think he was capable of doing something like that, and I did not want to make a baseless accusation. After all, I could have miscounted the vials. But after I saw the news yesterday and I saw what Jerry was capable of doing, those thoughts that I had resurfaced. Could he have poisoned his wife with succinylcholine?"

Roberto looked at Lizzy, wide-eyed. He was stunned by the words coming out of Lizzy's mouth. "So, how does this drug work, and why was this not found during the autopsy?" Roberto asked.

"It paralyzes all of the muscles of the body. The muscles used to breathe are paralyzed, and if the individual does not receive breathing support, that individual will die from a deprivation of oxygen. The challenge with this drug is that it is very short-acting. There is an enzyme in the body that breaks down the drug almost immediately. This makes it very difficult for the crime lab to detect because all of the succinylcholine will be metabolized. The breakdown products are naturally occurring. In a nutshell, if Jerry murdered his wife with succinylcholine, there would be no way for us to prove it."

Roberto was disheartened by the information. Could Jerry have actually poisoned his wife, and was Lizzy telling him that if Jerry indeed committed murder, there was no way to prove it? He thought to himself that at least Jerry would be indicted for the three charges. However, there was no actual hard evidence to prove that he'd committed the rape and murder of Sofia Valadez. He had not actually admitted to it, though it was clear that he was the culprit. Surely, the jury would see that he was guilty, given the circumstantial proof. All of the information that Giselle had provided against Jerry could not all be a coincidence.

He realized that he was deep in thought, and Lizzy was looking at him. "Lizzy, what you're telling me is very suspicious. I really wish that we could prove it, but from what you're telling me, it's virtually impossible."

"I'm sorry that I could not be of more help, but I just had to share this information with someone. It's really been weighing heavily upon me."

"Thanks for sharing the information. If Jerry indeed murdered his wife, she and her family need justice. I just don't know where to start." Roberto crossed his arms and looked up at the ceiling as he entered into deep thought. After a minute or two, he thanked Lizzy for her courage for coming forward with the information.

"Thank you for your time," Lizzy responded. She got up, and Roberto followed her to the door that led into the lobby.

Roberto sat back at his desk and thought deeply about the information that Lizzy had shared. Could Jerry have murdered his wife? It was not out of the question, as he had shown what he was capable of doing. Roberto's next reaction was to call Giselle.

Giselle answered the phone on the second ring. Roberto relayed to Giselle the information he had obtained from Lizzy, and she was shocked to learn of the possibility that Jerry could have been involved in his wife's death. Giselle was also dismayed to find out that the investigation would be a dead end given the fact that the poison would not be detected. Roberto and Giselle spoke on the phone for almost thirty minutes before terminating the conversation.

While Roberto was at work, Giselle was at a coffee shop downtown. She surfed the internet as she bit into a strawberry cheesecake and sipped on a caramel latte. She tried to get her mind off of the ordeal that had occurred the night before. When her mind revisited the kidnapping and near-death experience, the moment did not seem real. It had been such a scary, horrific moment that just the very thought of it caused the hair to raise on her body and goosebumps to form on her skin. She thought about the information that Roberto had shared with her. It was strange that a woman in her twenties had died from a cardiac arrest. What was the underlying cause? Had she suffered from a heart condition that could have gone unrecognized by the forensic pathologist? It was just strange that Jerry had fallen into a $500,000 life insurance policy. Giselle was determined to get to the bottom of the situation. She called Roberto to find out whether he would be able to gather more information on Jerry's wife. Roberto assured Giselle that he would do some digging and would get back to her as soon as possible.

About half an hour later, Roberto called Giselle back. He'd found out that Jerry's wife's name was Morgan Elaine Walters and she'd been twenty-three years old at the time of her death. She'd been a social worker and had worked in a facility with mentally and physically handicapped children. Morgan was born in Phoenix and she'd lived in Phoenix before moving to Shreveport. Her father, Isaiah Walters, and her mother, Farrah Walters, resided in Phoenix. Her older sister, Hannah Walters, also resided in Phoenix. Roberto had been able to obtain the contact number for Morgan's parents and also her sister. Giselle thanked Roberto for the information and hung up the phone.

Giselle stared at the phone numbers that she had written on a piece of paper. She was uncertain how to approach the family. How would Morgan's parents act towards the possibility that their daughter could have been murdered? Giselle decided to just bite the bullet and call.

The phone rang, and after the fourth ring, a male answered the phone. Giselle asked to speak to Isaiah Walters, and the voice confirmed that Isaiah was speaking. Isaiah's voice was deep and came across as authoritative. Giselle introduced herself and stated that she was a forensic scientist. Giselle stated that she had learned about his daughter's death, and she offered her condolences. Isaiah accepted her condolences, but he wanted to know the reason for her call. Giselle admitted that the reason for her call was to ensure that there'd been no foul play involved in his daughter's death. Isaiah revealed his shock, and he demanded to know why foul play was in question. His tone of voice had gone up a notch. Giselle could hear a female voice in the background asking what was going on. She assumed that it was Isaiah's wife, Farrah.

Giselle informed Isaiah about the arrest of and charges made against his former son-in-law, Jerry Frye. Isaiah became infuriated, and he acknowledged that he'd never trusted Jerry, though he had never met him. Isaiah admitted that he and his wife had been hurt and crushed when they'd learned of the courthouse marriage after only four months of them dating. He acknowledged that the quickie marriage had affected his relationship with his daughter. Isaiah felt that Morgan had not given herself time to get to know Jerry, and he'd just had a bad feeling about the whole relationship. Morgan had been upset that her father would not accept the relationship and recognize that she was happy. Isaiah stated that he'd been heartbroken when he'd heard about his daughter's death, and he was regretful that he'd not been able to mend fences.

Giselle asked Isaiah whether Morgan had suffered from any heart problems, to which he replied no. Giselle went further, asking whether Morgan had ever had any medical problems.

Isaiah stated, "When Morgan's appendix was removed, the doctors had difficulty getting her off the ventilator. The doctors were surprised that she required an extended amount of time on the ventilator. About three years later, she had a similar occurrence when her gallbladder was removed. She remained on the ventilator for an unexpectedly long period of time. The doctors questioned this, and they decided to run further tests. She was found to have a pseudocholinesterase deficiency." Isaiah added, "Morgan's body was not able to break down a lot of these medications administered with anesthesia, so the effects lasted a long time. Morgan was supposed to wear a bracelet to indicate her condition so if she was ever hospitalized, the medical staff would be aware of it."

Giselle could not believe what her ears were hearing. This could be the information that she needed to solve the case. If Morgan had indeed been murdered with succinylcholine and she'd had this deficiency preventing her from breaking down the medication, could her body still have evidence of this agent? She could not wait to share this information with Roberto. She thanked Isaiah Walters for the information, and she promised justice if his daughter had indeed been murdered.

As soon as Giselle hung up the phone with Isaiah Walters, she called Roberto. The phone went to voicemail. She called the number again, which went a second time to voicemail. Giselle found herself frustrated, as she desperately wanted to share the information she had gathered. Roberto called her back a couple of minutes later, and Giselle immediately answered the phone. She shared the information she had learned, and Roberto was both shocked and excited at the same time.

They spoke on the phone for about twenty minutes. Now that she had begun to put the pieces together, Giselle was almost certain that Jerry had poisoned his wife. The next step was to convince the family to request an exhumation of the body through the court for the purpose of an autopsy.

Giselle called Isaiah Walters back the same night of their initial conversation, and she told him everything she knew. Giselle informed him of the pharmacist's visit to the Shreveport police station. She stated that the pharmacist had a suspicion that Jerry may have stolen a vial of a medication from the pharmacy to murder Morgan. Giselle tried her best to explain the drug succinylcholine and why there might still be traces of the drug in Morgan's system, given her enzyme deficiency. Isaiah seemed overwhelmed at the information he was receiving. The thought of his baby girl being murdered was a hard pill to swallow, but he wanted to get to the bottom of it and ensure Morgan received justice.

Isaiah and his wife, Farrah, did not sleep much that night. Isaiah experienced a wave of different emotions. One moment, he was angry, and the next moment, he was despondent. He would weep inconsolably. Then he would gain the strength to move forward for Morgan's sake. Isaiah and Farrah reminisced about their daughter, and they shared fond memories. They also vowed to bring their daughter justice if she had, in fact, been murdered. Deep down, Isaiah felt that his daughter's life had been taken away from him by the hands of Jerry Frye.

After a night of unrestful sleep, Isaiah arrived at the police department at 7:45 am. The department was not open to the public until 8 am. He waited around in his car, and he entered the building at 8 am sharp. Isaiah reported a suspected murder to the authorities, and he inquired about the process of exhuming a body to determine the cause of death. He relayed the information he had obtained, and given the odd circumstances surrounding Morgan's death and Jerry's current charges, the authorities took Isaiah's request seriously.

The process took six weeks, and the wait time seemed almost like an eternity for the Walters family. A court order was granted, and a disinterment permit and license were obtained to legally exhume the body. Giselle flew from New York City to Phoenix to support the family and to attend the exhumation.

The exhumation took place at the cemetery at 6:45 am on Monday, November 5th. The sky was painted a soft shade of blue, with a glimmer of yellow light peeking through on the horizon. The air was cool and crisp, and the dew clung to the blades of grass. Morgan's parents and sister were in attendance, including some other family members and friends. They held hands, and Isaiah Walters offered up a prayer asking God to watch over the exhumation process and guide the hands of all those involved. Isaiah asked God to bless the soul of his daughter. He prayed that her soul be allowed to rest in peace again after being disturbed from the ground. Also in attendance were the environmental health officer, a state police officer, and a forensic pathologist.

Giselle approached Morgan's mother, Farrah, and gave her a hug. Farrah was a dark-skinned, slender lady of average height, and she wore a classic black dress with patent leather black shoes. Her dark sunglasses covered her eyes, and Giselle could only imagine the pain that was hidden behind the sunglasses. Farrah's husband, Isaiah, was a fair-skinned black male of average build, and he was about five foot ten. He wore a dark suit with a white shirt and a black tie. He was standing a few feet away, and he was talking to the forensic pathologist. Isaiah appeared very dignified in the way that he carried himself, and the patch of gray hair that stood out from his black hair added to his distinguished appearance. Morgan's sister, Hannah, approached Giselle and introduced herself. Hannah would easily fall in the category of being overweight. She had a brown complexion that seemed to be a perfect mix between her parents. She had beautiful facial features, and despite her obvious pain, she was able to give Giselle a warm smile. Hannah thanked Giselle for her help and support, and she gave her a tight hug.

The excavation equipment was in place, and the man who operated the backhoe began to plunge into the earth. The backhoe bucket removed the dirt overlying the corpse, and the operator poured the dirt away from the grave. The bucket plunged again into the earth, and the operator added the dirt to the pile. Isaiah Walters watched closely as the dirt was removed and the mound that was created became larger and larger. It was a traumatic experience, and he was reliving the hurt and pain all over again. He thought to himself that no parent should have to bury a child. Isaiah heard the sniffling of his wife next to him, and he reached out and held her hand. Farrah responded to his action, and she squeezed his hand to show a sign of love and support. Isaiah experienced some guilt for disrupting his daughter's resting place, but the guilt was short lived as he reminded himself that the exhumation was to bring his daughter justice. A film of tears formed over his eyes, and his vision became blurry. The whole experience seemed unreal, and each moment appeared to move in slow motion until everything became a blur.

CHAPTER 23

THE CRIMINAL CHARGES SET AGAINST JERRY FRYE BECAME NATIONAL NEWS, AND EVERY media outlet was covering the story. Jerry Frye was also being charged with the murder of his wife after traces of succinylcholine had been found during the second autopsy, and he was facing the death penalty.

Giselle turned on the news as she was getting ready for work. The trial of Jerry Frye was expected to begin in one week, and she was scheduled to be in attendance. The news anchor reiterated the charges against Jerry Frye, and she provided details about the impending trial. Giselle watched intently as a picture of Jerry appeared on the screen. The sight of his face created an uneasy feeling inside of her body, and she reflexively looked away for a few seconds. The thought that she knew that person on the screen and the fact that she'd once been romantically involved with him was mind boggling and quite chilling.

The news anchor introduced her guest, who was a former NSA agent. The anchor inquired about the method with which Jerry Frye had been able to change his identity. The agent informed the viewers that Jerry never confessed to the authorities the manner in which he'd been able to commit federal identity theft and hack into a university system. The former NSA agent made speculations about the manner in which Jerry Frye was able to successfully change his identity. The agent also gave the viewers advice on how to protect their identities. Giselle reached for the remote and turned off the television.

Giselle exited her apartment building, and she walked to the train station. She stopped at a newsstand, and she picked up the *New York Daily News*. There was a picture of Jerry Frye with the caption "Did he do it? His day in court awaits him." She picked up another newspaper that also had a picture of Jerry Frye on the front page. The caption under Jerry Frye's picture read "Life or death? His fate to be determined." A gossip tabloid had a picture of Jerry that appeared very mysterious and eerie. The title read "Cycle of deception. The Shreveport saga continues." Giselle purchased a copy of the *New York Daily News*, and she made her way to the train station. She wanted to know as much about the case as possible, though she also felt very troubled as new details unfolded.

Giselle managed to get a seat on the packed train, and she opened the newspaper to the page on Jerry Frye. She read through the article that detailed his juvenile charges and his time in the detention center. The article mentioned Jerry's difficult upbringing, but it did not go into specific details. The article made mention of Jerry's ambition during his college years but noted that he'd somehow become sidetracked. The paper detailed the charges against him. It mentioned the kidnapping and attempted murder of Giselle Bellamy, and Giselle was shocked again to see her name mentioned. Her reaction was the same every time she saw or heard her name mentioned in a news outlet. She just could not get used to the idea that she was a part of this huge media ordeal.

Her colleagues at work were very considerate and supportive. Her parents were also very supportive. They were concerned about her well-being, and after Giselle had refused to come back home to New Orleans, her mother had offered to come up to Manhattan to stay with her for as long as she was needed. As much as Giselle appreciated her parents' love and support, she'd declined the invitation. She'd convinced her parents that she was doing fine given the circumstances. She'd also reminded her parents that Jerry Frye was thousands of miles away and behind bars. Giselle's good friend Valerie, who had set her up with Jerry Frye, was devastated at the news. Valerie felt remorseful for introducing Jerry into her friend's life, and for that, she felt partially responsible. Giselle had repeatedly told her friend that she was not at fault, but despite her words, Valerie still carried around a weight of guilt.

A woman seated next to Giselle looked over at the newspaper and commented on the article that Giselle was reading. "Can you believe this man," the stranger remarked. "You would have to be a monster to do the things that he did. Killing your own wife to get a payout. Kidnapping a woman and holding her hostage in a motel. I really think the death penalty is an easy way out. I hope he rots in jail." The woman shook her head in disgust. Giselle was thankful that she hadn't been recognized as the woman who'd been kidnapped and held hostage. Occasionally, a stranger would recognize her, but most of the time, she would go unnoticed. The stranger continued, "Did you know that he is also being accused of a rape and another murder in Louisiana?" The stranger looked at her, expecting a response.

"That's what I heard."

"What do you think about the case?" the woman asked.

"Well, it's absolutely horrendous," Giselle replied as the train slowed down to a stop. "I'm sorry, but I have to go. This is my stop."

Giselle folded her newspaper, and she quickly exited the train. As usual, there was a rush of people in the station during her commute to work. She walked up the steps and emerged above ground. The yellow cabs were the first sight she beheld after emerging from the station, and the horns were blowing in succession. The pedestrian timer started its countdown, and Giselle crossed the street with the other pedestrians as she made her way to her workplace.

Fortunately, she was able to concentrate on her work. She was afraid that she would not be able to do her job effectively given the distressing circumstances, but this turned out to be untrue. Her work was a blessing, as it occupied her mind and allowed her to refocus her energies. Her idle mind allowed undesirable and unwanted thoughts to enter.

It was 5:45 pm when Giselle left her job, and she walked in the direction of the train station. She expected Kate and Valerie over at her apartment around 7 pm. She could have foregone the company, but Kate had been insistent. Kate had informed Giselle that she and Valerie were bringing over Chinese food.

It was minutes after 7 pm when Kate and Valerie arrived at the apartment. They both held white plastic bags from Hong Kong Garden Express. After resting the plastic bags on the kitchen counter, they both gave Giselle a hug.

"Are you okay?" Valerie asked with a sympathetic look on her face.

"I'm fine, guys. Don't worry about me. I'm doing just fine."

"Well, you know if you ever need us, you can call anytime, and we'll be right here at your side," Kate stated as she gave Giselle another hug.

"Thank you," Giselle replied with a smile. "I'm very lucky to have friends like you. Now, let's dig into this Chinese food. What did you guys get? It smells amazing."

"We got General Tso's chicken, beef with broccoli, chicken fried rice, vegetable lo mein, and egg rolls. Can't forget the egg rolls," Kate stated as she licked her lips. "We also got a liter of Coke."

"Sounds yummy," Giselle replied. "I'll get some plates and utensils, and you guys can set up the food at the table.

The friends sat at the table to eat, and Valerie took the initiative to pray. "Dear Lord, we thank you for this food that we are about to eat, and may it provide nourishment despite the large amounts of MSG it contains." The two friends snickered as they listened to the prayer. Valerie continued, "On a more serious note, we thank you for all of the blessings of this life. We thank you for friendship, and may you continue to strengthen the bond between us. I ask a special blessing on Giselle at this time. May you continue to guide her, guard her, and protect her. Give her the strength and courage to confront the challenges that she is facing. Send your angels to watch over her and keep her safe. I pray that justice will be carried out next week in the trial of Jerry Frye. I pray that you will bring all trickery, dishonesty, and deception to light. We pray for justice in the case of Sofia Valadez. We pray for justice in the case of Morgan Walters. We pray for justice in the case of Nathaniel Wellington. We also pray for justice in the case of my dear friend Giselle Bellamy. We thank you for sparing her life in that motel room and bringing her back to us safely. This cannot be said of the families of Sofia, Morgan, and Nathaniel, whose loved ones were taken away from them prematurely and coldheartedly. We ask that you console the families of those innocent lives that were tragically lost. May the families remember the warm and heartfelt memories, and may they provide them solace and comfort. Life is so precious, and it must be acknowledged as a gift. It can be taken away from us at any moment. Help us to love and appreciate life and not take one day for granted. Amen."

"Amen," Giselle and Kate responded in unison.

"That prayer was powerful," Kate remarked as tears formed in her eyes. "You're right about life being precious and not taking a moment for granted. It is important to appreciate our loved ones and tell them that we love them, because we don't know when they could be taken away from us. I have also come to the realization that it's important to forgive." Kate could not conceal her emotion. Her face turned red, and tears rolled down her cheeks.

"Are you okay?" Valerie inquired.

"What's wrong?" Giselle asked as she reached over to give Kate a hug. Kate's nose started to drip, and Valerie handed her a tissue.

"You already know that I have not spoken to my mother in almost five years despite her living in Brooklyn. I just found out that she has metastatic pancreatic cancer and she has less than three months to live."

"Kate, I'm sorry," Giselle and Valerie stated almost in unison.

"Yeah. My brother called me this morning with the news. She went to the hospital because she was vomiting. Apparently, she has not been feeling well for almost a month. She was very nauseous, and she just did not have an appetite. She wasn't eating solid foods, and she barely drank liquids because her stomach always felt full. My brother tells me that she has lost thirty pounds in one month. Yesterday, she had multiple episodes of vomiting, and her belly was distended. My brother called the ambulance, and she was brought to the emergency room. They initially did an x-ray, and whatever they saw, they placed a tube down into her stomach to give her relief. They did a CAT scan, and my brother said that she had a large pancreatic mass that was causing obstruction."

Kate wiped her eyes and blew her nose. "My brother said that the cancer was everywhere. He said that her kidney function was very abnormal, most likely from being severely dehydrated. He also said that a lot of her other labs were grossly abnormal." Kate paused for a few seconds. "My brother said that she still has her mind to be able to make decisions. She does not want anything done, and she just wants to be comfortable. My brother is preparing himself to take her home with hospice."

Kate reached for a clean tissue, and she wiped her eyes again. "Almost five whole years I did not talk to my mother, despite her trying to reach out to me. She's sent me cards on my birthday and holidays, and I have never responded. I always thought that she was a bad mother, and I still think that was the case. My brother was able to forgive her, but I was not able to find it in myself to forgive her. She reached out to me for forgiveness, and I shunned her. Who am I to deny someone if they yearn for forgiveness? Now she is dying." Kate paused again for a few seconds. "I always thought that I wouldn't care if my mother died, but this news has torn me apart. I can't have things end like this."

"Then go and make peace with your mother," Valerie responded. "Allow yourself to forgive her. This is not only for your mother. Do it for yourself. Lifting that weight off of you will set you free."

"Thank you, Val," Kate replied.

"Go to the hospital and wipe the slate clean with your mother," Giselle added. "Life truly is precious."

Valerie stood up from her chair and lifted up her glass, which was halfway filled with Coke. "Cheers to life!"

Kate and Giselle stood up with their glasses. "Cheers to life!" they exclaimed as they clinked their glasses together.

CHAPTER 24

IT WAS THE DAY OF JERRY FRYE'S TRIAL, AND THE SCENE OUTSIDE OF THE COURTHOUSE was a media circus. There were news reporters and cameramen stationed outside of the courthouse, and there were numerous spectators that congested the area in front of the building. Some of the spectators held up signs that supported the death penalty, while others were clearly against capital punishment.

The inside of the courtroom had a different atmosphere. The rigidity and tension were palpable, and all those present in the courtroom could have heard a pin drop. "All rise," the bailiff commanded, cutting through the silence. Everyone present in the courtroom obeyed the bailiff's orders. "The Court of Shreveport is now in session, and the Honorable Judge Mason Carter is presiding over the case of the State versus Jerry Frye."

Judge Carter, draped in his black robe, made his way to the bench. He was a black male who appeared to be in his early sixties. He had a receding hairline, and most of the hairs on his head and beard were gray. "Is the prosecution ready, and is the defense ready?" the judged asked.

"Yes, Your Honor," the prosecutor and defense attorney said in unison.

The prosecutor stood up to make his opening remarks. "Good morning, Honorable Judge, people of the jury, and all present in the courtroom. My name is Noah Larkson, and I am the prosecutor in this case against Jerry Frye." Mr. Larkson was a white male who appeared to be in his late fifties. He had black hair without a hint of gray, but his face told his age. He walked with assertiveness as he approached the jury. "It is an honor and a privilege for me to represent the people of this state." Noah Larkson looked at the twelve jurors in front of him. There were seven women and five men. Six of the jurors were white, five were black, and one was Hispanic. "Ladies and gentlemen of the jury. These are facts. Jerry Frye, the defendant, murdered his wife by poisoning her with an agent called succinylcholine, and he collected a $500,000 life insurance policy. Another fact. Jerry Frye manipulated the system, and he stole the identity of a fellow American who unfortunately died in a train crash. Jerry hacked into the system of a renowned university and awarded himself a degree of the highest honor. He then used the identity of his victim to obtain a job on Wall Street, where he handled the money of fellow Americans. Another fact. Jerry Frye abducted Giselle Bellamy at knifepoint and forced her into his car. He then tied her up to a chair in a motel room with the intent to kill. Had it not been for the quick response of the police officers, there is no telling what would have happened."

Roberto Sanchez was seated on the right side of the courtroom. Noah Larkson's words started to fade into the background as Roberto focused instead on those present in the courtroom. He observed Jerry, who was seated with his representation towards the front-left side of the room. Jerry, dressed in a black suit, looked straight ahead, and he did not angle his head at any point to look at the prosecutor. Roberto observed Isaiah and Farrah Walters, who were seated two rows in front of him. Their daughter Hannah sat on the other side of Farrah. On the left side of the room sat the parents of Sofia Valadez. One row behind the Valadez family was Daisy Lane, the grandmother of Nathaniel Wellington. Roberto had contacted the Valadez family and Daisy Lane a few weeks before the trial, and he had indicated to them that he had very strong reason to believe that Jerry was responsible for Sofia's murder.

He'd shared with them the reasons behind his strong suspicion, and both families had taken the news differently. The Valadez family had been devastated, and the news had opened up wounds that had not yet healed. Daisy, on the other hand, had felt a sense of relief and validation to know that her grandson was innocent. Roberto had indicated to the families that there was not enough proof to charge Jerry Frye with the murder of Sofia but he hoped that some incriminating evidence would manifest itself during the trial. The glimmer of hope had been enough to draw the Valadez family and Daisy Lane to the courtroom.

Michael Bricks was seated on the right side of Roberto, and Michael's eyes were fixed on the prosecutor. Roberto refocused on the words coming out of the prosecutor's mouth. "Ladies and gentlemen of the jury, we will call witnesses to the stand. We will call Elizabeth Henson. Ms. Henson worked with Jerry Frye, and she will attest to the fact that Jerry Frye stole a vial of succinylcholine. This is the agent that was used to murder Morgan Walters." A sniffling sound was heard from the direction of Farrah Walters, and Isaiah placed his arm around her. "We will call an expert witness to the stand. Dr. Leslie Benson is a forensic pathologist who performed the second autopsy on Morgan Walters and found succinylcholine in her body. She will educate us about succinyl-choline. She will tell us how the drug is used in a medical setting and, in this case, how it was used to commit murder. We will call to the stand Lorraine Summers. Ms. Summers is a very good friend of Morgan Walters. She will give us an insight into Morgan and Jerry's tumultuous relationship. We will call Mr. Timothy Ellis. Mr. Ellis was a former neighbor of Morgan Walters and Jerry Frye when they were married, and Timothy lived in the apartment next to them. Through the thin walls separating their apartment, he often overheard their intense arguments, and he witnessed the couple in the aftermath. We will also call to the stand Giselle Bellamy. Ms. Bellamy will detail to the jury how she was kidnapped by knifepoint and dragged to a motel room. She was tied up to a chair, and a piece of duct tape was placed over her mouth. A knife blade was placed to her neck. The words 'I'll kill her' came out of the defendant's mouth as he was barricaded by the police. The prosecution will call another expert witness to the stand. Dr. Justin Wang is a psychiatrist. He will walk us through the sociopathic nature of the defendant, Jerry Frye. This antisocial personality and deranged behavior were seen earlier on in Jerry Frye's life. As a teenager, he stabbed his mother's boyfriend, and he committed theft. He was sentenced to a juvenile detention center for rehabilitation, but he was still the same after he departed the walls of the facility. He often concealed his true nature with charm and charisma, but his true character could not be hidden for too long. His manipulative and aggressive behavior emerged, and extreme violence was the end result."

Noah Larkson paused briefly to let his words take effect. Then he resumed his remarks. "Ladies and gentlemen of the jury, the defense may try to argue insanity. They may even bring up his difficult childhood, but don't let this overshadow your judgement. We are dealing with an unconscionable, deceitful individual who has no regard for the rights and the lives of others. He exercises no remorse, and he is, in fact, an extreme danger to society. At the conclusion of this case, we will ask for a guilty verdict and the death penalty. Thank you." Noah Larkson took his seat at the table located up front and towards the right side of the room.

The defense attorney was a white man who appeared to be in his early forties. He had dark brown hair, and his face was clean shaven. He wore eyeglasses with dark brown frames that complemented his tan suit. The defense attorney stood up, and he walked towards the jury bench. "Good morning, Honorable Judge, members of the jury, and those present in the courtroom. My name is Ian Silver, and it is my pleasure to represent Jerry Frye in this case. Ladies and gentlemen of the jury, the prosecution has painted a rather gruesome and horrid picture of my client, but the truth is, my client was molded into the person he is today by his unfortunate past, and psychology indeed plays an important role in this case. Prior to my client being sent to a juvenile detention center, he had no record of being in trouble despite the environment in which he was raised. He grew up in a home where he felt no love or connection to his mother, and he dealt with constant rejection. He was verbally, mentally, emotionally, physically and sexually abused by his mother's boyfriend, who was, frankly, a drunk. In an enraged state and a drunken stupor, this abusive man revealed to my client the identity of his father, and he taunted my client when he told him that his mother was raped by his father. Jerry was young. He felt threatened and victimized, and the horrid news that he was the product of a rape sent him into a rage in which he stabbed the arm of his mother's boyfriend. Jerry could not have stayed in the house, or he likely would have been dead. He ran away, and he had nowhere to go. He sought a temporary hiding place at the home of his mother's friend. Jerry was scared and helpless. He was afraid to admit to what he had done, as he was fearful of the consequences. He was only a child. A child who had to turn to survival mode because going home was not an option. Going home meant further abuse and punishment. In order to survive, Jerry needed money. He took money from his mother's friend in order to survive. All he had on him were the clothes on his back. He did not go with the intent of stealing. My client had no history of theft. He was then arrested and placed in jail, and he was sent to a juvenile detention facility. My client grew up with an extreme fear of rejection, which is a pathology. He felt helpless and hopeless. His life seemed like a fruitless dead end, and in his mind, the only way to give himself a chance in life was to become a different person. My client has admitted to identity theft. The taking of Giselle Bellamy against her will stemmed from fear and rejection from someone he knew and loved. This triggered a psychotic episode. I will call to the stand Dr. George Berkinshire.

Dr. Berkinshire is a renowned and well-respected psychiatrist who performed a mental evaluation on my client. The other charges against my client are speculative."

Ian Silver paused briefly. Then he continued. "Ladies and gentlemen of the jury, what my client needs is mental health treatment and rehabilitation. He does not deserve the death penalty. Thank you." Ian Silver concluded his opening remarks, and he walked towards the defense table located at the front-left side of the room. Mr. Silver sat next to Jerry Frye, who was staring straight ahead.

"Would the prosecution call their first witness to the stand," the judge said authoritatively behind the bench.

Noah Larkson stood up. "Yes, Your Honor. The prosecution calls Elizabeth Henson to the stand."

Elizabeth Henson was ushered to the stand. She was wearing a cream blouse and black slacks, and her hair was combed into a right-side ponytail. "Would you raise your right hand," the bailiff ordered. Elizabeth obeyed. "Do you swear to tell the truth, the whole truth, and nothing but the truth?" the bailiff asked.

"I will," Elizabeth responded, and she took her seat on the witness stand.

Noah Larkson approached the witness. "Ms. Henson. Can you tell us what you do for a living and how you know the defendant?"

"Yes. I'm a clinical pharmacist, and I worked in the same hospital as Jerry Frye. He was a patient transporter."

"Could you bring us to the night preceding the death of Morgan Walters? You worked the night shift with the defendant, Jerry Frye. Is that correct?"

"Yes, I did."

"Tell us about your encounter that night with the defendant," Noah Larkson urged.

"Well, as you stated, I worked that night at the hospital with Jerry. I was surprised to see him in the basement. That's where the pharmacy is located. I always got the sense that he was trying to avoid me, but that night, he was a different person. He seemed thrilled when he saw me, and he was awfully interested in my job. He had never seemed interested before. He wanted a tour of the pharmacy, and he wanted me to show him 'the cool drugs,' as he put it. He specifically asked about the drugs used when running a code. Later that night, I counted the vials in the code cart, and there was a vial of succinylcholine missing."

"And that's the same succinylcholine that was found in Morgan Walter's body that was used to murder her?" the prosecutor asked.

"Objection!" Ian Silver shouted out from behind the defendant's table. "The witness could not possibly know if the vial in her pharmacy was the agent found in Morgan's body."

"Could you please rephrase the question, Mr. Larkson?" the judge asked.

"I will make a statement, Your Honor. A vial of succinylcholine was found missing in the code cart of the pharmacy. Jerry Frye was the other person in the pharmacy. Ms. Henson had stocked the code cart before Mr. Frye's arrival, and she realized that there was one vial of succinylcholine missing after Jerry Frye left the pharmacy. Morgan Walters was found dead the following morning, and traces of succinylcholine were found in her body on the second autopsy." Noah Larkson paused briefly. "I have no further questions, Your Honor." He made his way to his seat.

Roberto Sanchez turned his attention to the stenographer, who was seated at a small table in front of the bench. The stenographer was a petite Asian lady who appeared to be in her early fifties. She wore dark-rimmed glasses, and her brown checkered tweed pantsuit appeared a size too large. Her dark straight hair was cut into a short bob, and her bangs terminated midway down her forehead.

"Would the defense like to cross-examine the prosecution's witness?" the judge asked.

"Yes, Your Honor." Ian Silver stood up and walked towards the witness. "Ms. Henson, you mentioned to us that you got the sense that the defendant was trying to ignore you. How did that make you feel?"

"Objection!" Noah Larkson called out. "This trial has nothing to do with the witness's feelings towards the defendant."

"Sustained," the judge responded.

"You stated that you stocked the vials in the cart and when you recounted the vials, there was one missing. Is that correct?" Ian Silver asked.

"Yes. That's correct." Elizabeth answered.

"Is it possible that you could have made an error when you counted the vials?"

Elizabeth Henson appeared confused. "I suppose it's possible, but I don't think so. I'm very meticulous when it comes to my job."

"But it is possible that you could have made an error?" Ian Silver pressed on.

"I suppose. We're all human."

"Who else was in the pharmacy that night between the time you stocked the cart and the time that you claim to have noted a vial missing?"

Elizabeth Henson thought for a moment. "Well, there was the pharmacy technician, Stephanie. The pharmacist who was starting the day shift had already arrived."

"So you have two other people in the pharmacy who had legitimate access to the cart. Could medications have been rearranged or moved?" Ian Silver questioned.

"The technician and the pharmacist coming on had no reason to have moved medication from the code cart."

"Why not? They have access, and medications are handled all the time." Ian Silver stared at the witness, and he realized that she was getting flustered.

"We follow strict policy and procedure in the pharmacy. All I'm saying is this. I stocked the code cart, and I'm very careful and diligent when I do this. Later on in my shift, I recounted the medications, and there was a vial of succinylcholine missing."

Ian Silver changed his line of questioning. "Ms. Henson, there has been talk by your colleagues that you were very interested in pursuing a romantic relationship with Mr. Frye. Is it true that your husband left you for the babysitter?"

"Objection!" Noah Larkson called out.

"Your Honor, my line of questioning is pertinent to the case," Ian Silver responded.

"I will allow it, but please get to your point, Mr. Silver," the judge ruled.

"Ms. Henson, did your husband leave you for your babysitter, who was almost half your age?" Ian Silver continued.

"Yes," Elizabeth answered almost hesitantly.

"Did you ever mention to your colleagues that you were interested in finding a young lover?"

"I don't know if I actually put it that way. I may have mentioned that it would be nice to date someone of a younger age."

"Is it true that you wanted to date someone much younger than you because your husband left you for someone much younger than you?" Ian Silver continued.

"Sure. Why not? If my ex-husband did it, then why can't I?"

"So you then had your eyes set on Jerry Frye? Is that correct, Ms. Henson?"

"I wouldn't say I had my eyes set on him," Elizabeth responded. "Did I find him attractive? Sure."

"Attractive enough where you wanted to take the place of his wife?" Ian Silver asked.

"Heavens no!" Elizabeth blurted out.

"A colleague of yours, on record, stated otherwise. Ms. Stephanie Chambers, a pharmacy technician who you work closely with, reported that you said the following: 'I wish I could get rid of his wife and take her place.' I want to clarify to the jury that this is a statement that the witness reportedly made in regards to the defendant's wife. Remembering that you are under oath, is this a statement that you made, Ms. Henson?"

"I didn't mean anything by that. What I said has been twisted to mean something that it's not," Elizabeth replied. It was evident that she was flustered.

"Just for clarification, did you make that statement? Please answer yes or no, Ms. Henson," Ian Silver urged.

"Yes, but I was just joking. Sometimes I joke around."

"You joked about getting rid of his wife?" Ian Silver asked in a perplexed manner. "It just seems like something odd to joke about." Ian paused for a moment as he allowed the jury to digest the information. "Your shift ended one hour before Jerry Frye's shift ended. You had access to succinylcholine. You wanted to get rid of Jerry's wife and take her place. Did you murder Morgan Walters?"

"Objection, Your Honor!" Noah Larkson stated in a raised voice. "The witness is not on trial here."

"Overruled. Please answer the question, Ms. Henson," the judge ordered.

Elizabeth Henson's body was shaking, and she appeared to be on the verge of crying. "No, I did not murder her," Elizabeth answered. "I could never do something like that."

"Where did you go after you left work the morning in question, Ms. Henson?" Ian Silver continued.

"I went straight home," Elizabeth replied.

"Where was your son?"

"He was spending the week with his father. We have joint custody."

"Is there anyone who can attest to the fact that you were home between the hours of questioning," Ian Silver pressed on.

"No. I live alone."

"I have no further questions, Your Honor," Ian Silver stated. Ian walked over to the defense table and sat next to Jerry.

Noah Larkson stood up from his seat and approached the witness. "Ms. Henson, did you murder Morgan Walters?"

"No, I did not," Elizabeth answered.

"I have no further questions, Your Honor," Noah Larkson stated as he returned to his seat.

Roberto looked in the direction of Isaiah and Farrah Walters, who were seated two rows in front of him. He could not see their faces, but he could only imagine the grief that they were experiencing.

"The witness may be excused," the judge reported. Elizabeth Henson got up, and she was ushered out of the courtroom. Roberto observed Elizabeth as she walked out of the room. She appeared shaken up, and he felt very sorry for her. He knew that Elizabeth was not responsible for Morgan's murder, and it had been difficult watching the defense attorney attack her as though she was a suspect. "The prosecution may call the next witness," the judge stated.

Noah Larkson stood up. "The prosecution calls to the stand Dr. Leslie Benson." Dr. Benson was sworn in, and she took her seat on the witness stand. Dr. Benson was a white lady who appeared to be in her late fifties, or maybe early sixties. She had strands of gray hair scattered throughout her dark hair, which was combed into a French twist. She wore a black pantsuit with a burgundy blouse underneath. Dr. Benson sat erect as she waited to be questioned.

"Dr. Benson, please tell us what you do," Noah Larkson asked as he began his line of questioning.

"I am a forensic pathologist, and I've worked as a forensic pathologist for over thirty-three years."

"And you were the forensic pathologist who performed the second autopsy on Morgan Walters after the body was exhumed. Is that correct, Dr. Benson?"

"That is correct."

"Please lead us though the autopsy," Noah Larkson requested.

"It would be remiss of me not to first mention the first autopsy that was performed on Morgan Walters. I thoroughly read through the documents, and it was a very methodical and comprehensive autopsy. The agent succinylcholine is not a compound that is tested for during an autopsy. Succinylcholine is a muscle relaxant used in general anesthesia to facilitate tracheal intubation and to provide muscle relaxation during mechanical intubation or surgery. It results in respiratory depression or cessation of breathing so that respiratory support is needed. The agent succinylcholine is rapidly broken down by plasma cholinesterase so that the succinylcholine can no longer be detected. In order to illustrate this further, I have put together a poster to add more clarity. May I proceed, Your Honor?" Dr. Benson asked as she looked up at the judge.

"You may proceed," Judge Carter replied.

The bailiff brought over the large poster, and he mounted it on the easel that was situated lateral to the witness stand. Dr. Benson stood up and walked over to the poster. It was difficult to see the content of the poster from where Roberto was seated, but the members of the jury had a much better view. Dr. Benson explained the content of the poster, and she tried to simplify the information as much as possible. There were red and green arrows scattered throughout the poster. There were some words underlined and some words that were encased in bubbles. Roberto listened as Dr. Benson gave a combined biology and chemistry lesson. The presentation, though informative, appeared to be exhaustive, and Roberto wondered if it was starting to exceed the attention span of the jurors. He looked at the jury, and a couple of the jurors appeared bored. An elderly white male in the jury box was nodding his head as he tried to fight off sleep.

Dr. Benson tried to illustrate how Morgan's body reacted to the succinylcholine. "In the case of Morgan Walters, she had a pseudocholinesterase deficiency that inhibited her body from metabolizing exogenous choline drugs such as succinylcholine." Dr. Benson pointed to some words on the chart, and she used her index finger to draw an "X" in the air to illustrate that a pathway was interrupted. "When I did the second autopsy, I was looking for evidence of succinylcholine given the information I had obtained. Because Morgan Walters had this deficiency, there were traces of succinylcholine found in her body during my autopsy." Dr. Benson looked at the jurors almost as if to confirm their understanding. The elderly juror seemed to have fought off the sleep, as he was now staring directly at the expert witness. "May I now sit back on the witness stand?" Dr. Benson asked the judge. Judge Carter nodded his head, and Dr. Benson took her seat on the stand.

Noah Larkson walked towards the witness stand. "Would you conclude that Morgan Walters was murdered?" Noah Larkson asked.

"Morgan Walters had no recent procedures, surgeries, or emergency visits. To my understanding, the last time she was administered an anesthetic agent was when she had her gallbladder removed five years ago. During that time, the doctors had extreme difficulty getting her off a mechanical ventilator, which was similar to a hospitalization in which she received anesthesia for an appendectomy. Morgan subsequently was discovered to have a pseudocholinesterase deficiency, and she was to avoid certain anesthetic agents due to this deficiency. There was absolutely no reason for this agent to have been found in her body."

"Morgan Walters was discovered by the paramedics in her home. She was experiencing a deadly heart rhythm called ventricular tachycardia. Given the information provided, it can be deduced that Morgan Walters was administered the succinylcholine shortly before the paramedics' arrival. Would that be an appropriate conclusion, Dr. Benson?" Noah Larkson asked.

"Given all of the details in the case, that would be an accurate conclusion," Dr. Benson responded.

"How long before the paramedics arrival would you approximate that Morgan Walters was injected with succinylcholine, given the fact that there was still some cardiac activity detected?"

"Certainly a very short period of time. I would say a few minutes," Dr. Benson stated.

"The defendant had access to succinylcholine. He had access to the apartment that he lived in with Morgan Walters. The defendant was present when the paramedics arrived, and as Dr. Benson stated, the succinylcholine administration had to have happened minutes before the paramedics arrived. The defendant collected a $500,000 life insurance policy. He fell off of the grid shortly after, and he resurfaced after he stole the identity of a fellow American who was killed abroad in a train crash." Noah Larkson looked at the jury, and every eye was focused on him. "I have no further questions, Your Honor." Noah Larkson took his seat at the prosecution table.

"Would the defense like to cross-examine the witness?" the judge asked.

Ian Silver stood up. "No, Your Honor," Ian replied. Then he took his seat.

"It is now 11:48 am," the judge acknowledged. "We will break for lunch, and we will reconvene and begin promptly at 1 pm sharp." The judge struck his gavel. The jury were led out of the courtroom and through a side door by a clerk.

Roberto Sanchez exited the courtroom with Michael Bricks. They decided to grab lunch at a Creole eatery that was located a block away from the courthouse. The crowd was just starting to form, and fortunately, they were able to be seated without a wait time.

"I've been craving chargrilled oysters," Roberto commented as he browsed the menu. The waitress introduced herself as Maggie, and she took their orders. Michael Bricks was the first one to bring up the trial, as he'd been drawn in with deep fascination. It was almost as if he'd been pulled in like a magnet. He was intrigued that a college dropout had been able to change his identity, award himself a bachelor's and MBA degree, and secure a sought-after job on Wall Street. He just could not wrap his head around the intricacies that had needed to be overcome for the process to have run smoothly. Michael wondered if Jerry Frye had gotten outside help or if he'd accomplished the feat on his own.

Maggie, the waitress, brought out two bowls of gumbo and placed a bowl in front of each. She then placed a plate of a dozen chargrilled oysters in the center of the table. Roberto pulled the plate of oysters closer to him, and he wasted no time in consuming his appetizer. He scooped the oysters out of their shells, and his facial expression changed to pure delight as he ate one after the other. Roberto placed each shell to his mouth and tilted his head back as he ingested the garlicky buttery liquid. After Roberto ate about half a dozen of the oysters, he offered an oyster to his companion. Michael Bricks took him up on his offer and reached for one. To their satisfaction, the entrees came out rather quickly, as they were well aware that they were on the clock.

Roberto was enjoying his shrimp and grits, and he barely came up for air. Michael Bricks delighted in his alligator po' boy, but he could not ignore the aroma originating from Roberto's plate. Michael wished he could pluck the piece of shrimp that appeared to be lonely on the rim of Roberto's plate, but soon afterwards, Roberto's fork plunged into the piece of shrimp, and he devoured it. Michael wondered if this was the first meal that Roberto had eaten for the day or if Roberto just had a ravenous appetite.

Michael Bricks looked at his watch, which read 12:46 pm. He then waved down the waitress, who instinctively brought the check. Michael and Roberto paid for their meal, and they exited the restaurant.

There was a crowd in front of the courthouse, and the reporters were on the prowl for any useful information. Michael and Roberto maneuvered through the crowd and entered the courthouse after following strict procedure.

At 1 pm sharp, Judge Carter pounded his gavel, and the court was in session. All were seated, and there was silence. "Counselors, are you ready?" the judge asked.

"Yes, Your Honor," Noah Larkson and Ian Silver responded in unison.

"Great. Would the prosecution call their next witness?

"Yes, Your Honor. The prosecution calls to the stand Lorraine Summers."

Lorraine was led to the witness stand, and she was sworn in. Lorraine was a black woman who appeared to be in her early twenties. She was slender and of average height. Her hair was cut very flat, and she had beautiful, striking features. "Ms. Summers, please tell us your relationship with Morgan Walters," Noah Larkson asked.

"Morgan and I worked together with disabled children. We instantly became friends after our first encounter."

"Ms. Summers, can you tell us a little bit about Morgan Walters?" Noah Larkson urged.

"Morgan was such a beautiful person inside and out. She was very positive and always tried to see the good in people. Her warm, friendly nature is what first attracted me to her. She was definitely someone I felt that I could trust and rely on."

"Were you acquainted with Jerry Frye?" Noah Larkson asked.

"I've never met Jerry Frye, but I've heard a lot about him from Morgan."

"What kind of things did Morgan share with you?"

"Well, at first, she was very captivated by him. Soon after meeting Jerry, she felt like she was in love with him. She thought he was a nice, respectful guy. She said he was a gentleman. I tried to be supportive of her and her feelings, but I was very shocked to learn of the proposal and the court marriage. Everything happened so quickly and unexpectedly. Morgan once shared with me her dream of a wedding when she found the right guy. She envisioned all of her family and friends being present and her father walking her down the aisle. She once bought a bridal magazine and made cuttings of wedding ideas, so it was quite surprising to me that she would go along with a court marriage. I do know that she had some regret afterwards, as it seemed to have caused tension with her family, especially her father. I knew it hurt her more than she let on. From what I gather, soon after Morgan's marriage to Jerry, things started to go downhill. I noticed that Morgan was not the same. She seemed a little withdrawn, and that light that was shining brightly within her was almost extinguished. That smile that she always carried around with her was no longer visible. I remember one specific instance where a group of us had planned to meet up for dinner to celebrate a colleague's birthday. Morgan was excited to celebrate that evening, so I was surprised when she did not show up. I called her, but she could not talk, and she said that she would speak to me at work. That following Monday, we met up for lunch, and Morgan told me that she was not happy. She said that when things were good, it was good, but when it was bad, it was very, very bad. She used the word trapped.

"She said that she felt trapped in the marriage and she did not know how to escape. She actually was not sure if she really wanted to escape. She didn't think he would ever allow her to escape. I truly feel that deep down, Morgan hoped that things would get better. I know that she felt conflicted. She loved him, but she could not continue in the direction she was going in. She even started to blame herself, and she thought that if she changed to the person that he wanted her to be, things would work out and they would be happy."

"Did Morgan share with you the instances where things were very, very bad in the marriage? Did Jerry Frye abuse her?" Noah Larkson inquired.

"I don't know whether he physically abused her, but I do know that there was mental and emotional abuse. From what Morgan told me, Jerry constantly made her feel inadequate. He constantly made her feel guilty, and he constantly questioned whether she truly loved him. She told me that she did not know Jerry had a temper until they got married. Morgan once told me that she did not know which Jerry she would get when she entered their apartment. I never wanted to be that person who would encourage a friend to get a divorce, but I urged her to leave him."

"And what did Morgan Walters tell you when you encouraged her to leave Jerry Frye?"

"Well…" Lorraine paused for a few seconds. "Well, she basically just said that he would never let her leave. She made excuses for him, and she said that he loved her too much." Lorraine's voice had started to quiver, and she covered her eyes with both of her hands.

"Do you need to take a break?" Noah Larkson asked.

After several seconds, Lorraine uncovered her eyes, and she used her hands to wipe the tears that had formed. "I wish I had asked her more. I wish I had done more. Maybe she would still be here if I had done more."

"You can't blame yourself, Ms. Summers. It's not your fault," Noah Larkson said empathetically. He gave Lorraine a few more seconds before launching in to his next question. "You, however, mentioned that you wished you had done more. Do you believe that Jerry Frye killed Morgan Walters? Do you think she might have tried to leave Jerry Frye, which may have led to her death?"

"Objection!" Ian Silver called out behind the defense table. "The witness should not be asked to make that assumption."

"Mr. Larkson. Could you please rephrase the question or move on to another question?" the judge ordered.

"Yes, Your Honor. Ms. Summers, did Morgan Walters ever tell you that she was planning to leave Jerry Frye?"

"She never specifically told me that she had plans to leave. Did she consider it? Yes, she did. But again, I sensed a reluctance."

"When was the last time you spoke to Morgan Walters?" Noah Larkson asked, continuing his line of questioning.

Roberto listened intently to Lorraine Summer's testimony. He felt sorry for her, as it was apparent that she blamed herself to some degree for Morgan's death. Roberto hung on to every word exchanged between the prosecutor and his witness. After an exhaustive testimony, the defense was given an opportunity to cross-examine the witness.

Ian Silver stood up and approached the witness stand. "Ms. Summers, you mentioned that Morgan Walters felt inadequate. She felt trapped. Is that correct?"

"Yes," Morgan replied.

"Would you say that she was depressed?"

Lorraine's eyes were affixed on Ian Walters. She likely did not know where he was going with his line of questioning. "I think she became depressed."

"Depressed to the point where she did not want to live anymore?"

"Objection!" Noah Larkson called out. "The defense is trying to imply that Morgan Walters could have committed suicide when there is evidence to suggest that she was murdered with the agent succinylcholine."

"Overruled," the judge stated. "The court would like to see where the defense is going with this."

Roberto was uncertain where the defense was going with their line of questioning. The questions seemed speculative and full of hypotheses, which led to objections called out by the prosecution. After the conclusion of the cross-examination, Roberto thought that the whole interaction had been ineffective. It appeared as if the defense attorney was pulling scenarios out of thin air, which likely further confused the jury and subtracted from his credibility.

Lorraine Summers was excused from the witness stand. The prosecutor called his next witness, Mr. Timothy Ellis, who was a short white male and looked to be barely over five feet. He appeared reserved as he timidly walked to the witness stand. He was sworn in, and the prosecutor wasted no time in starting his questioning.

Roberto wondered how much coercing it had taken from the prosecution to secure Timothy Ellis as a witness, or maybe he'd been subpoenaed. Roberto was pleasantly surprised when Timothy spoke with assertiveness. His assuredness was quite unexpected given his appearance and the way he'd walked towards the witness stand. Timothy recounted the many times that he'd overheard Morgan and Jerry arguing, and Timothy certainly was not short on words. He was very colorful and detailed in his descriptions. Timothy's testimony was lengthy, and it went on for much longer than Roberto had anticipated. Ian Silver declined to cross-examine the witness, as it was likely futile given the previous cross-examination.

Roberto felt drained at the end of the day. The first day of trial was over.

———————————

It was the second day of the trial, and court was in session. Judge Carter asked the prosecution to call their next witness.

"The prosecution will call Giselle Bellamy to the witness stand," Noah Larkson remarked.

Giselle Bellamy was ushered to the witness stand, and she was sworn in. Giselle was aware of her heart beating fast as she looked at the individuals present throughout the courtroom. She spotted Roberto Sanchez and Michael Bricks seated towards the back of the room, which gave her a sense of ease. She briefly locked eyes with Jerry Frye, which again caused her heart to race. Giselle had planned to avoid eye contact with Jerry unless forced to do so, but she had not been able to resist at that moment. She took a deep breath, and she tried to relax her body.

"Ms. Bellamy, please tell the court your relationship with the defendant, Jerry Frye," Noah Larkson urged.

"I briefly dated Jerry Frye in New York City after being set up by a friend."

"And just for the record, you knew him as Anthony West?"

"Yes."

"So you were deceived throughout the relationship?" Noah Larkson continued.

"Yes, I was."

"Ms. Bellamy, please tell us about your relationship with Jerry Frye, who pretended to be Anthony West after stealing the identity of the real Anthony West."

"At first, everything seemed great. He was polite and charming. Quite the gentleman. I was attracted to his intelligence and ambition. He had a great sense of humor. He just seemed like an all-around great guy at first."

"At first?" Noah Larkson seemed to be pondering his question. "What changed throughout the course of your relationship with the defendant?"

"I discovered several things throughout the course of the relationship that just made me feel uneasy and made me question Anthony. I mean, Jerry," Giselle stated.

"Such as?" Noah replied as he encouraged Giselle to elaborate.

"Well, it was little things here and there. It started off more with an intuition. The way he would respond or his uneasiness when I asked him certain questions first made me suspicious. He was particularly uneasy when I asked questions about his family or background. It was all very odd, and it just did not add up. I became increasingly suspicious that something was not right when he was over at my apartment one evening. We started talking about my job in forensics, and I brought up a case that I was involved in. It was a case about a female student that was raped and murdered in her apartment. It made him very uneasy when I spoke about the case."

"Ms. Bellamy, could you please tell the court the female student that you are referring to?" Noah Larkson asked.

"Yes. The female student was Sofia Valadez, who was raped and murdered in her apartment in Shreveport."

"Okay. Please continue, Ms. Bellamy."

"Yes. It was a case that has stuck with me since my training as an intern in the crime scene investigation department in Shreveport. It was determined that a student by the name of Nathaniel Wellington committed the rape and murder. Nathaniel lived in the same apartment complex as Sofia, and his fingerprints and DNA were found in Sofia's apartment. I was trained to believe the evidence, but when I visited Nathaniel in the jail, I was not so sure of the meaning of the evidence. His eyes told a different story, and I started to believe him. I am fully aware that lies are told to hide the truth, but I questioned whether he was truly guilty. Nathaniel was convinced that he'd been set up, but he had no idea who would set him up or why. That question has been present in my mind since my meeting with Nathaniel Wellington."

"You mentioned that when you were talking about the case, it made the defendant Jerry Frye uneasy. Please go on, Ms. Bellamy," Noah Larkson stated.

"Well, I could see it on his face that he was very uncomfortable. His body seemed tense. I did not know why at the time. He also made mention that Nathaniel lived in the same apartment complex as Sofia Valadez. I never told him that Nathaniel resided in the same apartment complex, and he gave me no indication that he had heard of the case. It was all very strange and suspicious. I tried to dismiss my feelings, but the apprehensive thoughts were overpowering. After he left my apartment, I noticed a fingerprint on his glass, and I decided to run his fingerprints at my work."

"And what did you discover?" Noah Larkson asked.

Giselle looked in the direction of Jerry, and their eyes locked again. Her heart rate, which had slowed down, increased again, and it felt as if her heart would beat out of her chest. "I discovered that he was not who he claimed to be. His name was not Anthony West. His name was Jerry Frye. I flew from New York to Shreveport to look more into the case of Sofia Valadez. I did some more digging and questioning, and then I learnt that Jerry Frye lived in the same apartment building as Sofia Valadez. I also found out that Jerry Frye was the person who gave the detectives a statement implicating Nathaniel Wellington as a suspect."

"You liar!" blurted out a young male in the spectator area as he stood up. All present in the courtroom turned their focus towards the commotion. The judge banged his gavel, which was ignored. The young male pointed his index finger angrily in the direction of Jerry Frye. "You set my cousin up and made him kill himself. I hope you die and rot in hell, you bastard!"

"Order in the court!" the judge said with a raised voice as he banged the gavel. "Order in the court! Bailiff, please remove this man from my courtroom!"

Roberto Sanchez observed Daisy Lane seated on the bench. She held onto the young man's arm as she begged him to sit down. Two law enforcement officers obeyed the judge, and they escorted the young man out of the courtroom.

"Need I remind you that we are in a court of law," the judge stated authoritatively. "I will not tolerate any further disruptions or outbursts. From now on, anyone who chooses to make a spectacle will be fined heavily or thrown in jail. I hope I have made myself clear." The judge's eyes moved across the room, and he kept a stern demeanor. "Counselor. You may proceed."

"Okay. Where were we?" Noah Larkson asked rhetorically as he stroked his chin. "Ms. Bellamy, you were telling the court that the defendant Jerry Frye gave a statement to the detectives implicating Nathaniel Wellington as a suspect."

"Yes," Giselle responded as she tried to regain her composure.

The interrogation went on for what seemed like an endless period of time. Noah Larkson seemed to leave no stone unturned.

Finally, Noah Larkson decided to switch gears. "Ms. Bellamy, please tell the court how the defendant followed you from New York City to Shreveport and stalked you. Please tell the court about your terrifying experience in which the defendant, Jerry Frye, kidnapped you at knifepoint and held you hostage in a motel while threatening your life."

Giselle dreaded this part of the interrogation, as she was now forced to relive the gruesome memory of her kidnapping and near-death experience. The memories of her capture were still vivid and intense when she recalled the events. As she spoke about her tragedy, she noted a discomfort in her throat, and she fought hard to fight back the tears. The tears could no longer be contained, and the salty drops rolled down her cheeks. Noah Larkson asked Giselle twice whether she needed a break, but she declined. She opted to push through the interrogation, as she did not want to revisit the subject again. Giselle wiped her eyes with a tissue periodically throughout the questioning, and she was able to make it through to the end of the interrogation.

"Would the defense like to cross-examine the witness?" the judge asked.

"I will, Your Honor." Ian Silver walked towards the witness stand. "Ms. Bellamy, are you authorized to run fingerprints in your department for personal use?" Giselle was speechless as she stared into the cunning eyes of Ian Silver. "I'm sorry, Ms. Bellamy. I did not hear you."

"No."

"So you violated your work policy and used it for your own personal use?"

"Objection, Your Honor!" Noah Larkson called out. "The defense is trying to deflect blame when it was their client who committed a federal crime by committing identity theft."

"That was the only time I ever ran fingerprints outside of my job," Giselle interjected. "I only ran them because I had a strong suspicion that Anthony West was hiding something about himself, and I was correct. He was living a lie. His name was Jerry Frye. He was hiding his true identity not only from me but from his job and from others. I accept responsibility for my actions, but I did it with worthy intent. My actions were not done for fun or to take advantage of the system." Giselle realized that she'd spoken with firmness as she'd stood up for herself.

Ian Silver changed the direction of the interrogation. "Ms. Bellamy, my client had a very rough life and a life that most people can only imagine. My client admits to changing his identity, as he thought he would get a fresh start on life. This does not excuse his actions, but he wanted a clean slate. I've listened to your testimony, and I must admit that I'm a little confused. You spoke a lot about intuition, hunches, suspicions, inklings, or whatever you want to call it. My client has denied any involvement in the rape and murder of Sofia Valadez. What concrete proof do you have to indicate otherwise?"

"Jerry Frye lived in the same building as Sofia Valadez, and he was the one who steered the detectives in the direction of Nathaniel Wellington, which led to him being a suspect."

"Ms. Bellamy, are you referring to the same Nathaniel Wellington whose DNA and fingerprints were found at the scene of the crime?" Ian Silver asked.

"Yes, but I know that his DNA and fingerprints were planted there," Giselle stated defensively.

"How exactly do you know this, Ms. Bellamy? Because my client happened to live in the same apartment building, and he gave an account to the detectives of what he witnessed. What about the other witnesses in the building who gave an account? Are they guilty too?"

Giselle realized that she'd been backed into a corner. She really did not have any hard evidence to substantiate her claims. "I may not have the answers you need, but I honestly don't believe that Nathaniel Wellington committed the crime."

"And why is that? Because he told you he didn't do it? Is it because you saw it in his eyes? Well, Ms. Bellamy, I thoroughly reviewed the police and forensic reports. I know the documents like the back of my hand. The only evidence that was found were the fingerprints and DNA of Nathaniel Wellington. Nathaniel lied when he stated that he was never in Sofia Valadez's apartment when the evidence clearly stated otherwise. We cannot base this on hunches and intuitions. We have to let the evidence speak for itself, and the evidence spoke loudly." Ian Silver looked in the direction of the jury. "I have no further questions, Your Honor." Ian Silver made his way back to the defense table.

Giselle was excused from the witness stand. She felt that she had let down the families of Sofia Valadez and Nathaniel Wellington, and she wanted to cry again. However, she managed to maintain her composure. The judge called for a lunch break, and the court was to be back in session at 1 pm sharp.

Giselle met up with Roberto Sanchez and Michael Bricks for lunch at a small café located less than a block away from the courthouse. They took a seat at one of the tables in the corner of the room, and a waitress immediately came to take their order. Giselle ordered half of a turkey sandwich and a cup of tomato soup. Roberto ordered a foot-long meatball sandwich, and Michael ordered half of a ham and cheese sandwich with a cup of broccoli cheddar soup. The companions spoke about the case, and Giselle was congratulated for her bravery.

"I don't feel brave," Giselle lamented. "I'm so glad my part of the trial is over, but I feel as though I've let down the families of Sofia Valadez and Nathaniel Wellington."

"Are you kidding me, Giselle?" Roberto responded in disbelief. "It is because of you that this criminal will be brought to justice. If it wasn't for your intuition and bravery, this criminal would be walking the streets of Manhattan freely and living a life that was not his to live. I don't care what the defense had to say about your intuition. It is because of your intuition that we are here today. Even if the jury does not see his guilt in the Sofia Valadez case, the jury will surely see his guilt in Morgan Walters's wrongful death. If it wasn't for your intuition, Morgan's family would not be in the position to receive the justice that they deserve."

"Not to mention your strength in dealing with the kidnapping. You're much stronger than you give yourself credit for," Michael Bricks chimed in.

The companions ate lunch and spoke more about the trial. The time was approaching 1 pm, and the three companions made their way back to the courthouse. The outside of the courthouse was very similar to the scene that had been present on the first day of the trial.

The Honorable Judge Mason Carter took his place behind the bench, and court was in session.

"Would the prosecution like to call their next witness to the stand?" the judge questioned.

"Yes, Your Honor," Noah Larkson replied. "The prosecution would like to call Dr. Justin Wang to the stand."

Dr. Wang was sworn in, and he took a seat. Dr. Wang was an Asian male who appeared to be in his early forties. His dark hair was combed in a side part, and he wore round spectacles.

Noah Larkson approached the witness stand. "Dr. Wang, please tell the courtroom what you do and please give us an overview of your background."

Dr. Wang introduced himself as a psychiatrist who had practiced in the field for fourteen years. He listed his training background and the numerous articles that he had published in the field of psychiatry. Dr. Wang spoke extensively about antisocial personality disorder. Roberto again looked at the jury, and the elderly man who he'd previously seen nodding off was at it again. The juror's head lowered in sleep, and his body jerked, causing him to rouse again. The juror sat up straight, and he tried to focus his attention on the witness. Roberto turned his attention back to Dr. Wang. He felt as though he was at a psychiatry conference as he listened to the drawn-out details about mental disorders and antisocial personality disorder. Dr. Wang applied the diagnosis to Jerry Frye, and he labeled the defendant as aggressive, impulsive, unremorseful, and as having no respect for the law.

"Dr. Wang, in your professional opinion, would you say that the defendant Jerry Frye is a danger to society?" Noah Larkson asked.

"In my professional opinion, I would say that the defendant is a danger to society."

"I have no further questions, Your Honor." Noah Larkson walked back to the prosecution table, and he took a seat.

"Would the defense like to cross-examine the witness?" the judge asked.

"Yes, Your Honor." Ian Silver stood up, and he walked towards the witness. "Dr. Wang, have you had the opportunity to sit down with my client and do a full mental assessment?"

"No, I have not."

"But yet you're making a diagnosis?"

"Jerry Frye exhibits all of the signs of someone with antisocial personality disorder. He's a clear textbook case," Dr. Wang stated.

"I see that you're always quick to make a diagnosis. Just as in the case of Cheryl Woods, where you misdiagnosed her as having major depression when she actually had bipolar II. You prescribed her an antidepressant instead of a mood stabilizer, causing her mania to get out of control, and she committed suicide. The signs of her disease were all there, but you missed it. You ended up settling with the family outside of court. Isn't that correct, Dr. Wang?"

"Objection!" Noah Larkson shouted. "Dr. Wang, you don't have to answer that. Your Honor, the defense if trying to run a smear campaign on my client, when he has proven to be a very worthy and experienced psychiatrist in the medical community."

"Has he?" Ian Silver interjected sarcastically.

"Yes, he has!" Noah Larkson stated defensively.

"Are you sure about that?" the defense attorney retaliated.

"Counselors, that's enough!" the judge ordered. "Both of you, please approach the bench." Ian Silver and Noah Larkson obeyed the judge's command. "I will not have you turn my courtroom into a three-ring circus. Moving forward, we will stick to the facts at hand. The witnesses are not on trial."

"Yes, Your Honor. But the witness's work history is pertinent to him being justified to make this claim about my client," Ian Silver replied.

"Well, find another way to present it so the witnesses don't feel like they're on trial. Do I make myself clear, counselors?" the judge asked sternly.

"Yes, Your Honor," the attorneys replied in unison.

Noah Larkson took his seat at the prosecution's table, and Ian Silver continued his line of questioning.

It was a long day, but eventually the second day of trial was finally over.

CHAPTER 25

THE CROWD HAD ONCE MORE GATHERED IN FRONT OF THE COURTHOUSE. THERE WAS A coolness to the air from the rain that had fallen overnight. The inside of the courtroom bore a similar feel, and the atmosphere was rigid and tense. The hands of the clock were getting closer to 8 am, and the twelve jurors were seated in the jury box. Shortly after the jury was seated, the bailiff instructed all individuals present in the courtroom to stand as the judge, draped in his black robe, made his way to the bench.

"Good morning," the judge greeted to those present in the courtroom. "We will get right into it. Is the prosecution ready, and is the defense ready?"

"Yes, Your Honor," both attorneys replied.

"Good. The defense will have the opportunity to call their first witness."

"Thank you, Your Honor." Ian Silver stood up from his chair. "The defense would like to call Dr. George Berkinshire."

Jerry Frye stood up from his seat before Dr. Berkinshire could be ushered to the stand. "I would like to take the witness stand, Your Honor," Jerry announced.

There were gasps and whispers heard throughout the courtroom. Giselle watched in disbelief as the judge banged his gavel and requested order in the court. Ian Silver sat down with his client and began whispering into his ear. Two other members of the defense team also hovered over Jerry Frye.

"Counselor, who will you be calling to the stand?" the judge inquired.

"May I have a couple of minutes with my client, Your Honor," Ian Silver asked.

"You may have a couple of minutes with your client."

Giselle observed the defense attorney as he continued to whisper into the ear of his client. She observed Jerry's posture, and it did not appear as if the defense attorney was getting through to him. Jerry shook his head from side to side, and he covered his face momentarily with his hands. Ian Silver continued to whisper in Jerry's ear, and the defense attorney was using forceful hand gestures.

A couple of minutes elapsed, and the judge demanded an answer from the defense attorney.

Jerry Frye stood up, and the whispers continued throughout the courtroom. "Your Honor, I have great respect for the court, and I apologize if I seem out of line. I am also extremely grateful for my defense team, who have worked tirelessly on this case. I cannot move on with this heavy weight on my shoulders. If you will allow it, I think it is my time to take the stand."

"Counselor?" The judge looked in the direction of the defense attorney.

Ian Silver raised his hands in the air almost as if to indicate that he had given up. "The defense calls to the stand Jerry Frye."

Jerry walked towards the witness stand. He was wearing a gray suit, white shirt, and black tie. He was sworn in, and he took his seat.

Ian Silver walked towards the witness stand. For the first time since the trial had commenced, the defense attorney appeared perturbed and ruffled. He had evidently been thrown off of his game, and he had to decide on a new play.

"Jerry Frye, you have many accusations against you. You have admitted to identity theft. You have also admitted to kidnapping Giselle Bellamy, though you claim that your intent was not to murder her. You gave a statement to the police claiming that your objective for kidnapping Giselle Bellamy was to find out why she was setting up a trap for you. With that said, you have vehemently denied any involvement in the murder of Morgan Walters and the rape and murder of Sofia Valadez. You have wholeheartedly denied any sort of interaction with Nathaniel Wellington. Please tell the court your side of the story."

Jerry gazed forward, and he observed the individuals who were seated in the spectator region. He observed Isaiah Walters, who had his arm around his wife. He was saddened that this was the venue in which he first saw his father- and mother-in-law in person. He had seen pictures of them from Morgan. He knew that he would never be able to refer to them with the title of father- and mother-in- law. Seated a couple of rows behind the Walters family was Giselle. Jerry looked at the grief and sadness on her face. He truly did love her. He wished that they had met in another place and time where he did not have such a disgraced and defiled background and he did not have to pretend to be someone that he was not. He observed Daisy Lane, who was seated in the spectator area. He recognized her from the news from a few years back as being the grandmother of Nathaniel Wellington. He could never forget the hurt and the sense of loss in her voice as she'd spoken lovingly about her grandson.

Jerry then noticed the individual seated behind Daisy Lane. He was stunned, and his heart skipped a beat. It was his brother, Robert. Jerry had not seen his brother since Robert had left for college, but the man seated in the courtroom was undeniably his brother. Jerry felt a lump in his throat as he got increasingly emotional. He'd never thought that he would ever see his brother again. He'd experienced extreme hurt and abandonment when his brother, the person he most loved and admired, had left him. Jerry had been only a teenager when he'd had to deal with the abuse of Fletcher and the rejection of his mother. His brother had left him when he'd been most vulnerable and had most needed him. Jerry had hoped and prayed that his brother would come back for him, but he never did. The absence of his brother had created a huge void in him, and his life had just spiraled out of control. It had been one adverse event after the other that had dug him deeper into the ground. Jerry had come to the harsh realization that in order to move on, he had to forgive all those who had hurt him in life, especially his mother. He also had to take responsibility for his actions.

"Please tell the court your side of the story," Ian Silver repeated himself.

Jerry breathed a deep sigh, which was audible to some who were present in the courtroom. "I speak to all of you with a heavy heart. I am living in a mental and emotional prison, and it is far worse than being locked up behind bars. It is worse than the poison that could be injected inside my veins to end my life. I have had a difficult and painful life, and I have allowed it to rot me to the core. I don't even recognize myself anymore. I despise the reflection of the person in the mirror. I have gone through life blaming and condemning others for my misfortune. I have allowed the fear of rejection to take over my life and to lead me to do terrible and horrendous things that I am not proud of. I have carried a hatred and disdain for my mother all of these years, and today, that ends."

Jerry's face started to turn a light shade of red as the tears escaped his eyes. "Mother, I forgive you." Jerry's voice was breaking as the words came out of his mouth. He had difficulty controlling his breathing as the tears flowed unhindered. "I forgive you, mother," Jerry repeated.

He looked out into the spectator region of the courtroom, and he saw his brother. "My brother is here today in the courtroom. I was thirteen years old when my brother left the house. I lost my friend and my mentor. He was all that I had in the world. He was everything to me. When my brother left the house, I felt that I lost everything. Aside from one letter that I received, I have never heard from my brother again. Not even on holidays. I grew to resent my brother. I felt unwanted and rejected my entire life. First, it was my mother. I later learned that my existence was the product of my mother being raped. Maybe that's why my mother rejected me. Maybe I reminded her too much of the past. But when my brother rejected me, it was like a knife had pierced through my soul. Today, I want to tell you, my brother, that I forgive you. I know it was not easy for you growing up and you had to make a way for yourself. I hope that you are happy and fulfilled."

Jerry looked again at his brother, who was also crying. "Today, I want to break free from all lies and deception. My fears have bound me like a chain, and it is time for me to remove them. I am going to take responsibility for my actions, and I am ready to accept whatever punishment is placed upon me."

Giselle realized that she was holding her breath as she waited for Jerry to continue speaking. She looked around the courtroom, and all eyes were fixed on Jerry Frye.

"I raped and killed Sofia Valadez," Jerry confessed.

The noise in the courtroom escalated at quick speed. Gasps and loud talking were heard throughout the courtroom. Mrs. Valadez screamed out, and her husband instinctively wrapped his arms around her.

"Order in the court!" the judge shouted as he banged the gavel. "Order in the court!" The noise in the courtroom settled down after the judge was forced to bang his gavel again. Giselle was stunned at Jerry's confession, and she felt as though her body was momentarily paralyzed. "You may continue, Mr. Frye."

"I am so sorry," Jerry declared as his voice cracked. "I am so sorry. Sofia was such a nice girl, and she did not deserve it. I wanted desperately to be with her, but she did not want to be with me. I could not handle the rejection. I wanted her to pay for rejecting me. I wanted to be in control. That is when I raped her and killed her. I broke into Nathaniel Wellington's apartment when he was not home, and I obtained strands of his hair and his fingerprint. I planted the evidence in Sofia's apartment."

The noise in the courtroom escalated again, and the judge banged his gavel again. Giselle looked over at Daisy Lane, who was wiping her eyes with a handkerchief.

"Order in the court! Order in the court!" the judge shouted out again. "I understand that this is all very emotional to those present in the courtroom, especially the families of the victims, but order must be kept in the court." The noise started to subside again. "You may continue, Mr. Frye."

"I am so very sorry. Nathaniel did not deserve any of this." Jerry's voice quivered, and he wiped the tears from his eyes. "I killed my wife."

The noise in the courtroom erupted again. "Murderer!" someone shouted in the back of the courtroom. The judge banged the gavel again. The noise started to calm down again.

"I loved Morgan, but I was so afraid that she was going to leave me. I admit that I was at fault. Morgan was such a good person, but by that time, I was so rotten inside. I was vile and hateful. I did not kill Morgan to get the life insurance money. I did, however, use the money to start a new life. I wanted to escape. I wanted to get away from everything that was holding me back in life. I wanted to be a better person. I wanted another chance."

Ian Silver had been speechless from the moment Jerry Frye had opened his mouth on the stand. Ian was finally able to break his silence. "How were you able to change your identity?"

Jerry opened up about his introduction and meeting with Regulator. He acknowledged that he knew very little about Regulator, but he confessed to the court what had transpired. Jerry opened up about his meeting with Regulator in New York City. He revealed that he'd been handed documents with his new identity.

Jerry proceeded to tell the court about his relationship with Giselle Bellamy. He admitted that he had followed Giselle to

Shreveport by using her phone as a tracking device. He detailed the kidnapping and his confrontation with the police at the motel. Jerry looked out into the spectator region, and he spotted Giselle, who was staring directly at him. "Giselle, I hope that you can find it in your heart to forgive me. These may seem like just words, but I just want you all to know how deeply sorry I am."

The courtroom was silent aside from a few sniffles. The judge asked the prosecution whether they wanted to cross-examine the witness. Noah Larkson declined, as he was likely also speechless.

"Does the defense or the prosecution want to bring any other witnesses to the stand?"

"No," Ian Silver responded.

"No," Noah Larkson replied.

"Well, since there are no more witnesses or evidence to be presented, the jury can be excused to reach a verdict," the judge reported.

The twelve jurors were led out of the courtroom to the jury room, where they discussed the case. The jurors deliberated for almost an hour before informing the bailiff that they had reached a decision. The judge was notified by the bailiff that a decision was made by the jury, and the court was back in session.

"The jury has listened carefully to the evidence, and the jury has reached their verdict in the murder trial of Jerry Frye," the judge stated. "Would the defense please rise." Jerry Frye stood up with Ian Silver and the rest of the defense team.

The jury clerk stood up and addressed the jury. "Would the foreperson please rise and state your seat number for the record."

A female juror stood up and announced her seat as number two.

"Madam Foreperson, how do you find the defendant, Jerry Frye, on count one of felony first degree murder of Morgan Walters?"

"We find the defendant, Jerry Frye, guilty of felony first degree murder of Morgan Walters."

There was crying heard in the spectator region. Giselle observed the Walters family as they hugged and comforted each other.

"Madam Foreperson, how do you find the defendant, Jerry Frye, on count two of felony life insurance fraud?"

"We find the defendant, Jerry Frye, guilty of felony life insurance fraud."

"Madam Foreperson, how do you find the defendant, Jerry Frye, on count three of felony identity theft?"

"We find the defendant, Jerry Frye, guilty of felony identity theft."

"Madam Foreperson, how do you find the defendant, Jerry Frye, on count four of felony kidnapping of Giselle Bellamy?"

"We find the defendant, Jerry Frye, guilty of felony kidnapping of Giselle Bellamy."

"Madam Foreperson, how do you find the defendant, Jerry Frye, on count five of felony attempted murder of Giselle Bellamy?"

"We find the defendant, Jerry Frye, guilty of felony attempted murder of Giselle Bellamy."

"All members of the jury, please rise," the jury clerk ordered. "I will now ask each juror individually to give their verdict. "Juror one. Is this your verdict?"

"Yes."

"Juror three. Is this your verdict?"

"Yes."

"Juror four. Is this your verdict?"

"Yes."

The jury clerk asked each juror individually for their verdict, and each gave a guilty verdict. The bailiff approached Jerry and placed him in handcuffs. Giselle was relieved by the guilty verdicts, and she was pleased that justice was served. Jerry, however, had not been charged for the rape and murder of Sofia Valadez or for the falsification of evidence against Nathaniel Wellington due to a lack of evidence at the commencement of the trial. Giselle was disappointed that Jerry had not been rightfully charged for these offenses, but she was comforted by the fact that the truth had been revealed. Nathaniel Wellington was vindicated, and the true identity of Sofia's rapist and murderer had been disclosed. All of the darkness had now been brought to light.

Judge Carter addressed the jury. "Members of the jury, this was a very emotional case. I have not seen a case like this in all of my years of practice. On behalf of the court, I want to thank each and every one of you for the sacrifices that you have made for serving on this jury. This case has garnered extensive media coverage, and there will be members of the media who may try to interview you. You may speak to the media if you choose to do so. If you choose not to, the media should honor your request." The judge turned his attention to the clerk. "What is the sentencing date?"

"The sentencing date is scheduled for March 24th," the clerk responded.

"You are all discharged and free to leave," the judge stated as he hit his gavel on the bench.

Giselle watched as Jerry was led away in handcuffs.

CHAPTER 26

JERRY SAT ON A COT BEHIND THE STEEL BARS OF HIS PRISON CELL. AN ORANGE JUMPSUIT clothed his body. He'd been given the death penalty. Jerry opened his Bible and read 1 John Chapter 1. Verse nine of the chapter resonated with him: "If we confess our sins, he is faithful and just and will forgive us our sins and purify us from all unrighteousness." Jerry lay on his pillow and reflected on the words of the passage. He looked through the bars of the prison cell, and he smiled to himself, as he was finally free after all of these years.

He thought about his brother, Robert, who had visited him twice since his incarceration. The first visit was very emotional, and it was filled with apologies and tears. There were also words of love and forgiveness. Robert informed Jerry that their mother was not doing well and she was suffering from major depression. Robert went on to say that he'd recently visited their mother, and he'd been saddened to see her emotional state. It was almost as though she was empty inside. The trial had taken a toll on her. Mrs. Jackson apparently checked up on her frequently. Robert stated that he made it a duty now to call their mother every day to lift up her spirits. At Robert's encouragement, she was now seeing a counselor. Jerry inquired about Fletcher, and Robert informed him that Fletcher had died almost a year ago from complications of alcoholic liver cirrhosis. Towards the end of their encounter, Robert told Jerry that he was married and a father to fourteen-month-old twins, Randall and Courtney. Jerry was indeed thrilled to learn that he was an uncle. Robert's second visit was more lighthearted. He shared stories about the twins, and Jerry was thoroughly amused. Randall and Courtney appeared to be a handful but yet an absolute joy. Robert promised to send Jerry a picture of the twins.

"Frye. You have a visitor," a burly guard announced, which interrupted Jerry's thoughts. Jerry wondered about the identity of his visitor. Was it Robert? Could it be Giselle?

Jerry was led by the burly guard to the visiting area. He was astonished to see who was sitting on the other side of the partition glass. Jerry sat on a plastic navy blue chair within the confines of the cubicle, and he looked his visitor in the eyes. The moment seemed surreal, and he felt a myriad of emotions springing to life in his body. Jerry picked up the phone, and his visitor followed suit.

"Hello, Mother," Jerry stated through the receiver. He was in absolute disbelief that his mother had come to visit him, but he was also very appreciative. The stress and burden were evident on her face, and she appeared to have aged quite a bit throughout the years.

"Hello, son," she replied.

Jerry was sentimental on hearing his mother acknowledge him as her son. He had yearned to hear those words for years. "How are you doing?" he asked.

"I'm not doing so well, but I am more concerned about you," his mother replied. "How are you doing?"

"I'm okay given the circumstances. I just have to take it one day at a time. I have prayed for God's forgiveness, and I am trying every day to be a better person. I want to get rid of all of the negativity inside of me and fill that space with positive energy."

Jerry looked at his mother's face, which appeared very deep in thought but extremely saddened. "I'm so sorry, Jerry," she stated as tears formed in her eyes. "I'm so sorry that I've allowed this to happen to you. I should have been there for you. I have failed you as a mother, and I'm so sorry. Please forgive me."

Jerry looked at his mother, who was consumed with emotions. The tears streamed down her cheeks, and the tissue that she used to dab her face was soaked. "Mother, for the longest time, I hated you. I despised you. I loathed every part of you. But I realized that it all stemmed from extreme hurt. I wanted so much to be loved and accepted by you, but all I experienced was rejection. It made me feel undeserving and just worthless. It made me feel like there was something wrong with me, and I felt powerless. I learned that you were raped and that I was the product of rape. Mother, I am so sorry that you experienced that. It must have been the most terrifying experience of your life. I know that for a fact because I experienced it. I also saw the terror in her eyes. I have dissected the meaning of my actions. That dreadful moment that I committed that rape, I wondered if it was a part of my DNA because my so-called father was a rapist. I also wondered if maybe I just became that person because Fletcher molested me. But that was only an excuse. I was fearful of rejection, and she rejected me. I was a coward. I wanted to feel powerful, because, all of my life, I'd felt powerless. It was because of my own selfishness that she is not here with her family today. It is because of my own disdain for myself that my wife is not with her family today. I have lived my life blaming others and not taking responsibility for my thoughts and actions."

Jerry looked at his mother, who was still crying. "You asked me to forgive you. I am working on forgiving myself and forgiving those who have hurt me, but I want to say to you now at this moment that I forgive you. I forgive you, Mother, and I want you to forgive yourself."

Jerry looked at his mother, who was still crying. He wished that he could have given her a hug, but this was made impossible by the glass that separated them.

His mother managed a smile despite the sadness that she was experiencing. "I love you, my son."

"I love you too," Jerry replied with a smile. "Promise me that you will continue the counseling. Promise me that you will forgive yourself and move forward."

"How can I move forward when you are locked up behind bars? How can I move forward when you are on death row?" She wiped her eyes with her soaked tissue.

"Don't cry for me, Mother. I am paying the price for my heinous actions. I'll be okay. I plan to do good within the walls of my confinement. I hope to change a life for the better or have a positive impact in some way. I continually pray for God's forgiveness, and hopefully, my freedom will one day be in heaven."

Jerry and his mother spoke a few minutes longer before the guard indicated that time was up. Jerry looked at his mother, and his heart was overjoyed. "Mother, thank you for visiting me. I love you."

"I love you too, son." Jerry placed the palm of his right hand to the glass. His mother reciprocated and placed her left palm over Jerry's palm.

The guard led Jerry back to his prison cell.

May 4th 2015

Dear Valadez family,
My words could never ease your pain or comfort you in any way. For the brief time that I was blessed to be in the company of your daughter, I was able to witness her kind and gentle soul. She was truly a beautiful human being. My own selfishness and bitterness allowed me to rob this beautiful soul of the bright future ahead of her. I wish that I could rewind time and take my actions back. I wish that Sofia was still here. I wish that I could even take her place. I know that she is smiling in heaven and watching down over you. I hope and pray that you can find it in your heart to forgive me.

Jerry

May 4th 2015

Dear Ms. Daisy Lane,
I pray that you are well. I know that these words seem audacious of me given all that I have put you and your family through. I want you to know that I am very, very sorry for your heartache and pain. Nathaniel was innocent, and I took his hopes and dreams away from him. I know that he wanted to make you proud. He did not deserve any of this. For years, he was labeled as something he was not, and he is finally vindicated. I am so sorry that you had to endure the pain of your grandson being falsely accused. I can't say enough how sorry I am, and I hope and pray that you will find it in your heart to forgive me.

Jerry

May 4th 2015

Dear Walters family,
I don't know where to begin, but I will first start by telling you how sorry I am. To the depths of my soul, I am truly, truly sorry. I know that these words don't offer you comfort. I know that these words will never bring your daughter back, but I pray that you will find it in your hearts to forgive me. I was Morgan's husband. I should have been the one to love her, care for her, and protect her. As the Bible states, husbands are to love their wives as their own bodies. The truth is that I did not love myself. It is hard to give something that you don't have. I am not making excuses for my actions. What I did was horrendous and indefensible. I deserve to be sitting in this jail cell. I wish that I could take back what I did and you could be holding your daughter right now. I wish that I could take back many things in life, but I know that I can't. All I can do at this moment is to learn to forgive myself and pray that God, too, will forgive my sins. I hope that you can forgive me also.

Jerry

May 4th 2015

Dear Giselle,
I hope that you are doing well despite all that I have put you through. I want you to know how truly sorry I am, and I hope you can find it in your heart to forgive me. I want you to know that the good moments that we spent together were not a lie. I loved you, and I still love you. You are a beautiful person inside and out. You deserve only the best in life. I pray that you find someone who will love you and treat you the way that you deserve to be treated. Please don't let me ruin your hope for love. There are good people in this world, and there is someone out there designed for you. Keep smiling and continue to be the good person that you are. God bless.

Jerry

ABOUT THE AUTHOR

Juelle Christie is a board certified Internist with a profound love and passion for writing. She is fond of suspense thrillers that generate excitement and take the reader on an adventure. Dr. Juelle Christie enjoys traveling, and she has a long list of countries to visit on her bucket list. She resides with her husband in metro Atlanta.